Praise for Anne Strieber's *An Invisible Woman*

"Incredibly exciting, fast-paced, and involving, *An Invisible Woman* puts Anne Strieber in the class of writers like Nora Roberts and Sandra Brown. Like them, she imbues her thrilling rollercoaster of a story with lots and lots of heart."
—Peter Straub

"This entertaining thriller pits a Fifth Avenue matron against a shattering conspiracy that blurs the line between friend and foe. Upper-crust New Yorker Kealy Ryerson . . . receives an urgent call from her lawyer husband to grab the kids and run. Overnight, all she has known and loved has become sinister. As Ryerson's comfortable world crashes around her . . . Kealy discovers that without the glitter and makeup that's her usual uniform, a middle-aged woman can simply disappear."
—*Publishers Weekly*

Forge Books by Anne Strieber

An Invisible Woman
Little Town Lies

LITTLE TOWN LIES

Anne Strieber

TOR®

A TOM DOHERTY ASSOCIATES BOOK
NEW YORK

This is a work of fiction. All the characters and events portrayed in this book are either products of the author's imagination or are used fictitiously.

LITTLE TOWN LIES

Copyright © 2005 by Anne Strieber

A Tor Book
Published by Tom Doherty Associates, LLC
175 Fifth Avenue
New York, NY 10010

www.tor.com

Tor® is a registered trademark of Tom Doherty Associates, LLC.

ISBN 13: 978-0-765-34945-3
ISBN 10: 0-765-34945-0

First edition: November 2005
First mass market edition: September 2006

Printed in the United States of America

0 9 8 7 6 5 4 3 2 1

To my late mother
(in some ways, Sally's story is the same as mine).

The men will all hurt you
Their hearts you may despise,
But you cain't get away from those
Little Town Lies

—*Agnes Pontrelle, from her 1949 recording,*
"Heartsick in the Hills"

LITTLE
TOWN
LIES

1

Sally Hopkins gave up trying to find an NPR station. They didn't make that kind of radio out here, not on the long road back home . . . and maybe that was just as well. She stopped twisting the dial when she heard the faint sound of country music coming through the static. It was impossible to make out the words, but she imagined that she was hearing Tammy Wynette, singing "D-E-F-E-A-T," which had become Sally's theme song in Houston.

She didn't know what she would have done—maybe something desperate—if Ed hadn't told her he could use her back home in Maryvale. She hadn't felt needed for a long time, and frankly, his words had caused grateful tears to come. He'd alluded to a problem that he considered "kinda strange," that was, according to him, connected with her line of work. Which fascinated her, of course. Actually, it also kind of worried her, because little old Maryvale was not the kind of place that had strange problems involving family issues. Surely it was just strange to him— an alcoholic twelve-year-old or something, the kind of thing she saw in Houston every day.

A restless sort of depression had rolled over her like a bitter fog about a month ago, when one bleak night it had hit her: she'd used up Houston . . . which was a pretty damn big place. She was on a collision course with that dreaded milestone, her fortieth birthday, and there were no princes showing up in her life—not even any frogs to kiss. She'd long ago stopped thinking that sex with strangers was exciting, but lately she wasn't even getting any offers.

Her first thought had been, *Let's shake things up a little. Get a hot new job.* But there were no fast-track jobs to be found online or in the classifieds or anywhere else for a gal with a master's in social work. In fact, the number of slow-track jobs was about zero, as well.

When a social worker finds her idealism is all used up, she ends up just like Sally was right now, driving down a long, long road in a beat-up old car.

So here she was, sure enough, clattering along the one road that led to some sort of home. At the end of it was her own private heaven, the town of Uncle Ed and the sweet summers of her childhood. Here, in the one happy place of her heart, she intended to find out if it really was possible for a gal on the last frontier of youth to find some real fulfillment.

The car hummed right along. You'd think that the suitcases and boxes and books of a lifetime would put a strain on an old Camry. But after toiling for fifteen years in the big city, it came down to this: she could fit everything she owned into a very elderly compact car and not even make it groan.

It scared her to think how easy it had been to drive away from her old life. When she finally decided to make the break, her first impulse had been to hike up to Dallas and see if maybe they had painted the offices of the Department of Social Services something other than Navy-surplus gray. Maybe, if she played hard to get, she could wrangle an office with a window, even.

She sat at her workstation staring at the transfer request application so long that people started to worry that she'd gone into a coma or died.

All of a sudden, she'd picked up the phone and dialed a number she'd remembered all these years, from the age of twelve. Even the ring—*brrring-brrring*—sounded like old times. And, oh, that gentle, familiar East Texas twang of his—when he answered she'd choked up so completely that he was just about to hang up before she heard herself say, "Ed, hi, it's Sally."

He had been the sheriff in Maryvale for what seemed like forever. After an initial silence, his voice had vibrated frank surprise. "Why, Sally—well, darlin' . . . hello. Hello, there!"

She'd left Maryvale behind as the only good part of a hard childhood. He hadn't heard from her in years, and had no reason to expect to. So she'd just plunged in. "Ed," she'd said, "I've been missing Maryvale for too long. I'm coming home."

Another silence, then, "You're in social work, aren't you?" She told him she'd been working for Texas for all these years. That digested, the old, welcoming smoothness returned. "Why, Sally, darlin', I think that's just real fine."

She'd asked him if there was any work like that in Maryvale, maybe with the county.

He had been surprisingly quick on the uptake. There was indeed money in his budget to take her on. "Heck, Sally, your call came at just the right time," he'd added. "The truth is, we can use someone with your skills. Most of our troubles are right up your alley, like alcoholism, families beating up on each other and hurting their kids, young people watching too much violent TV and running wild."

Oh, yes, those were a social worker's problems, all right. "Seems like those kinds of sins are the same just about everywhere, Uncle Ed."

Then he'd added the little something that she hadn't expected. "Well, we got kind of a special problem here."

A tone had entered his voice that she didn't like to hear. Really did not like. "What problem?"

"Might be your kind of problem. I'll tell you about it when you get here."

What could trouble Ed so much his voice would get all tight like that? She knew stress when she heard it. "I hope Maryvale's not turning into South Houston."

He'd chuckled, and his old East Texas style slipped back into place like a well-kept old Ford pickup sliding through its gears. "You'll still find a lot of the old Maryvale around here, darlin'. I'll be waiting for you."

The closer she got to Maryvale, the clearer the radio station became. Where was it from? Not Maryvale itself, surely. There couldn't be more than two thousand people in the whole county, if that. Somewhere farther down the road, then. East Texas is a big stretch of country that contains some of the most isolated corners of the whole United States.

She hit the scanner on the radio, and it swept right around to the same station again. Fine, she'd loved country and western when she was a girl. Who knew, maybe there were still square dances on Saturday nights. Course there were, what could she be thinking? Texas was still Texas, at least out here.

With Johnny Cash rumbling in the background, she thought back to her last week on the job, when the truth about her life had just plain struck her in the face. She had just visited her favorite client, Rashanda Martins, spent half an hour more than she should, sitting across from her in her cigarette-choked little kitchen with that rotted green curtain on the window and the screen door that let the flies in.

Why not get another curtain? A couple of bucks at Wal-Mart. Or fix the damn door, a project of an hour, maybe two?

Sally knew what Rashanda's monthly check was— about two hundred bucks less than her own salary. It was all in the attitude, and Sally's job was just that: change their attitudes.

She didn't know why she enjoyed talking to Rashanda so much, since her life was pretty much the same as all of Sally's other clients. Rashanda's project was a disintegrating warren of concrete block apartments along dark halls scarred by eerily beautiful and violent graffiti. "DOS EZE," in fluorescent purple and orange, with blood falling from the letters. "Git me Rad Ate," whatever that meant.

Rashanda supplemented her aid with a little drug peddling and hooking on the side, so she did have a flat-screen TV in the living room and a curious, round bed with satin sheets, so crammed into the tiny bedroom that it looked like it had been grown in there.

The state of Texas wanted Rashanda to get off her rear and quit spending all her time smoking joints and watching daytime TV. It was Sally's job to inspire her.

"Miz Hopkins! How you doin'?" she would crow, her smile too wide to mean anything but "Hello, enemy."

Most of Sally's clients were so hopeless and glum that giving them suggestions was about as effective as kicking a snail. They couldn't wait for her to write up her damn report and get the hell out. However well she might conceal it, they knew that she felt contempt for the way they'd screwed up their lives. Texas wanted these people to get off their tails and get a job scraping dishes or rendering fat or something. The nobility of labor—minimum wage, minimum benefits, no unions need apply.

Sally, however, could relate to Rashanda, largely because she was so refreshingly straightforward. When she started her standard lecture about the pride to be gained from earning an honest living, Rashanda said, "Hell, Miz Hopkins, I know I've messed up by playing around, but that don't mean I got to be punished in this life by going out to clean public toilets. Ain't no way what I do's gonna make any difference in this world, so I may as well enjoy myself as best I can. Trouble is, I like men too damn much, and they ain't never been any good for me."

She had left that last visit in a sour funk—and not because Rashanda was stubborn. For another, darker reason: as she bypassed the broken elevator and walked down the long flight of stairs to the parking lot, she reflected on the idea that maybe Rashanda was dead-on right.

Truth be told, Sally's middle-class life was, in fact, no

better than Rashanda's poor one, and it was certainly a lot less fun. She lived in a tiny, sterile hole of an apartment with a grouchy roommate, and she had the same problems with men that Rashanda did. She liked them too damn much, and they were never any good for her.

This new realization was the little flutter of breeze that brought the whole house of cards down. She'd done a slow-motion meltdown in the office, erasing files, pulling records, doing whatever she could to make her clients disappear into the system.

Texas was planning to abandon them sooner than they thought. Texas was getting real uneasy about folks supping at the public trough, yes ma'am, she surely was. But now these few, these precious few, were going to be real hard to find. Their checks would keep coming for years, probably, maybe unto death. Maybe after.

She'd been working there long enough to know she'd better leave before she got canned, so she handed in her resignation prior to somebody figuring out that her clients had all been "ghosted" off the rolls.

She'd gone home to find her roommate pounding away in her bedroom with her latest sex toy, a guy named Harry or Frankie or Seth or Jason or whatever. Whoever. She'd listened to the jungle drum of it, her roomie's transparently fake cries, the guy's gasping and yelling, and had decided there was no choice: she had to leave here and she had to do that right now, this instant.

She'd pulled down her suitcases and started packing, and then realized that she wasn't just leaving this apartment, she was leaving this whole life, Houston, her job, everything.

As she packed, she'd sort of assumed that this would be the first of three or four days of moving, during which her friends would find out and try different ways to make her stay.

In fact, the packing was done in an hour and over the three days until her Friday departure, the only comments she'd gotten had been good-byes.

Her roommate could scarcely conceal her delight. She could ask Will-Mark-Todd to move in. Think of it, he could get drunk and slap her around right here at home instead of doing it out behind the bowling alley on Riverside and Old Spanish Trail.

Actually, when her last day arrived, the office gained an atmosphere of celebration. She faced a hard reality: people were relieved to be rid of her and her dark moods.

Sally had told herself, *It's okay, you will get through this, you will not break down and cry.* She should be used to feeling unwanted. That had been the story of her childhood, after all.

She was always kind of baffled by the way people congregated, by all the friends they seemed to have, by the laughter and the delight with which they greeted each other. Before Sally spoke, she would compulsively clear her throat. And if she was in a crowd, she'd feel the need to first tap the shoulder of anybody she wanted to address.

Shyness, she thought, attributable to a lonely childhood and a lack of parental affection. Until she'd left home, heading for the University of Texas in Austin, she hadn't realized that most children didn't get up in the morning unsupervised, get dressed and make breakfast by themselves, without glimpsing an adult, then go off to school without so much as a wave good-bye. She'd learned from the way people talked about their pasts that her own family had qualified way high on the Dysfunctionality Scale.

Her parents had been like ghosts drifting in a ghost world of their own that only intersected with hers in the deep of the night, when long, drunken arguments, pitched low in the wee hours, would ebb and flow through her dreams like a poisonous smoke. But that had only been at first. Later, it was not as good.

When she came home after school, she'd let herself into a dark and empty house. After a makeshift supper scrounged from whatever she could find in the refrigerator, she'd do her homework to the droning accompaniment of the television, then get herself ready for bed. Sometimes her dad would look in on her when he came home, some-times—precious memories—actually kiss her good night.

But an atomic bomb had gone off in the family when she was seven: the simple horror of it was that her mother had killed herself.

To this day, she remembered the moment she'd found her, the strange coolness of the room, the way her hand lay along the bed, soft late sunlight gleaming on the empty skin. She had touched her face, and it had felt like the cool rubber skin on a doll.

In her college psych courses, she'd learned that her mother had been "bipolar," a nicer term than "manic-depressive." But manic-depressive gave a more accurate picture of what life with Mother was all about. There were long, slow storms of weeping, when Sally couldn't comfort her and Daddy stayed away, and the desperation came to seem like a sort of weather, with gray clouds forever.

Then there were the times when, all of a sudden, the sun would come out, and Mother would enter the living room dressed and ready and sing out cheerily, "Sally, let's *go*!" Off they would go to see a movie, assuming there was an old musical at the Texan or a comedy at one of the multiplexes.

Afterward, they always stopped at Baskin-Robbins and had hot fudge sundaes and fed each other and fought over the cherries. Occasionally, while channel surfing late at night, Sally would come across one of the films they'd seen together and her heart would be struck as if by a blow.

One afternoon when her father was away on a business trip, Momma had come into Sally's bedroom and said, "Promise me that if anything happens to me, you'll go next door to the Trumans."

The Trumans were a strange little couple who had built their house themselves. It was a fifties-style box with a flat roof, and they were kind of box-shaped themselves. The house leaned a little to one side. Years later, Sally drove by and noticed it looked sort of okay since the new owners had put on a traditional peaked roof.

That evening, her mother was unusually quiet. When Sally went into her bedroom and called her, then touched her hand, she remained eerily still. Then that other touch, the one that still lived in her fingers and always would, of her cool, lifeless cheek.

She promptly went next door, just as she had been instructed to do. After going over to check on her mother's condition, Mr. Truman got hold of her father, who rushed home. The funeral was held a few days later. Sally could not remember crying. Her father had been polite, shaking hands with family members. And there had been those low voices again, murmuring the incantations of loss that seemed to her a special, secret adult language, a language that meant only one thing: the little girl will now be completely alone. Momma had taken so many sleeping pills that she'd died. To this day, Sally refused to take them, even when the ghosts of the past sobbed in her memories and sleep would not come.

Uncle Ed was her mother's brother. She had begun visiting him in Maryvale during the summers, because her father didn't know what to do with her once school was out. Ed was a lifelong bachelor, but nevertheless he was happy to entertain his little niece for a couple of months every year.

That had been happiness—looked forward to from the moment she had to leave in the fall to the moment she came back after school was out. Then, by the grace of God and the calendar, she would return to her wonderful little room that looked out on the old elm with its squirrels and its mockingbird who would trill on moonlit nights with a sweet demon's fervor.

Maryvale, named by its founder for his long-lost wife. Sort of English-sounding for a Texas place. But so lovely: the Vale of Mary. Orange Indian Blanket swarmed the roadsides, and bluebonnets marched the long valley itself, and on stormy nights, the hills around conversed in their ancient, rumbling tongue.

Her father remarried two years after Mom died, and if

her suicide had been an atomic bomb, this was like opening a flamethrower on the broken little soul that still survived, because her stepmother just plain hated her.

During the courtship, it had been "Oh, Sally, love, come sit over here with me." She'd smelled of Arpege and Camels, and her nails were blood red.

Before the coming of her stepmother, Sally had never doubted she was loved, because children have a hard time doing that, but afterward, she knew what it was to be despised. She'd never been cared for, but her poor momma had certainly loved her—and her dad, too, in his dry and distant way.

Once the new woman entered her world, though, Sally made a horrifying discovery: this was someone who could not be pleased. Suddenly Sally wasn't athletic enough, didn't clean her room well enough, read the wrong kinds of books. Babies poured out of her stepmother like an avalanche, and Sally soon found herself caring for howling twins and a curly haired little boy who understood by the time he was three that this house contained a real-live Cinderella to kick around.

As Sally reached her teens, it became clear that everything would be perfect if she would simply vanish.

She tried to oblige by running away from home. Time and again, she took off from the house, from school, from wherever she happened to be, heading for vaguely imagined nirvanas like the streets of New Orleans or New York or San Francisco, dreaming of passage to India, of the byways of Paris . . . but always ending up in the backseat of a cop car on her way home.

When at last she got her letter of admission to UT, she took off for real and with their full and complete approval.

"Be good," was how they put it. Sentimental to the end.

She never returned home again, not even for Christmas. She tried not to hear the relief in her father's voice when she told him she'd be visiting Uncle Ed for the holidays instead.

The Maryvale exit came up suddenly, and she had to

brake hard to avoid passing it by. She made it though, tires squealing as she turned. Once off the highway, she slowed the car, rolled down the window, and sucked in the country air, rich with summer heat.

That scent, the dry grass of high summer, the faint tang of sweating East Texas pine, filled her with a burst of emotion so powerful and so unexpected that she sobbed. She almost had to stop the car. But there was no way she would do that. She went on down the road, toward the one place in the world that had always treated her well.

Maryvale dribbled along the roadside at first, an abandoned farm here, a working one there. Then came a big metal prefab with a neat new sign on it, "Wilson Stamping." On the door, a smaller sign: "For Lease." Nothing to stamp, apparently.

Then came the true border of Maryvale, the Simpson Funeral Home with its Venetian blinds forever drawn and its hearse in the parking lot, summer heat shivering up from its black metal body.

Then she was in the middle of town.

When she saw the old place again, the first thing she thought was, *Thank God it hasn't changed much.* But how could it? There weren't many local jobs that brought money into town—which was, maybe, just as well. Money changed things, didn't it, making people decide to tear down lovely old buildings and put up ugly new ones in their place? Maryvale's charm had been preserved by its poverty.

The wonderful old courthouse built of red stone, with its crenellated tower and its turrets, still stood right in the cen-

ter of the town square. It was set behind Confederate
Square, a grassy little park that, to Sally's delight, was now
bordered by wonderful beds of roses. A neatly painted sign
had been placed near the flower beds: "Courtesy of the
Maryvale Ladies' Garden Club."

Now, *that* was new. There had been no garden club in
Maryvale in the old days. Must be some new blood in the
old town after all. Darned nice new blood, too.

Small stores with overhanging awnings surrounded
Confederate Square on three sides. Some of them were
alive, but more were boarded up than she remembered
from her childhood bike riding around this square on the
old green Raleigh that belonged to her mother.

The Western Auto where she used to get her flats fixed
was closed, but Flagg's Grocery Market was still function-
ing, and so was Rank's Emporium. Could old Miz Rank
still be running it? She'd sold boots, work clothes, and
things like Rudd's Hog Flush and Horse Liniment, and
anything else that might be needed in a rural community.
Kelsey's drugstore had become a Rite Aid, but she could
still glimpse the dark old interior behind the new orange
and blue plastic front.

There were plenty of signs of life, actually. The town
seemed a little like a stage set, though. For example, the
Dascola Barbershop still had its pole out front, but there
were antiques in the windows where once old Bill Dascola
had held court, and a little girl could sneak a peek at the
latest issue of *True Detective*. The Mode O'Day, which had
once sold frilly dresses for Sunday wear, seemed to have
been transformed into a crafts shop. The window where
headless mannequins had stood in delicate poses was now
full of intricate needlepoint kits.

There was one place that Sally was sure was as un-
changed as Rank's appeared to be. Had to be, or Ed
would've mentioned something about it.

She came to the end of West Front, took a right onto
Main, and there was Cantor's, and boy was it ever totally
the same. The gold lettering in the two broad windows,

"Cantor's Steak and Seafood," was a little more flaked, but the old screen door, still painted dark green, hung at the same exact angle as it had when Sally had come running in to get a Cherry Coke and a slice of pie, or have a hamburger for lunch with Ed.

If her uncle wasn't in his office, he would be there transacting business over coffee. Nothing got decided in Maryvale except over a cup of Cantor's coffee, usually accompanied by a slice of lemon pie topped with meringue so fluffy they called it "cow slobbers."

Even though it was after two, she had decided to stop at Cantor's first, on the theory that it was the most likely place to find Ed at any hour.

She nosed her car into the high curb, got out, stretched her back, then stepped up onto the raised sidewalk and put her hand on the door. The sun blazed down. Cicadas cried in the big old live oak behind the restaurant. From the dark interior there came the clink of dishes and the murmur of conversation.

As soon as she pushed back the screen, she could feel the attention of every person in the place zoom right in on her. The murmur abruptly ceased. She entered, and there was the long black lunch counter against the back wall, the red vinyl booths under the windows, and the tables standing between, each a four-top, all set with glass salt and pepper shakers and sugar dispensers—and now, also, little white boats of NutraSweet packets.

And men, men in straw Stetsons and boots, in western shirts, in T-shirts, even a few in white shirts and ties, guys from over at the courthouse.

Not only was she a stranger, she was the only woman in the place—aside from Beatrice the waitress, who looked like she'd had a pretty rough battle with gravity, which had flattened her feet and pulled her bosom practically down to her waist. How many miles had Bee walked on this floor, over what must now be at least thirty years?

Many of the men sitting at the tables looked vaguely familiar to her, but nobody recognized her, that was clear, not now that she was grown up.

She hadn't seen Ed in so long she was afraid they might not know each other anymore, either. But when she saw a tall man push his chair back and stand up, she knew it was him right away, and ran over and threw her arms around his neck.

He pulled away awkwardly, as soon as he could. She'd forgotten how formal he could be. "Sally, I didn't expect you so soon. I'm sorry I wasn't back in the office yet." He introduced her to his friends who were sitting around the table. "Gentlemen, this is my niece, Sally Hopkins." His courtly Texas manners hadn't changed one bit.

The two other men at the table rose to their feet. Sally could see by the cowboy boots they wore under their suit pants that they were in the only business that meant something in this part of the world—the buying and selling of livestock, trading in feed and seed. Their weathered faces told her they led hard lives.

After a few polite phrases, they prepared to take their leave. "Think about our talk and get back to me, will you?" one of them murmured to Ed. There were handshakes all around, then suddenly they were gone.

Sally was brimming with enthusiasm. "It's so good to see you again, Uncle Ed."

He looked after the two men. "I'm never gonna sell my place," he murmured.

"Oh, no, Ed, never do that!"

He laughed. "I'm glad to see you too, darlin'. Just real glad! Have you had any lunch yet?"

Sally remembered the awful hamburger she'd thrown down her gullet two hours ago when she took a fifteen-minute break at a drive-in. So far, her stomach had refused to deal with it, and it was still sitting there, solid as a brick. "I couldn't eat anything right now. Tell me how you've been."

"Oh, I've been fine, just fine. But let's talk about you.

What made you decide to come down here to visit us poor folks?"

Sally started to explain again that she wasn't coming to visit, but to stay. Ed seemed to read her mind. "I sure am glad to have you, Sally, but what kind of life can you make for yourself in a little town like Maryvale?"

After signaling to Beatrice to bring them coffee, he went on. "There's nobody much in town anymore, except poor, uneducated folks living in trailers, with nothing to do but drive out to buy beer at the 7-Eleven. On weekends we got the city folks visiting their 'ranches,' who like to poke through the shops looking for antiques."

According to Ed, catering to these city folks had become the main industry in Maryvale, far more important than livestock. The antiques in the windows of the cute little shops had sat in the living rooms of generations of Maryvale natives, until they sold off their old homesteads to folks from Houston. Once they found themselves living in a double-wide, they also found there was no room for grandpa's big old rocker.

"They ain't real sad about it, though," Ed said, with a wink. "Those trailers are a blessing—easy to clean, and they even come complete with furniture and curtains. All you got to do is grab your TV and move on in."

Sally felt an evil little prickle at the back of her mind: she wasn't sure she'd fit in here. Ed saw her worried look, and changed the subject. "Come on back to the office," he said cheerfully, "and we'll see about that job."

They strolled out to Sally's car and she gave him a lift back to the sheriff's office. He always walked to Cantor's, which must have been what kept him so lean, since she had never seen him participate in any sort of exercise or organized sport.

As they drove along, Sally realized that she was looking at her uncle with adult eyes, really, for the first time. She wondered if the citizens of Maryvale kept electing him because he projected such a perfect image of a small-town sheriff. His shirt had pearl snaps instead of buttons, and he wore a string tie. His slim khaki pants were flared at the bottom, so they flowed past the tops of his boots without a break. He didn't neglect his headgear, either—he wore a felt Stetson during the cold months and switched to a straw one in the summer, like now.

She had never seen him wear jeans on the job; in his world, jeans were reserved for ranchers. Professional men only wore them on weekends, when inspecting their purebreds or mucking out the barn. His craggy gray eyebrows completed the picture perfectly, giving him the look of someone who'd just stepped out of a western movie.

As they strolled into the police station together past the dusty receptionist's desk, he checked to see if he had any messages. The town budget didn't allow for a receptionist these days, but everyone who wanted to contact Ed knew to leave a note on the desk for him.

She looked at him affectionately as he leaned back in his chair and put his boots up on his desk in what had always been his "thinking position."

"I've arranged for you to take a room for now at Elizabeth Lerman's house. It's only a couple of blocks from here."

Sally nodded, trying to hide her surprise. She'd assumed she would stay in her old room at Ed's house. Being a boarder in some strange woman's house wasn't part of her daydream. But she forced herself to shut up and keep listening.

"Elizabeth's a psychologist who grew up here. You may remember her. She's come back home to practice after her divorce. She lived in Houston for a while too, so I thought you two might get along."

So she was about to be thrown together with the town's other middle-aged female failure.

Before she could protest, Ed moved on to a more interesting subject. "The truth is, I need you here in Maryvale, Sally. Some things have been going on for the past six months that I don't know how to cope with."

Now it came. Was she ready? Of course she was. She kept the smile out of her voice as she asked, "Like what?"

"Well, nothing real serious. Lots of little disturbances, you might say. The trouble is, we can't find out who's doin' 'em. People's pets—dogs and cats—have been found tortured and killed—maybe two or three a month. You can imagine how riled our city folk get when they come out to their country place and find their pedigreed dog strung up from a tree with its genitals cut off."

So much for any sort of a smile in her voice, and boy, was that ever not a Maryvale kind of a problem. She listened to the alarm bells it set ringing in her mind and did not like them, not one bit. She grasped at a straw: "Maybe it's kids from Houston. City kids acting out their resentment at being forced to vacation in a little one-horse town instead of Cancun or somewhere."

Ed sighed. "I wish I thought so. But a lot of these things have happened on weekdays, when our part-timers aren't around. I expect one of the motives is jealousy."

"Local trailer trash envy the rich folks' cars and stereos, so they kill their pets?"

"That's my theory."

She suspected he had more to say, but there was no rushing Ed. She waited, careful to leave the line slack on the water of conversation.

"We've had fires too—abandoned shacks burned down, then a barn and now old Mrs. Crew's little house. That was done while she was away at the hospital, which was real mean. She had to go live with her sister when she came out."

She felt sick inside. But she asked, "A youth gang?"

"Nah, I'd know. They'd be parading around, showing their colors."

Sally nodded. He was more up-to-date than she'd thought.

But he wasn't up on everything. Animal torture and arson were two of the three signs of "the unholy trinity," indications that a seriously disturbed person was out there. These monsters are created by repeated cruelty and sexual abuse throughout their childhoods. The third sign of the trinity is wetting the bed, which, Sally had to admit, would be a tough one for the sheriff to check out.

"You've got trouble all right," she said. "It's likely that one person, probably an adolescent, is doing all of those things. You've got to catch him before he grows up and moves on to a higher level."

"What happens then?"

"Well, that's when he quits torturing dogs and starts in on people."

Ed's eyes widened, then his lips became a tight line. "You're full of all those ideas they stuffed into you at that university."

"You don't understand, Ed. These are cries for attention. There's someone out there who can't help himself."

"Don't tell a man who's been sheriff as long as I have that he doesn't understand criminals! *Everybody* can help himself. I've got to believe that, Sally, or I couldn't continue in law enforcement."

"Not these guys. They can't help themselves and they can't stop." Ed's face got darker. She could see that he was bottling up a powerful reaction. She'd never seen him angry, but she thought he was now. She thought he didn't want to hear one more word of this. She needed to back off, here. He was not ready for this. "Look," she said carefully, "some of them get it out of their systems and stop all by themselves, usually before you can find out who they are. You're left wondering who did those awful things. Was it the postman? That nice young man at the convenience store?" She shook her head. "We can hope for that. And if we don't get it, then I can handle this, Ed. I can catch this guy."

He looked sick, now, his face ashen. He opened his mouth, then snapped it closed as if thinking better of what he was about to say. Then he leaned forward, stared straight at her. "OK, Sally, if you think you can take care of it, then just damn well do it!" Then he smiled, as if apologizing for his outburst.

She concluded that he wanted to dump it in her lap and forget it. And that was fine with Sally, since she needed a job. But she hoped she was up to it, because she hadn't told him the truth. She'd said what she needed to say, to calm him down. She had no idea how to investigate a crime.

The truth was that psychopaths like the kind she suspected was at large in Maryvale generally didn't ever stop. Oh, they might pause for a while, sometimes even for years, but they always struck again eventually. And during that second wave, their targets were almost always human.

But Maryvale was a small town, a tiny town, really, if you didn't count the newcomers. It would be easy to drive around and check everybody out if you knew what you were looking for. It might be hard to catch a serial killer in Houston, but surely she could spot the culprit here before things got to that final stage. And when she found him, she would make sure to get him the kind of serious psychiatric help he needed. Yes, there was definitely a place for her here.

"I'd like to go meet Elizabeth now, so I can unpack and settle in."

"Sure thing, darlin'. Get your car and follow me."

Elizabeth was not the bitter, failed city girl that Sally had expected. She'd pictured a rail-thin woman, lips pursed in permanent disappointment, sucking cigarette after cigarette and crying in her heart.

Instead, she was plump and soft, like a comfortable couch. There was an openness to her smile that suggested that she'd been out of the city for quite a while. You felt as if you could curl up on her broad and cushioned lap like a purring cat and never have to worry about anything ever again.

Appealing though all this was to another woman, Sally could understand why she'd had marriage trouble. Guys liked their females slim and coltish these days. They only appreciated Elizabeth's sort of beauty after they finally returned home from the dating wars, beaten down and ready to retire. Until then, they required a companion who got looks of envy from the other guys when you took her out to the local wine bar. Sally had plenty of friends who had been dumped by men like that. She'd escaped only because she had never gotten attached in the first place.

Elizabeth, it turned out, had come back to Maryvale after her father died and she had inherited the little house
she'd grown up in. "I never thought I'd see this place again
after my parents were gone," she told Sally. "I was so
bored here when I was growing up. I thought my life in
Houston was working out perfectly, just like I'd always
dreamed it would. Even after my divorce, I was still coping
fine. I had a good profession, lots of friends, and an active
cultural life." She smiled wryly.

Sally's own East Texas background told her the hidden
meaning behind that smile. Words like that, coming out of
the mouth of an understated East Texas lady, actually
meant that she'd had a walloping good sex life.

Sadness followed the smile, though, and Sally knew,
also, that there was a lot more to Elizabeth's story.

She continued, her voice lilting with the soft, deceptive
music of the South. "Then I found out I couldn't sell this
house. Nobody from Houston wants to live in a little place
like this, so close to town. None of the locals wanted it either. Then all of a sudden I realized I wanted to come back
home more than anything else in the world."

A surprisingly familiar story. Ed was no fool. He'd chosen Sally's new roommate better than Sally ever could
have, by herself.

She glanced around the living room, which was tiny if
measured by modern standards. There was barely enough
room for a small sofa and matching chair. Elizabeth had
pushed a scuffed old coffee table close to the couch so you
could put your feet up on it. A TV was in the corner and
next to it was a bookcase crammed with well-worn paper-
backs. Familiar psychology texts lined the shelves, inter-
spersed with heavily read romances.

The walls were made of the old-fashioned kind of plaster that builders used before the invention of sheetrock. In
those days, walls stayed where they were put. An alcove
had been carved in the hall especially for that newfangled
contraption called the telephone, with just enough room
beside it for a straight-backed wooden chair. Phone calls

were still a luxury in the days when this house was built, and since you wouldn't be talking long, there was no need to get comfortable. Your neighbors were probably listening in on the party line, anyway. Real gossip was conducted in person, over homemade cookies and cups of coffee.

The windows were small so as not to let in too much hot Texas sun. This gave the house a restful, cavelike atmosphere, so different from the harsh, sun-filled rooms that had become popular with the advent of air-conditioning. A table fan blew the warm air around listlessly. For Sally, being here was like traveling back in time, to a safe place that existed long before evil stepmothers, worthless boyfriends, and useless jobs had started shadowing her life like a flock of buzzards.

This was a good beginning, for sure. She couldn't wait to find out what the rest of the house looked like. Trying not to seem too eager, she picked up her bags and headed upstairs.

"Your room's the one on the right!" Elizabeth called after her.

The windows in her room were hung with sheer white ruffled curtains tied back at the corners, the same kind Sally would have chosen. There was a quiet here, a peace, even, that drew her to the bed.

She lay down on the chenille bedspread and closed her eyes, just for a second. The world drifted on a gentle tide of warm summer air and the lazy calling of the cicadas in the tree outside. She told herself to get up and not just fall asleep on this nice lady. She had to work out living arrangements with Elizabeth, had to get a key, had to learn about her kitchen privileges. She didn't even know how much rent she was being charged, for God's sake.

Later, when Elizabeth leaned into the room just far enough to switch off the lamp on the dresser, Sally didn't even hear her . . . or know that it was already sunset, that two hours had passed in her new life, in the form of deep and renewing sleep.

When Sally woke up, it was as if she'd landed on another planet. She was still dressed, still lying on the bed-spread. At first, she couldn't believe that it was morning. She sat up into a chorus of mockingbirds and cardinals celebrating the new day.

Shocked at just how deeply she had slept, and how impossibly long, she showered and got some clean clothes out of her suitcase, a pretty pink blouse from Lands' End and some black slacks. Not very country and very wrinkled, but she couldn't do a whole lot better at the moment, and it ought to be conservative enough to pass Ed's muster when she reported for duty.

She went downstairs feeling more than a bit bashful. Elizabeth, who was sitting at the kitchen table over a big mug of coffee, laughed and told her to help herself to the refrigerator. Sally had been used to staking out her own territory in the refrigerator and kitchen cabinets. Once she had even drawn smiley faces on her eggs so her gluttonous roommate, who was always on a new diet, wouldn't dump them into the frying pan and then pretend not to know what happened to them.

"I hate silly fights," declared Elizabeth, when Sally told her about it. "We're both professional women who can afford to treat each other to a yogurt now and then. Whoever gets home first and feels like cooking can make enough dinner for both of us. If one of us doesn't make it home, half of whatever gets made can be eaten as leftovers the next day. I only cook dishes that make good leftovers, anyway. Some foods, like meat loaf, are even better after being left in the refrigerator overnight.

"Whoever's in a domestic mood can shop. If you do the shopping, you get to buy the kind of junk food you like, but you have to make sure there's always Coca-Cola in the house. Don't ever drink up the last can. And don't get me any of that diet stuff, either—it tastes like rubber."

Now came the big question: "Who cleans the house?"

"Don't worry, honey. Mrs. Fernandez takes care of that. It's included in your room rate. She'll iron for you too if you slip her a little extra now and then. As for washing, there's a washer and drier in the basement. They're museum pieces, but they work great. It's dark and damp as a cave down there so be careful not to slip on the steps." She smiled. "Last but not least, I make a fair cup of coffee."

As she got a mug out of the old-fashioned glass-fronted kitchen cabinet that hung above the long drain board beside the sink, Sally considered that maybe she'd died and gone to heaven. Elizabeth's speech had been more than a set of instructions. It came from a deeply noncompetitive place, and for the first time in a much longer time than she'd realized, she felt free from same-sex competition. Elizabeth's house was an all-girl world, reminding Sally of those blessed days before the Houston roommate wars.

After Elizabeth had dressed and hurried out to her office, Sally sat at the kitchen table and finished off the rest of the coffee. She rummaged in the cupboard and found a box of cereal that was way too sweet for her taste, but the milk was fresh, so she was able to make breakfast out of it.

She washed up the dishes, including the ones Elizabeth had left in the sink, then made her way upstairs to freshen up before reporting for duty at the sheriff's office.

On her way out, Sally couldn't resist peeking into Elizabeth's room. It was the biggest of the two bedrooms and had clearly once belonged to her parents. Framed baby pictures still lined the walls, including studio portraits of a rosy-cheeked little girl who was obviously Elizabeth at various stages of development. The gaudy old wallpaper was both striped and flowered, lending a feminine feel to the room. There was something kind of amazing about just how intact this house was. It could have been a time capsule. It was nice, too, very nice. The past had known how to bring peace to a home.

She knew she shouldn't, but she peered in deeper, until she could see into the closet. It looked like Elizabeth had a serious weakness when it came to shoes. There were at least forty pairs in there, most of them hopelessly impractical high heels in colors like fuchsia and lime-green, stashed in a shoe holder that looked custom-made. Did Elizabeth lead some kind of very different life that required sophisticated shoes like that? Maybe she drove up to Houston and club-hopped.

It was a strange, discordant note.

On the bedside table was another surprise: a framed snapshot of a young boy. Elizabeth must have a son. Funny that neither she nor Ed had mentioned this. Her divorce wasn't a secret, so why had she left out this child?

She looked into the bathroom, tempted by the medicine cabinet. But no, that was just plain too nosy. She turned and, feeling actually a little proud of herself, left the bathroom.

It was time to start her first working day with Ed, and if she didn't leave right this minute, that day would start late. Ed was a stickler on time, always had been. You could call him easygoing, but he had always kept to a schedule.

When she stepped outside, she was greeted by a beautiful blue sky, scattered with the lacy white clouds they'd called "mare's tails" when she was a kid. She decided that she'd found her future here, almost certainly. Sure, she'd had to go back to her own past to do it, but maybe that wasn't such a bad thing, after all.

4

It was a nice, brisk walk from Elizabeth's house to the sheriff's office, so she could avoid wear and tear on the Camry.

When she turned the corner and saw the new sheriff's office again, Sally stopped and just stared. It was a squat, flat-roofed structure made of cinder blocks painted green. There was gold lettering on the glass front door: "Mary-vale County Sheriff's Department." On the wall beside the door was a brass plaque with the county seal on it. Out front, the Lone Star flag of Texas snapped in the morning breeze. Somewhere inside, there'd be an American flag, probably in Ed's office. Official Texas showed the local colors first, always.

The old office had been wood, with tall windows and an Old West appearance that made it look like it had been moved straight from Dodge City. If the newcomers had had anything to say about it, that old wreck probably would have stayed. But she suspected Ed probably loved the new place, dreary and sterile though it was. He'd see it as a sign of "progress," whatever that might mean around here.

Inside, the walls were a darker green—sure enough, it was the same hateful color that covers the interiors of public buildings everywhere in Texas, the same color she'd run away from in Houston.

Uncle Ed's office was the last door on the right, with the words "Sheriff, Maryvale County" stenciled on the frosted glass window.

Well, here we go. She raised her hand, made a fist, tapped lightly on the glass. The response was immediate, "Come on in."

As Sally entered, she noted that he was in the exact same position he'd been in the day before, with his long legs stretched out, his boots up on the desk.

The instant she appeared, he went into action. His feet hit the floor with a bang and he unfolded from his chair. He stood up to greet her, all six lanky feet of him.

"Hi there, darlin', have a good night?"

"Ed, I slept from four in the afternoon until an hour ago!"

"You did look kinda all-in. Did you get a chance to say hello to Elizabeth before you crashed and burned?"

"I sure did, Ed. Elizabeth is wonderful. Thanks for sending me to her."

"Well, I knew she could use the income and I thought you two would have a lot in common. Maybe she can help you get adjusted to little town life again, if that's really what you want."

"I don't know what I want, Ed. I'm just going to try to see what works for me right now."

"Well, we can surely find something for you to do around here."

"That problem you mentioned certainly needs attention, Ed."

He looked embarrassed. "I was wondering if you could start off by doing a little paperwork for me. We've got so many federal and state forms to fill out these days. I'm afraid I've gotten somewhat behind."

She was rather stunned. She'd expected to come in here and start dealing with an urgent situation, a serial killer in the making. "Every social worker is an expert at filling out government forms," she said carefully.

"Great!" He sounded terribly relieved and Sally soon saw why. It looked like he'd been "somewhat behind" for a good six months. The stack of papers to be dealt with was so big he couldn't pick it up without individual sheets escaping and fluttering down to the floor. As Sally bent over to retrieve them, she felt panic. This was insane, to ask her to waste her time on this when there was somebody out there who could turn into a killer at any moment.

Ed gave her a sheepish sort of a look. "I thought you could work at the reception desk out front. That way you can get to know all my deputies and the state cops, as well as anybody who comes in with a problem."

So that was it. Unholy trinity or not, Sally was slated to become the new receptionist.

Very different from yesterday, and a sort of false note. Very false note. Yesterday, he'd wanted to dump the whole problem on her. Now he seemed to want to keep her away from it, in fact, to bury her in busy work. With this mess to face, she wasn't even going to be able to spend her days chewing gum and filing her fingernails, like her predecessors undoubtedly had. Nope, she was going to use her master's degree to wade through stacks of forms while answering the phone and expressing sympathy to people who came in to report a lost dog.

"Shall I make the coffee in the morning too?" she asked sweetly, hoping he'd notice her ironic tone.

"Thanks, sweetie, but there's no need to do that," he replied, "I always get here about eight, so I put the first pot on. You could see that a fresh one gets made later on, though. I'm sure the boys would appreciate it."

She wasn't getting through to him. She tried again. "Aren't there any other women here, besides me?" She managed to use that sugary southern tone again, but she knew she couldn't keep it up much longer.

"Not right now. We have a state mandate, like everyone else—we have to hire more women and African-

Americans. But there are never any applicants, so you're it for us."

So she was slated to fill another role as well: the token femme. But she also realized that the gulf between Houston and Maryvale was incredibly wide, and she loved Uncle Ed too much to try to educate him after all these years. She'd play her assigned part for now, and maybe he would eventually realize that a woman's professional opinion could be worth taking seriously.

Trying hard to unpurse her lips and plaster a smile on them, she went out to the lobby and used a paper towel to dust off the steel receptionist's desk. She sat down, stared across the bleak lobby toward the doors. Then she picked up the phone, just to be sure it had a dial tone. Ed came in with the forms, and dropped them on her desk with all of the indifference of a postman on his rounds. As she stared at them, he said, "I gotta leave now, hon. Wouldn't you know, there's been another animal mutilation."

Then he turned and strode out. "Let me go with you, I can help!" she called, but before she could run after him, the door had swung closed.

Before her were the forms. She silently mouthed a curse, then snatched the first one off the stack. County of Maryvale, Department of Animal Control. Wonderful, a skunk under a house, sheriff's department called to remove.

Forty-five minutes later, she was still separating the hateful forms into piles. She looked up in relief when the front door opened, but it wasn't a case at all, but one of the four state troopers assigned to Maryvale County. His black plastic name tag identified him as Rob Farley and he was handsome in a hick sort of way. He was also spit and polish neat, with straight creases pressed into his uniform pants. He wore his hair in a military-style buzz cut and had given himself a shave so close, his cheeks looked polished.

"Where's Ed?" he asked abruptly. "He called and said he wanted some help, but he's gone off the air."

"I'm afraid I don't know where he went," Sally said. "He told me he was checking out a new animal mutilation. I didn't get a chance to find out any details." Although Trooper Farley didn't seem too interested, she decided to introduce herself, anyway. "I'm his niece, Sally Hopkins, by the way. I'll be working here as his assistant."

This made him pause long enough to notice her, but all he said was, "Aren't you supposed to be the new reception-ist around here? It's your job to know where everyone is so we can touch base when necessary."

"I am *not* the new receptionist!" she flared. "I'm only using this desk to sort out some forms."

He turned around and tramped out without another word. Sally found his military bearing amusing because according to the forms she'd been reading, in Maryvale a state trooper's job consisted mainly of issuing speeding tickets.

She had discovered that traffic fines must be one of the main sources of Maryvale's revenue. Visitors who neg-lected to slow down to twenty-five immediately after exit-ing the highway would find a trooper waiting for them just around the corner.

Sally imagined that the city folks in their Explorers and Land Rovers probably bitched like crazy and said they could prove the local pickup trucks hardly ever got tick-eted, but no one would be able to convince the county judge that such discrimination existed. Although their property taxes were much appreciated, city folks couldn't vote in the local elections, so they might as well be talking to themselves.

She could see from the forms she was sorting that the troopers performed other vitally important duties—like rounding up stray dogs, for example, mostly in response to angry phone calls from the same people who got all the speeding tickets. These folks would drive up for the week-end and find that their trash cans had been tipped over and their expensive new bushes sprayed during some wild doggy orgy that had taken place while they were away. Of course, the county was full of strays because they'd been left behind by other visitors, summer pets abandoned.

Another job assigned to the troopers was to knock on the doors of people who liked to play their music too loud. It looked like at least five different complaints had to be lodged before this happened, however. Again, the newcomers were the only ones who ever complained, because the locals figured it was more neighborly to live and let live, and simply turned up the volume on their own TV until it was loud enough to drown out the annoyance. If that didn't work, though, then they'd take another sort of neighborly step. They'd get out their shotgun and shoot a few holes in the offender's tires. That sort of solution generated a few police reports, too.

Sally suspected that they also assumed it was safer to look the other way when it came to "domestic disturbances." Folks would crouch down in their living rooms when the shouting and screaming began next door, in case any bullets came flying through the windows, but it was generally felt that what went on between a husband and wife was their own business.

If the screaming went on too long, the troopers were sometimes called. Sally guessed that this was definitely not the kind of call a guy was eager to take. Some crazed husband might be likely to shoot you if you knocked on his door at the wrong time, when all he'd been planning to do was shoot his wife.

As a kid, Sally had never thought much of the troopers, but from the forms, she could see that a couple of times a year, they were called on to do something important. Once, an escaped death-row inmate had headed this way, and they'd had to borrow bloodhounds from a neighboring town to search for him. A couple of times a retarded child or an addled old husband had wandered off and they'd dropped everything for those searches, too.

Once, an out-of-work citizen had gotten so desperate, he'd holed up inside his trailer and threatened to kill himself and everyone else in there unless he finally got a hearing. Rob Farley was the one who had sweated it out with him.

She eventually did manage to make some headway on

the pounds of paper in front of her. She located some phone numbers on the forms and sat through what seemed like hours of canned music until she reached a human being who grudgingly answered a few questions.

By the time Ed and Rob got back to the office, she had a pile of forms filled in and ready for Ed's signature, with a stamped, addressed envelope clipped to the back of each one. She spread them proudly across the desk in a dramatic display. The look of relief on Ed's face when he saw them almost made her morning worthwhile. The two men headed straight back to the sheriff's office. Sally followed them, eager to find out what was going on.

Rob poured out coffee for all of them, and the two men filled her in on the latest animal torture. Suzette had been Suzanne Chesterton's prized blue point Siamese. Suzanne was a local painter who had loved her kitty dearly. She had become hysterical and called the police when she returned home from grocery shopping that morning to find it hanging by its neck from a tree limb in her backyard.

Ed explained, "Suzanne is from the city, but she's been living in Maryvale full-time for a couple of years now." It turned out that once she had established herself as a permanent resident, a lot of things that hadn't bothered her before began to seem terribly important, such as the woman's screams she heard coming from the house next door.

"Suzanne's daddy had tried to buy that land years ago, so they could have a larger garden and more privacy, but it was left in a will to ten kids who couldn't stand the sight of each other, and none of them could stop hating the others long enough to sign the papers.

"Finally one day, without asking anyone's permission, the oldest son, Hank Sunderland, brought in a back hoe and scraped off the old family home, along with a big ol' weeping willow and three rusty trucks. He built himself a ranch house." Sally could picture it, covered in pastel aluminum siding, which was probably already beginning to stain, with a dirt driveway running straight out to the road from the shiny white plastic garage doors. "It don't seem to matter to Hank that he only owns a share in the land," Ed said. "He figured nobody in his family could afford to hire a lawyer all by themselves, and they'd never get along well enough to hire one together. Meanwhile, he has a nice place to live."

"Yeah," said Sally, "a place where he could beat up his wife in peace—until Suzanne started sticking her nose into his business."

To Sally's surprise, Rob seemed upset by her remark, but Ed plowed on. "Suzanne thinks Hank killed her cat to get even with her for all her noise complaints. The troopers told her they had never let on to Hank that she was the one causing all the fuss, but she says Hank could have figured it out for himself."

Rob took up the narrative. He had caught up with Ed at Suzanne's house, and they had both tried to explain to her that they couldn't just go next door and arrest Hank Sunderland until they had some proof he'd done it. She vowed to press charges and demanded that a trooper be stationed outside her house twenty-four hours a day. Rob said, "I told her we didn't have the manpower for that, and Ed suggested that she get a big dog and a shotgun, but that just seemed to upset her more."

Ed suddenly said, "Rob, we should hand this problem over to Sally. That's what I hired her for."

"What could she do about it?" He sounded genuinely curious. This was her cue.

"I was a social worker in Houston. Ed told me about the pet killings yesterday and I pointed out that we can assume, based on statistics, that one sick individual is doing them all."

Rob squinted at her. "And what exactly is it you'd be looking for?"

"The signs—the trinity," Ed broke in. "She said he'd be a bed wetter, for one thing."

Rob snorted. "So will you start by interviewing every mother in town, asking who had problems toilet training their kids?"

It was time to defend herself. "These crimes are being committed by someone who has been seriously abused all his life."

"Beaten up, you mean? We've got plenty of that, although most folks around here would call it discipline."

"I'm talking about adults having sex with kids."

"Sexual abuse? I've never heard of any of that around here. And wouldn't it be the kind of thing that's more likely to happen to a girl? I can't picture a female committing a crime this brutal. This is the kind of thing done by a gang of teenagers who've been watching too many horror films."

To her surprise, Ed cut him off. "Rob, I really want to pass this one on to Sally—at least for now."

Sally waited breathlessly until Rob finally agreed. "I guess she might as well give it a try." He didn't sound very enthusiastic.

After Rob climbed into his pickup truck for the drive home, Ed hitched up his belt and said, "Well, Sally, that's done. What do you say we amble on over to Cantor's for lunch? They always have pot roast on Thursday. A big meal like that'll last me until breakfast time tomorrow. That's something to consider when you're a bachelor like me."

"Great!" Sally replied. "We can drop off these forms at the post office on the way." She headed for her desk.

"Uh, Sally—don't you think you ought to wash the coffee cups before we go? If you leave dirty ones around, they attract bugs."

Sally was careful to keep a smile on her face as she filled up the bathroom sink with suds and dunked the cups.

Despite being used as a maid, she felt happy because she was now certain of her ground. The cat killing, with its ritual overtones, proved it. Somebody in this town was wandering out in those vast pine woods, dreaming of death. And it was likely he'd move on to killing women sooner or later.

Unless she missed her guess, the killer had been fantasizing about his first victim for some time now. Maryvale didn't know it, but this was a community hanging by a thread.

No matter how she was treated, she couldn't abandon them now.

In afternoon heat so intense it was like a thing alive, Sally drove over to Pinewoods Lane to interview Suzanne Chesterton. She planned to talk with Hank Sunderland, too. She would be very surprised to find out that it was him, but you never knew.

In the back of her mind was the knowledge that some serial killers start quite late in life, in their thirties and forties. No matter, it always came down to the same thing: dead women.

Maybe talking with an unfamiliar female, instead of a man he'd known for years, would unnerve him enough to get him to reveal something.

The long Chesterton driveway was no more imposing than those of the other ranches, harking back to a time when even rich Texans took a dim view of flaunting it. But when she came around a bend, she found something she hadn't expected: an electronic security gate.

"This is Sally Hopkins," she said into the speaker.

"Excuse me?" came the tinny reply, in a pleasant-sounding but very worried female voice.

After the high-tech gadgetry she'd had to go through to get in, Sally had been ready for the sort of French provincial mansion that in Houston was known as a faux château. Instead, she found herself driving up to a very attractive old ranch house built in classic Craftsman style, with an inviting wraparound front porch.

A short distance away was a barn that Sally guessed had been fitted up as an art studio, since air-conditioning compressors hugged its sides. Not even the rich around here spent good money to cool down their cows.

Suzanne Chesterton was standing out on the porch when Sally drove up. She was a lovely woman about Sally's age, with blond hair pulled back and wide eyes that, right now, eloquently communicated hurt and fear.

"You've got incredible security up here, for such a little house," Sally said as she got out.

"I know it seems excessive," Suzanne admitted. "Daddy was terrified of kidnappers when we were kids. Now that I'm living here alone, he's glad he did it."

She held the screen door wide, and Sally walked into a cool, flowered interior. The upholstery and curtains were made of flowered chintz in shades of pink and mint-green. There was matching wallpaper. Sally guessed that no males had lived here for a good long while. Suzanne had created a beautiful hideaway. But no way was it a guy place, not by a very long shot. There was even a scent of lavender in the air.

"Care for a lemonade? It's fresh-squeezed."

Of course, it would be. Suzanne wasn't the type to serve the powdered variety.

Sally accepted gratefully. From where she sat, she could see Suzanne adding a sprig of mint to each glass, before she brought them in from the newly remodeled open kitchen on a wicker tray.

Sally had brushed up against this type of woman one too many times in Houston, and was prepared to dislike her. She would be self-involved and into instant gratification. There was likely to be a burned-out husband in her past, too. At least she didn't appear to be bottle blond—her hair color looked real.

Sally sipped her drink, letting the mint brush her nose so she could suck up the smell. "No one comes up here now but you?"

Suzanne nodded. "This was our family's country house in the old days, but Mother and Daddy live at Hilton Head. My sister married a Wilbraham."

"Ah. Meaning?"

"She lives in Boston, of course."

There were subtle signals here that Sally wasn't picking up. Oh, well, better get straight to the point. "With a security system like this, I don't see how a cat killer got in here in the first place. I assume you have the doors and windows alarmed?"

"Oh, yes, and there's a glass breakage detector and a motion detector, set high enough so the cat wouldn't set it off, and a heat detector and a smoke alarm that's carbon monoxide sensitive. Everything reports automatically to a central station. The phone automatically dials out when any of the alarms go off." She smiled sadly. "None of that helped, since Suzette was killed when she was out in the yard this morning, while I was away buying groceries. I installed a cat door so she could go in and out on her own."

"Why do you suspect Hank?"

"Because of all the security—it had to be him. No one could have gotten around the gate while I was away, since somebody has to be home to buzz them in. It had to be someone who could sneak over here on foot."

"Lots of folks could do that. They'd drive up to the gate, then climb over the fence and walk the rest of the way."

"Yes, but since when was there a Maryvaler born who would walk a quarter mile if they didn't have to? And they would risk being discovered when I came back. Also, Hank can look out his window and see me leaving, so he knows when the coast is clear."

This did not look good for Hank Sunderland. Sally shuddered, imagining him over there staring at this house, turning over in his mind how he would kill this woman, working up his courage.

"Tell me more about Hank."

"A mean little redneck with the brain of a cabbage and the disposition of a scorpion."

"No redeeming qualities?"

"Well, he's patriotic, in the sense that he displays a Confederate flag decal in the back window of his pickup. I think his hobby is crumpling up beer cans and tossing them out the window of that truck into my property. He makes a living doing a few odd jobs here and there." She paused, frowning. "When I've had him over here to fix a few things, he's always been nice and respectful. I was never afraid of him, not in the least, until I started hearing the screams."

Sally sat up and listened carefully. She was coming to the important part of the story.

"He got married last summer to a local girl, very sweet, very East Texas, just made to spend her life behind the counter at a McDonald's or somewhere like that. In fact, before she was married, I used to see her there when I went in for coffee."

This made Sally smile. No women she'd ever known would admit buying anything at McDonald's but coffee—herself included. Truth be told, she didn't even know what McDonald's coffee tasted like, but she could tell you all about the fries and the exact taste sensation of a Big Mac with double cheese. "I love their coffee, too," she said.

Suzanne laughed a little, as if she recognized their shared secret.

"Tell me about the screams."

"They started late at night, mostly during the weekends. At first I thought they had the TV turned up too loud. I couldn't believe sounds like that could be coming from a real person, not an actress. Later, I realized it was that poor woman. Glynesse."

Sally tried not to get too worked up. She found men like Hank utterly loathsome. And as for their women—how could they allow themselves to be beaten up? If this went no further, she still vowed that she would not rest until Glynesse Sunderland was in a battered women's program. And if the county didn't have one, she'd start it herself.

"I started calling the troopers almost every night."

"Trooper Farley?"

"Whichever one was on duty! I couldn't let that kind of abuse continue next door without doing something about it. I called the County Social Service number and guess who I got—Ed! I might as well have been calling the moon."

"Until an abused wife agrees to give evidence, there's nothing any agency can do about it. Usually the cops don't get involved until she's dead on the kitchen floor."

"Well, I certainly complained to the sheriff. I let him have an earful, and I demanded action. That woman sounded like she was being killed! I figure Hank found out it was me and got even by killing Suzette." Her eyes filled with tears. "I feel like a real fool, crying about a cat while a human being is being tortured next door. But I'm all alone out here and that sweet little cat was such good company. I will miss her, very truly."

And there, in that last sentence, was the music of the South coming out, in the soft accent that was special to East Texas people, and the gentleness that characterized the best of them. Sally decided to forgive Suzanne her upper-crust ways. She couldn't help being rich, and her suffering was very real. So, she suspected, was her danger.

"Please understand, Suzanne, I'm on your side," Sally said. "But maybe you ought to follow the sheriff's suggestion and get yourself a watchdog. It'll warn you if anyone comes near the house, and it takes a brave man to kill a big dog. Hank'll probably head right back over that fence, once he hears the first bark. A man who beats up a woman isn't what I would call brave."

"Maybe I will get a dog. But I'm not going to get a gun! I don't believe in that."

"I'm not going to encourage you to. There are too many guns around Maryvale as it is." She hesitated. She needed to take this to another level. "I'm not just here about Suzette," she said carefully, "although I wish I could catch the guy who did it and string him up to a tree by his balls. There have been a lot of these animal mutilations around here lately and the sheriff has asked me to look into it, since I'm a social worker. It may be Hank who's doing all this, but as I listen to you, I'm finding that I'm still not entirely convinced. The type of person who does things like this is usually very quiet. The wife beating doesn't fit the profile."

"You're a real pro, Sally. Not like the Sheriff Dopey and his gang."

She decided not to mention that Ed was her uncle.

"I'm from Houston. I've done my share of criminal social work." More than her share, she thought, looking back on some of the beaten-up wives she'd interviewed, the crack-house babies she'd seen through detox.

"So you don't think it was Hank?"

"I'll form a professional opinion after I interview him. I'm going over to talk to him as soon as I'm done here. But he's probably just the kind of bastard he seems to be. I doubt if he has any hidden depths, good or bad."

"Is there anything I can do to help that poor woman? Or should I just butt out?"

Sally considered that. Maybe it would be good for Suzanne to reach out a little bit—if she was careful. "Don't go over there, obviously. But phone her. I'll pave the way. See if you can hire her to do some cleaning for you. If she comes, make an effort to get to know her better. Be sure to tell her that if she needs to get away, she can always come to you. But don't expect her to do it until things get much, much worse."

"I'll call her up right away. There's always something around here that needs doing. She drives the school bus part-time to earn money, but that job was over in June, so she must need some income right now." She blinked back tears of frustration. "I can't stand to see a woman so helpless. And on top of everything else, she's going to have a baby!"

Sally stood up. "One thing you have to promise me. Buy that dog. And don't get any friendly damn golden retriever, either." She was surprised at the harshness that crept into her voice, but she could feel anger and frustration burning inside her. Even if Glynesse was his only crime, that was bad enough. "I'll call you as soon as I've formed an opinion about Hank."

"Thanks, Sally. I'll be waiting to hear from you."

Sally went out across the wide porch, feeling not a breath of breeze even up on this hill.

Suzanne waved as Sally got back into her Camry. When she reached the gate, it opened automatically. At the end of the driveway, Sally forced herself to turn right, toward the Sunderland place.

His dirt driveway was rougher, and there were beer cans and trash along the side. The brush choked the sides of her car.

As she drove up, she noticed how very quiet the place was. She stopped in front of garage doors that had started out white, next to an elderly pickup truck. Since the truck was there, Hank must be at home.

She noticed that the aluminum siding on the house looked better from the road than it did up close. The light blue color was already starting to fade. A few window boxes filled with real flowers would have improved the place tremendously. The yard was covered with the weedy kind of grass that comes up naturally, if you just leave the dirt alone.

When she knocked on the front door, she was able to count to twenty before it was pulled open by a large man who looked like he'd gotten dressed in a hurry. Sally glanced at her watch—afternoon already. She said, "I'm Sally Hopkins from the sheriff's office. We're investigating the cat killing next door. Are you Hank Sunderland?"

He nodded and opened the door wider. As he did, she

heard a TV blaring away, and smelled stale cigarette smoke and bacon grease.

Surprisingly, the house was neat—almost pathologically so. There were knitted afghans stretched tightly over every inch of precious upholstery. The rugs were spotless, the floors gleaming with wax. Hank switched the blasting TV off before he sat down. There was no sign of Glynesse. Without the TV, the house was totally still. Sally felt a sharpening edge of concern.

"You're aware of the details of the death of Ms. Chesterton's cat this morning?"

"Yep, and I know she thinks I done it, but I didn't." He made the statement calmly, without any rancor. Sally knew well how violent men were generally passive until they exploded. The trouble was, you never knew just what was going to light that fuse.

In college, she'd learned that this type of reaction was the result of too much punishment during childhood. Because the only control in their lives came from the outside, these guys never learned self-control. They just went with whatever emotions happened to be swirling around in their heads at the moment, and God help the wife or child who was in their way—or social worker, for that matter.

"Listen, the troopers have already talked to me about it. I'd like to help, because she's a nice lady, but I really don't know nothing."

"She thinks you might have been getting even with her because of the complaints she's made about you recently."

"Naw, she's just a city lady. You've got to learn to put up with them these days, 'cause it don't look like they're goin' away soon."

"They bring money and jobs into the community, don't they?"

He shrugged. "Some do, I guess. They bring their own folks over from Houston to do the work for them, too, a lot of them." He grinned, or rather showed his teeth.

Sally decided to flatter him. "Did you build this house yourself? It's really very nice."

"I sure did, and I can always find work when I need it, not like some. That reminds me, I got to get ready to go trim some trees for the McCarthys down the road."

"Just give me another minute, here. I want to be honest with you, Mr. Sunderland. We've had a whole lot of animals tortured in Maryvale lately." Hank drew himself up in his chair and stared at her like he felt insulted.

She added, "I don't think you're the one who's been doing them. You've got no reason to go around town torturing people's pets." No, he was not the animal torturer. But he might be something else. "I think you may have killed Ms. Chesterton's cat, to get her to shut up and leave you alone." She leaned forward. "I'm a social worker, not a cop. Remember that nothing you tell me need go beyond these four walls. You can ask for confidentiality and get it. It's urgently important that I know whether or not the same person who's been torturing animals killed Suzette, or if you did it for revenge."

Hank looked at her for a long time. "I've been around," he said slowly. "I could kill a man if I had to, but I got no reason to stoop so low as to kill a cat." He got up. "It's time for us to leave, miss. I got work and I guess you do, too."

"Did you see or hear anybody over there this morning? They would have had to get up there on foot. Did you see anyone walking up the road?"

"I was working late last night, so I slept late and didn't see nobody. I already told Sheriff Ed that."

"What about your wife? She might have seen something when she got up to make breakfast. Can I talk to her?"

His lips formed a taut line. "She's not here."

"Well, give her a message for me, will you? Suzanne says she could use some domestic help up there and wonders if Mrs. Sunderland would like to come over. She'll be glad to pick her up and drive her home, so she won't have to walk up through the brush."

Hank's face opened into a very real smile, and suddenly he was no longer a sinister figure. "That'll be good. Real good. I can tell you right now, she will do that. Yes, ma'am."

As soon as the door was closed, the TV blasted on again. So much for getting ready to trim trees. Sally wondered again about Glynesse. She couldn't have gone out, since their truck was parked ten feet from where she stood. She considered looking in some windows, but all the blinds were drawn. She hoped to heck Glynesse wasn't lying in there dead.

She left the Sunderland place. She'd made some progress: she was fairly sure—almost certain—that Hank was not the torturer. He hadn't displayed any body language that suggested that he was even slightly afraid of her questions. He hadn't glanced away, his legs hadn't crossed, his skin had remained dry. He was a normal human being—poor, angry, and probably of below average intelligence. He certainly didn't have the charm that so many psychopaths did.

She arrived back to a sheriff's office that was just as silent as the rest of Maryvale in the thrall of a summer afternoon. She went toward the back.

"Ed?"

His office was empty—full of his personality, his career, his life, but the man himself was gone. It was getting late, and she thought that he must have gone home.

She went back to her desk, gathered the unfinished forms into a stack, and put them in a drawer. They were an education, certainly, but she hoped she'd be too busy to have to deal with them again anytime soon.

On her way home, she stopped at the Chevron station to pick up a map. In the morning, she planned to ask Ed to mark the places where fires and animal mutilations had occurred.

She pulled up to the Chevron. From inside, the old clerk raised his eyes. He had as sweet a face as you would ever see, burnt by the sun, deeply lined. When she stopped at the self-service pump, he returned to his newspaper.

It was all so normal, so Maryvale. She wondered what that innocent-looking old clerk had seen over the years, what he knew. Just then, the sun slipped behind the far hills. As she filled her tank, moths fluttered around her in the gathering dark.

She was glad to find Flagg's Market still open, and she stopped to get some ingredients for supper.

When she stepped in the door, the smell of the market, a mix of old produce and barrel candy and wax and a million other things, surprised her, its familiarity striking right to the center of her heart. For a moment she was twelve again, coming in here to buy a nickel's worth of candy corn and a comic book, the money Ed had given her clutched tight in her hand.

She moved like a zombie through the aisles, gathering ingredients for her self-invented spaghetti sauce. She bought her groceries from a girl of about twenty, so shy she could not look up into the face of a stranger. The entire transaction was silent, just the two of them in the old store with the brand-new cash register beeping as the groceries were scanned. She paid, smiled, and hefted her bag.

"Thankyew, ma'am, come again," came the polite phrase in the sweet, familiar drawl, barely audible even in the quiet, as she left the store.

Elizabeth came home while Sally's sauce was bubbling, and called out, "Hey, lady, that smells *go-o-o-d*," as she came rolling through the house.

They had a jolly supper together. When Elizabeth heard she'd been to Hank's she laughed heartily. "Mr. Niceguy," she said. "Piece of work."

Maryvale had no cable and Elizabeth didn't have a dish—something that Sally found she kind of appreciated. The satellite listings at her old apartment were so complex that she usually ended up watching nothing. After supper they found an old John Wayne movie on the one station they could get, the Gladewater ABC affiliate, and watched it until both of their heads were nodding against the back of the big old couch.

Sally was in bed by ten. She slept a deep and dreamless sleep, waking up suddenly when the smell of coffee rose up from below.

While she was dressing, she reflected that she might prefer a *little* more activity in the evenings. Question was, did Maryvale have a social life at all? She was inclined to doubt it, although there'd been weekend square dancing when she was a girl, and a roadhouse outside of town called Bruno's Curve that drew the local wild youth.

When she got to the office at eight-thirty, Ed, true to his word, had the coffee made.

"Well, good mornin,' darlin'," he said as she came into his office. "How was your night?"

"Very quiet," she said. She then reported her concerns about Hank and Glynesse. He listened, nodding from time to time, as she told him how Hank had probably lied when he'd said that Glynesse wasn't there. When she mentioned murder, the softest of smiles crossed his face and he shook his head.

"You know how many of those I've had here in Maryvale?"

"I'd assume not a lot."

"Give me a guess."

"Three a year?"

His eyes twinkled.

"Two? One?"

"Five—in my entire career. Just five in over twenty years."

"Am I bringing too much Houston with me, Ed?"

"Sure you are. But you'll get past it. You'll settle right in to this little world. What it's got a lot of is venial sins. Low-level drug use, public drunkenness, fights, that kind of thing. There's no murder here, no robbery, no muggers beating folks to within an inch of their lives."

She unfolded her map. "Could you show me where the fires and pet killings have taken place?" At this point, she was considering that she might find her man out in the woods in some old cabin, a reclusive Unabomber type.

There he would sit, in a tangle of dirty sheets, old newspapers, and used TV dinner trays, just waiting for Sally to come and get him under state control. His neighbors would later describe him as someone "quiet" who "kept to himself." It would turn out he never said much because he had to stay tuned to the voices in his head that kept telling him to do all those awful things.

But the marks Ed made on the map didn't suggest a marauder, a person who attacks from a central location. They suggested the presence of what was known as a "commuter," somebody who is purposeful, seeking to avoid detection by trying to make the crime pattern appear random. So there would be no cabin in the woods—at least not one centered on the crimes.

This was going to be a real challenge.

Ed ran two patrols a day, one in the morning, one in the afternoon. As he left for the morning look-see, as he called it, he told her just how happy he was that she was doing the forms.

She got the hint and opened her desk drawer and started to pull them out. But the moment the office door closed behind Ed, the desk drawer also closed. It was time to do some more investigating.

There had been three incidents along or near Pinewoods Lane, where Hank and Suzanne lived. Could it be Hank, after all? It was easy to make mistakes in cases like this. Sometimes a psychopath was such a good actor, he or she seemed entirely normal. And sometimes, a serial killer had a normal emotional life. The evil part was deeply buried in such people, and they were very, very hard to detect. Such a man had been Ted Bundy, who'd murdered thirty-six women before he was caught. Not even skilled professionals had been able to find any flaw in his personality.

To her knowledge, no correctly administered test had revealed anything except deep-seated anger in Ted Bundy. His childhood had been depressingly normal. His attempts in prison to portray himself as a soulless murderer, unable to feel except when killing, were unconvincing, at least to experts. No, in Sally's opinion, psychology had not yet fully penetrated the labyrinth of the human mind, and the mystery of Ted Bundy was proof of it.

She would have to be damn careful, or she might well end up as the killer's first human victim—assuming that it wasn't Hank and Glynesse was still breathing.

She decided to use the indirect, southern approach. She'd drive along Pinewoods Lane and other nearby roads, stopping to chat and get to know folks along the way. She would call herself the sheriff's new assistant, not a social worker. Plenty of people around here drew welfare checks, and her experience was that nobody who did would say one true word to a social worker, and she needed them to fill her ears with all the local gossip.

The day developed hot and sunny, cloudless and swarming with humidity and flies, typical of this part of the world at this time of the year. Later, there might be a thunderstorm, and it would be beautiful and grand in its passing, and fill the air with freshness.

She stopped her car frequently and talked to lonely old ladies living in silent old houses, who were out weeding their flower gardens, who offered her iced tea and pleaded with their eyes for her to stay. She met harried housewives in trailer homes who left off screaming at their kids just long enough to answer a couple of questions.

She met Tim Harrelson, a carpenter who had come home on his lunch break, who showed her the new house he was building, little by little, behind the tiny house where he now lived with his wife and mother-in-law. At the rate he was going, it looked like he might be finished by the time his unborn children were ready to leave the nest.

Besides the tea, she was offered coffee, beer, soda pop, and homemade pie. She ate it all, and pushed back her guilt by telling herself she needed to ingratiate herself with her new neighbors. Every place she went, she made sure to mention she was Ed's niece, so they wouldn't think she was an outsider and clam up.

She was especially successful with Joe and Florence Kravitz, a nice retired couple from Houston, who had lived on Pinewoods Lane for ten years. They were far below the level of the weekend ranchers, a couple of modest means who'd come here largely so that they could make ends meet.

It looked as if they couldn't resist a stray cat around their place. Still, their yard was well kept. It was a sea of felines, though, hanging from trees, hissing at each other, rolling around under bushes, and twirling about Flo's ankles. Sally could imagine the cattish orgies that must go on there at night, the howling and the furry grappling in the dark.

So far, none of their cats had turned up dead, but they were concerned that a couple of them seemed to be missing. Sally wondered how they could tell.

After making her promise to consider adopting a kitten, Florence inventoried the neighborhood for her. "You should stop by the Davis place," she told Sally. "Mr. Davis works for the state, inspecting home sites and septic systems and whatnot to make sure everything's according to code."

"He's a pill," chimed in Joe. "Last year he made me move my propane tank, said it was too close to our little swimming pool. Cost me a bundle. 'What does it matter if it blows up,' I told him, 'all it can do is blow a hole in the pool. If that happens, all the water will run out and douse the fire before it reaches the house.' But he wouldn't budge an inch. The code's the code, as far as he's concerned."

"It's because we're newcomers," Florence snapped. "But as I was saying, dear, go and talk to them. There are a lot of children in that family, including grown-up ones who should have gone off and gotten jobs by now. I think there's something wrong with some of them." She kept her voice down, even though there was nobody but cats around to overhear her. "I think his wife is also his first cousin. That's illegal, isn't it?"

Sally sighed. When Flo first mentioned the Davis household, she'd gotten interested, but now it looked like all she would find was a house full of inbred kids, some of them maybe mildly retarded. It sounded like there were as many kids over there as there were cats at the Kravitz place. Why did people whose genes didn't mesh keep on trying so hard?

She was surprised to find, when she left the Kravitzes, that it was already pushing seven. It hadn't even crossed her mind to stop for a break.

Her throat was sore from talking and her bladder felt like a balloon from all the liquids she had consumed. It was also Friday afternoon. She decided to wait until Monday to check out the Davis place. She'd do a little due diligence beforehand, look them up in Ed's files and the state's records, and, above all, ask Ed what he knew, which would likely turn out to be just about everything.

Twilight was coming on fast, as it did around here in the summer. She drove along the road, her car lights gently pushing away the gloom of evening. She had about twenty miles to cover, and it would be dark before she got home. She hoped Elizabeth was in the mood to do her own cooking tonight.

When she got back to the house, she noticed that all the lights were off. Everything was silent. Could Elizabeth be working late, also? To hear her tell it, her office over in

Gladewater was a busy place. She dealt primarily with troubled children, and many of her cases were court-mandated. Plus, Gladewater was a lot bigger place than Maryvale, and she could easily be running late.

On the other hand, maybe Elizabeth was out on a date, using a pair of dancing shoes from her collection. If she had a boyfriend, Sally was glad for her.

She stood in the middle of the dark living room. Boy, but this town was quiet. Not to mention this house. The walls sighed a little, contracting as the heat of the sun left them. She felt a stab of loneliness, more powerful than she would have expected. Also annoyance. She'd been eager to get Elizabeth's input about some of the folks she'd talked to.

She sat down and snapped on the TV, but she wasn't a sitcom person and Friday appeared to be a sitcom night on ABC, so she turned it off again. Maybe she'd catch the news at ten. One good thing, she was reading a great mystery, and her book, for sure, was not going to let her down.

She considered calling her Houston friends. But none of them had bothered to call her, even though she'd used Ed's office computer to e-mail her new phone number to all of them.

So Sally read. When the antique Regulator Clock in the hall bonged ten, she was kind of surprised.

When she watched the news, she found herself half expecting to hear about the first Maryvale murder, but there was nothing but the usual chronicle of car wrecks, a Stop-N-Go robbed out on the Interstate, but nowhere near Maryvale, a train stalled across a country road for six hours in Welasco.

East Texas was a land of milk if you were fast enough to catch the cows and agile enough not to get kicked senseless while milking them. It was a land of honey, too, if you could get it out of killer bees.

When it was close to midnight and Elizabeth still had not returned, Sally decided she might as well hit the sheets. She made her way upstairs. Although she knew she shouldn't, she glanced into Elizabeth's room for some clue

as to where she'd gone. The bedspread was tossed aside
and there were dresses and several pairs of shoes on the
floor, evidence that pointed pretty clearly to a date. She'd
gotten home tired, tried to repair that with a quick snooze,
overslept, and had to throw her clothes on.

Mystery solved: Elizabeth was out having fun.

Sally wondered if Glynesse was doing the same . . . and
what of the animal torturer, what was he doing right now—
lying on his back maybe, in his dark, hot bedroom, listening to the whispers of the night, planning his next move.

When she woke up the next morning, Sally was not surprised to find the house still silent. Now, however, Elizabeth's door was shut tight. Actually, it was a hopeful discovery. It meant that there was indeed, some way to raise a little hell around here. Somewhere there was dancing, there were men, music, life after sundown, praise heaven.

As soon as Elizabeth rejoined the land of the living, Sally would find out all about it. Maybe even go out tonight. It was Saturday night, after all. Surely whatever had happened on Friday night would happen again on Saturday night, and in an even bigger way.

She made coffee and threw down some toast, then called Ed.

She didn't just want to talk to him on the phone about the Davises, she wanted to do it face-to-face, at his house. She wanted to see her old bedroom once again, maybe make the ghost child within her walk again.

"I hope I'm not waking you up," she said.

"Don't even think about it, darlin'. You know I've been

lighting up the sun all my life. Come on over around noon. I've got chili brewing on the stove." Sally remembered how he used to always cook chili on the weekend. She also remembered, all too well, just how dubious Ed's culinary skills were. There was his tendency to want his chili meat to cure for a couple of days. That is to say, get just a little, as he put it, "rusty." She'd never actually collapsed from it. Probably high heat and all that cayenne pepper killed off most of the bugs. It did, however, as the old ladies would say, "repeat on you."

Uncle Ed's house was just out of town, down the Dimmit-Simpson Road, which was originally staked out between the ranches of two of the county's founding families. The big old southern red oaks alongside it had grown so tall that they formed a shade-dappled canopy.

How fond she'd been of this old road when she was a girl, strolling it in the moonlight with Uncle Ed, dreams of a future romance floating through her mind. When he was a very little boy, they'd had a buggy out here, and he'd driven it himself, behind an Appaloosa named Jane.

She'd imagined that buggy and that horse, with Ed at the reins and her mother sitting beside him, brother and sister singing as the buggy swayed through the sweet summer night.

She pulled up in front of the old white clapboard house. She had always loved the traces of her mother that could be found here.

She could picture her sitting at the big oak dining table with Ed and her grandparents, whom she had never known. The family had never been the kind to keep scrapbooks, but a few photos and letters had turned up here and there. Sally stared at these scraps for hours, trying to learn the secrets of her mother's mind.

She noticed that the front door was open a crack, so she went in. Country folk rarely knocked when they came to visit, and doors were never locked in Maryvale. Instead of knocking, you'd call out "whoo hoo!" as a warning before you walked on in. This gave the home owner about five seconds to get decent before guests came tramping into the living room.

"Uncle Ed? You still around?" She had picked three rolled-up newspapers from off the lawn on the way in, and she deposited these on the little hall table by the door. She put them down next to a couple of others that were lying there already, still tightly wrapped. Ed obviously didn't need to crack the local paper to get the news.

"I'm in the kitchen, darlin'."

Sally was almost knocked over by the pungent fumes. "Ummm, when will it be ready?" she managed to ask past her tears.

"In an hour. I invited Rob over too."

"Rob Farley?" She was disappointed. She had hoped to spend some time alone with her uncle, talking about old times . . . and the Davises.

"Yep. He's mighty interested in those animal mutilations. I knew he'd want to hear what you found out."

Would he? She guessed otherwise. "I just wish I'd had a chance to learn more. But I have learned a few things."

"Save it for now—no need to tell it twice."

"Is it OK if I go up to my room and look around before he gets here? I want to see if I left any dolls up there or anything." She could see Ed's back stiffen, his lips tighten. So she added, "Don't worry if it hasn't been cleaned, I don't care."

"Darlin', the truth is that it's just as it was the day you left." He stared at her like nothing so much as a deer caught in headlights. Then the smile came again, as soft as the East Texas night.

He hadn't so much as entered the room in all these years?

That surprised her. It was kind of eerie, actually. Why would the room be sacred to him? Or maybe he'd just never bothered to clean it up.

She ran up the stairs. On the way, she passed Ed's own room, and noted that it was still as sparsely furnished as it had always been. The bed was neatly made, with the sheets pulled tight, a technique he'd learned during his years as a Marine. Not a single photo or work of art adorned the walls. It could have been a monk's cell, except there was no crucifix on the wall.

And then she came to her old room. Moving softly, feeling like an intruder in her own past, she crossed the tiny floor and touched the coverlet on the bed. It was still turned down at the corner, just as she'd done as a girl, as her mother had taught her. "Turn the corner," Momma used to say, "it makes the bed inviting."

The coverlet was stiff and fragile, almost dust. She saw that she herself had probably been the last person to make this bed. She remembered pausing in that doorway, looking back saying, "See you again next summer, my room."

It had been nearly twenty years.

She trembled her fingers along the faded yellow cloth, touching the little flowers that had once shown bright but were now barely distinguishable. She shuddered. This was like seeing a ghost, and discovering that it was you.

Tears tickled her cheeks, the hurt of time ached in her heart. She felt a sense of having missed something, as if her girlhood should never have passed away as it did, lost in the maelstrom of adolescence and caring for her stepbrothers and stepsisters.

She went over to the pine dresser. Everything was so small! Bits and pieces of her mother's life in this room had always been discoverable in there. Wonderful old newspapers from the World War II years lined the drawers. She had learned more history from reading the inside of those drawers than she ever did from books.

An odd, choked feeling began to trouble her, almost as if she were allergic to the room in some way. She sat down on top of the old bedspread, took a deep breath. Like Flagg's, it smelled the same.

As a psychologist, she knew that smells bring back memories that can't be recovered otherwise. Once when she'd picked up a particular brand of hand lotion, simply by accident, she had suffered an agony of remembrance when she opened it, because it had been the kind her mother had used. She'd had no conscious memory of that.

She leaned down now to sniff the bedspread. It smelled of dust and just maybe a whiff of that barrel candy, the cherry sours that she'd loved. There was a subtle, almost animal scent there too that made her uneasy. She felt an impulse to look under the bed for monsters.

Then she heard "Hey there" coming from downstairs. It must be Rob Farley, belting out the male version of "whoo hoo."

She heard Ed's low-voiced answer, then the thudding of Rob's boots as he ambled on into the kitchen.

Might as well go down. She was hungry for company, as well as chili, after her lonely evening. Even Mr. Uptight Trooper Rob would do for now.

But when she saw him, a bark of surprised laughter escaped her mouth before she could stop herself. It was the first time she'd seen Trooper Farley out of uniform, but he might as well have been wearing his khakis, for all the difference it made. His short-sleeved plaid shirt was stiffly starched and pressed, and the seams in his jeans were arrow straight.

He looked at her, eyebrows raised. "Hello."

"Rob Farley, don't you ever relax?"

Yesterday when she'd mentioned his name, one old lady had alluded to a marriage that failed while he was away in the military. She wondered what his secrets were. What did he do for fun, attend Kiwanis meetings?

"Our social worker has been observing," Ed said.

"Oh?"

"I did a few interviews out along Pinewoods Lane. A number of the animal killings have taken place out that way, and the Kravitzes are missing a couple of cats as we speak."

"I know where all the others were found," Rob said. "I worked most of those cases."

Ed spooned chili into three big bowls. When Sally lifted

a mouthful to her lips, the fumes made her eyes water. She closed them and savored the complicated fury of the chili in her mouth. This recipe must have been used to kill varmints in the old days.

"Ed," she managed to whisper, "that is powerful."

"Know why chili's hot? The vaqueros used to carry it with them on the range, and the spices kept it from rotting. 'Course, the secret of it is, the meat's gotta be left out for a couple of days, otherwise it's never gonna get good enough to cook."

Rob went to the sink for a big glass of water. While he was busy there, Sally choked back her chili and asked Ed, "What do you know about the Davis family?"

"The building inspector?" Ed asked. He squinted. "He's got a raft of kids out there. Do you think one of 'em's been running wild, causing all this trouble?"

"I keep telling you, Ed, these aren't the acts of a juvenile delinquent. There's a very mixed-up young man out there. Very dangerous."

Rob finally came back to the table and sat down. "Explain your theory to me again."

How often did he need to hear this? "Serial killers have probably been around since before Jack the Ripper, but there seems to be more of them now. The truth is, most serial killers never get caught, or even discovered. Most serial killings are never even identified for what they are. The reason is that serial killers read crime stories too, and they know to vary their methods."

"But not every kid who tortures animals grows up to be a murderer," Rob protested. "I know this for a fact because I'm ashamed to say that me and my friends used to blow up frogs and torture cats occasionally. And a dry old woodshed is a natural magnet for a boy with matches."

"I agree with that," Ed said. "But if this was a group of ordinary brats, we'd have caught at least one of 'em by now. You know that yourself. So Sally's right about one thing: it's got to be just one smart kid. That's bad enough.

But if she says this kid's going to grow up to do worse things, we've got to try damned hard to catch him. Maybe she's wrong about that, but we can't risk it."

"Could it be an adult?"

"Good question. The short answer is yes. The long one is, probably not. I did think for a while it could be Hank Sunderland. But I think I'll be able to identify this person by his affect."

Ed raised his eyebrows, a little smile playing in his face. "What the ding-dong is that, college girl?"

"The way he acts. He'll be a psychopathic personality. I'll be able to recognize the signs. Hank's not a psychopath, incidentally. Just a bastard, excuse my French."

"He beats up on Glynesse," Rob said.

Sally was surprised to hear a sadness enter his voice. Men beating up on women made him feel for the women, that was clear. She was glad of it. Too many men just did not empathize, police officers very much included.

"He might have done Suzette and he might be a danger to Glynesse, but I don't think he's a budding serial killer. Which reminds me, when I was there yesterday, I couldn't manage to see Glynesse. I was thinking maybe you could drop over and just check on her, Rob." Since Ed obviously hadn't.

There was a silence. Then Rob spoke. "What'll we do if we catch this psychopath? We can't give a guy the needle for killing a few cats. If it's an adult, he might get a little slammer time. A child is gonna get a few sessions with somebody like your friend Elizabeth."

"None of which is likely to help, I know. But what else can we do?" Sally asked. "We can't wait around until whoever he is starts torturing and killing women. We've got no choice but to try and catch him now."

"Wait a minute, we're getting ahead of ourselves," Ed said. "Anyone want more chili?" He got up to get it. "What's important right now is that Sally's pretty sure this is all being done by a single person and she thinks she'll be able to identify him. So I say, let her look for him, and do that full-time. When she finds the guy, we can watch him, get the evidence we need to convict him. At least we can remove him from the community for a while."

"What's the main thing you look for, when you're trying to spot a psychopath?" Rob asked her.

"Signs of dissociation. Lack of emotional affect."

"And how do you know the signs when you see 'em?"

"That's why you need me. As a professional, I can recognize these signs."

She spoke so firmly, and with such self-assurance, that neither one of them tried to argue with her. Rob stood up and gathered up his dishes. As he clattered his bowl and water glass into the sink, he said, "I've got to be going now. Thanks for the chili, Ed, it was remarkable. I've got to get some shopping done before I go on duty tonight. Saturday nights can sometimes be busy."

"Why doesn't Sally go along so you can show her where to shop around here?"

Damn you, Edward Walker! Are you trying to get me out of here?

Ed took the bottle of dish soap out of Rob's hand and pushed them both toward the door. "Be sure to show her the stand where Miz Evans sells tomatoes and donuts and the places where you can get serious Mexican food. And don't forget Rank's, in case she needs to pick up some sundries."

As if she didn't remember Rank's. Admittedly, there had been no Miz Evans selling tomatoes in the old days, but most of the Mexican food around here was pretty serious, as she recalled. At least as serious as Ed's chili.

Rob didn't have his cruiser, since he wouldn't drive a state car on personal time. Sally got in the passenger side of his freshly washed truck and sat down. As they pulled away, she looked back at the house. It looked just as it had when she would leave it as a girl, silent and filled with memories.

"We'll do the fruit stand first," Rob said.

"Fine."

Why hadn't Ed wanted her to stay and talk?

8

Sally was happy again when she saw the roadside stand, which proved to be a vegetable heaven. "This is incredible," she said.

"Most of it's grown around here," Rob commented.

The tomatoes were deep red and you could smell them, actually smell them in their bin. Ditto the cantaloupes. Some of the onions still had soil clinging to them, and the corn was all dewy, as if it had been picked within the hour.

Sally was not normally a big vegetable eater, but she loaded up anyway. She'd cook corn on the cob slathered in sweet butter, tomato salad, and—gosh, look at this kale. She'd cook it with bacon and to hell with the fat content.

Rob smiled and Sally realized he was shy. She felt a kind of bubbly amusement at the idea. He was so unsophisticated.

They got back in the truck and passed a Mexican place called Fonda la Paloma. "Great cheese enchiladas and mojitos that'll settle you right down," he said. "You can get out for five bucks, if you stick to iced tea."

"Which you do, of course."

He gave her a look out of the corner of his eye, as if he knew she was mocking him. "Of course. And now, welcome to the fashion hub of Maryvale."

"Rob, I practically grew up here, remember."

"That's right, Ed told me that. Well, then you're gonna see a local phenom. Miz Rank might be seventy, but she's truckin' right along."

"I remember she could get pretty grouchy."

She followed Rob into the old store, past Stetsons stacked in groups of three, all gray or straw. She learned that Ed wore a straw Cinch hat in the summer, and given how good these hats looked, he could use a new one. There were racks of jeans and a little hutch full of boots—moderately priced boots, none of that fancy alligator and ostrich skin.

There were a few dresses here and there, and most of them looked like the sort of housedresses Ethel Mertz had worn on *I Love Lucy*.

There was movement back in the depths of the store, a shadow passing a display of cowboy-style shirts. Then Sally saw what could only be described as a heap of human flesh and, judging from its wrinkles and flaps, ancient. As Mrs. Rank had aged, she had also expanded greatly.

When the mountain of flesh asked, "May I help you?" Rob replied that they were just browsing. But Sally said, "I'd like to buy a hat."

"A hat. Well, we haven't kept ladies' hats for a little while." She squinted up at Sally. "We might have a few in the back." She didn't seem inclined to go look for one, however. Even the threat of a Wal-Mart opening nearby couldn't turn old Miz Rank friendly.

"No. A Stetson. Uh, a straw. Summer Stetson."

"A man's hat?" Miz Rank asked.

"Yes."

"For a man?"

"For me."

Miz Rank produced something called a Stetson Sonora Comfort, which fit perfectly, and which Sally bought. She thought she looked kind of cute in it, actually, although Rob seemed to stifle amusement when he saw her.

Their next stop was the drugstore. Sally was puzzled by this, since she figured Rob would realize she could find the Rite Aid on her own.

"Need anything?" he asked as he got out of the truck.

"I'm good," she said, following him in with her Stetson on the back of her head. He loped into the antacid section and went for a pink box of Pepto-Bismol tablets.

"Chili?"

"Chili. Every darned Saturday." He laughed. "This was the last time, though."

"Too hot?"

"He rots the meat!"

"That he does." She had no problem with it herself—she'd probably developed an iron stomach during her summer visits.

He went to the back of the store, and there, in a white uniform with her blond hair pulled back in a bun, stood one of the prettiest girls Sally had seen here or anywhere.

"Hi, Rob," she said, smiling like a jack-o'-lantern. Her voice was silk.

"Hey, Wanda." He put the Pepto-Bismol on the counter. "Don't tell Ed about this, please?"

"Sheriff Ed's chili?"

"You better believe it."

She laughed, her eyes sparkling . . . at him. She was no more than twenty-two and naturally pretty in an effortless way that made Sally feel helplessly jealous. Sexual heat radiated out of her every pore.

"Sally, this is Wanda Ellis. She was in kindergarten here when I was in high school."

She gave Sally a wide I-know-something-you-don't-know smile, just a hair too sweet. "I may have been behind him, but I know *everything* about him."

Rob reddened. Sally thought that Wanda was either already part of Rob's personal life or intended to be.

On the way back to Ed's house to get her car, she decided to test the waters. "Wanda's really beautiful."

"Very beautiful girl."

"What do you do around here for fun?"

"Fun? There's dances. The movies over in Gladewater. Couple of clubs."

"Sounds pretty quiet."

"That would be true."

And that would be that. They drove on in silence. When they arrived at Ed's, his car was nowhere in sight, and the garage door was shut tight. She was hoping to spend the afternoon with him, find out more about the Davises, and run the rest of the people she'd met through his encyclopedic mind. "You have any idea if Ed's home?"

"Could be doing Saturday chores, be my guess. If you want to wait for him, go on in. It'll be unlocked."

She got out and watched him drive away. Then she turned toward the house. She would go in, maybe even have a little more chili.

But when she tried the door, it was locked. She went around to the back, and it was locked too. On her way to her car, she thought she heard voices in the house. She stopped—and realized that it was the TV. So the mystery was solved. Ed must be napping in front of what sounded like a baseball game. Probably the locked doors were meant as a subtle signal: I'm an old guy and I need my quiet weekends. Okay, understood. She'd wait until Monday morning to talk more business.

As she drove home, she found herself wishing that Rob had at least told her where the dances were held.

"Whoo-hoo," she yelled as she entered their house. She stopped, listening for Elizabeth's response. She was rather surprised by the silence. Could it be that Elizabeth was still asleep? If so, she must have really tied one on last night.

She tiptoed upstairs and found the bedroom door still tightly shut. That could mean one of two things: either she was in there sleeping or she'd gone out. Her car was in the garage, but a date could have picked her up.

Sally told herself it was silly to creep around if nobody was home, but she wasn't brave enough to turn the door-knob to find out. Because maybe the date was in there with her. Or if Elizabeth was neither making love (very quietly) nor nursing the mother of all hangovers, then maybe she just wanted to be alone.

Sally went down to the living room, read for a while, turned on the TV and found, yes, the baseball game. She watched half an inning, but she couldn't get into the game. She walked back and forth until she realized that she was actually pacing. She flounced back into her chair, then hopped out of it like it was on fire. This was not fun. Mary-vale was about as lively as a crypt.

She found the paper in the kitchen where she'd left it this morning. There was only one movie theater in Maryvale, the Excelsior, but it was a two-dollar rerun job, and she'd seen the film. She could drive up to Gladewater, and maybe that was what she needed to do. There were films that started at five-fifteen. If she drove fast, she could make it.

It was a great feeling to get in the car and get on the road out of this tomb. She forgot to bring along the movie list-ings, but it didn't matter, she was bored enough to watch almost anything, as long as it wasn't an animated film star-ring animals.

Gladewater turned out to be a big antiquing center. In fact, it billed itself as the antiques capital of the world, and looking at all the shops, that might not be hype. Certainly it was better than Maryvale, with its few stores packed with treadle sewing machines, Tin Lizzie wheels, and wicker baby carriages.

But Sally didn't have the money to buy them or a place to put them, so she drove through town to the Cineplex. A picture was just starting—an action extravaganza. It wasn't animated, but everybody in it still seemed unreal to her. Her favorite movie was *When Harry Met Sally*. Still, it was noisy and there was lots of movement and the popcorn was kind of good. She found that explosions could actually put you to sleep, if you let them.

She arrived back in Maryvale just after nine, and found the house dark. Damn it, this was creepy, it was actually creepy! She went inside, turned on all the lights downstairs, and got out the gin that Elizabeth kept in the pantry. Then she put it away. That was a direction she did not need to go in.

She went upstairs and stared at the door. What if she was dead in there? Stranger things had happened. She put her ear against it. Maybe there was rustling on the other side, maybe it was her own heartbeat.

She put her hand on the knob. Took it off.

The woman had gone away for the weekend, for God's sake. She hadn't told her roommate because, well, why should she?

She flounced into her own room and threw herself down on the bed. Nine-twenty Saturday night and guess what Sally Hopkins was up to?

She brushed her teeth, put on her pajamas, and turned in.

Her bedside lamp formed a golden pool around the head of the bed, the leaves of the tree outside whispered with the night wind, and katydids argued their way across the reaches of darkness.

It was so beautiful, so very magical, the softness of it, the sense of mystery, the billowing elegance of the dark.

She tossed and turned in the elegance. Much later, she was dimly aware of thunder, but Sunday morning dawned sunny and full of cheerful birdsong. There was something that was just very damn nice indeed about waking up with the sweet smell of oleander coming in on a country breeze.

Elizabeth's door was still shut when she went into the bathroom for her shower. She told herself, *You will not go there, it's none of your business.* If it lasted past the weekend, then she would go in. By tomorrow morning, her concern would be entirely legitimate.

While she was drying herself off, though, she smelled something familiar. She cracked the door. Coffee fumes!

Elizabeth was alive and well! And boy was Sally glad. She was real eager for company, even more than she'd realized.

She found Elizabeth cheerfully preparing breakfast, gliding around the kitchen in her ratty old robe. "I got inspired to make blueberry pancakes, I assume you like 'em?"

"Died and gone to heaven."

While Elizabeth poured the batter onto the griddle, they chatted. Or rather, Sally did. She asked, "How was your ʳeekend?"

That got a shrug.

'Did you see my new hat hanging in the hall? I guess old Miz Rank's still the fashion leader around here."

That brought an amiable chuckle.

Then the pancakes were ready and they sat at the kitchen table and wolfed them down with plenty of syrup and sides of bacon. During the breakfast ritual, neither party spoke.

When Sally offered to clean up, Elizabeth accepted gratefully, and went upstairs to get dressed. When she came back down, Sally asked, "What's up for today?"

"For a start, I thought I'd drive out to the gas station and pick up a Houston paper so I can read the Sunday funnies."

Sally decided to take a little flier. "I'm going to interview the Davises, up on Pinewoods Lane—you know, with all those kids?"

Elizabeth nodded as if she knew all about them. Of course, strict confidentiality rules would prevent her saying directly if she had any of them under her care, but there were ways of telegraphing these things among professionals.

"I have a feeling they may know something about these animal mutilations."

"Ah. Any evidence?"

"Not yet. But the whole family should be home on Sunday morning. There's a lot of them, and I don't want to miss any."

Elizabeth stared off into space for a moment, then said, "I shouldn't tell you this, because it violates a patient-client relationship to some extent, but I think something may be seriously wrong in that family."

Pay dirt.

"I saw the oldest boy, Jeff, a couple of times, when I first moved here. The high school suspended him pending counseling, and since I'm the only game in town, he came to me. His insurance wouldn't pay for more than two appointments, so I didn't get a chance to learn much about him. I offered to see him for free, but the family was too proud to take me up on it."

"Twice—you only saw him twice? How are you expected to help someone in so short a time?"

She shrugged. "It's impossible, of course. You'd be surprised at how many patients I see under similar circumstances. If it was up to the insurance companies, they wouldn't pay for psychological sessions at all, but pressure has forced them to cave in to some degree. Their official policy seems to be that we can cure schizophrenia in four visits, paranoia in two."

"And what was wrong with this boy, Jeff?" When she said his name out loud, Sally realized he'd been named for Jefferson Davis, who had been president of the Confederacy during the Civil War. This was not a good sign.

"Ethically, I can't get into details, but I can tell you that I didn't learn a whole lot. I guess he shaped up, though, because the principal let him return to school. He graduated in June, and I don't know what he's doing now."

"Did you see any psychopathic tendencies?"

Elizabeth thought for a moment. "I can't say that I did."

"But you think I'm wise to go out there as soon as possible?"

"In all truth, I just don't know. But don't arrive until after one. They'll be at church."

"How do you know they go to church?"

"Hon, around here, *everyone* goes to church. They're Methodists, and the Methodists get out at twelve-forty on the dot."

"I don't see you putting on a hat and gloves."

"Since I'm a psychologist, I must be kin to Satan anyway, so I don't bother. I'd rather stay home and read the

Sunday papers, so I'd better get going before they're sold out. They only get four of them at the Stop-N-Go out on the highway."

Sally watched Elizabeth go. By what she had revealed—and what she hadn't—she'd actually said a lot. Sally thought she might be about to collar her killer.

Sally had guessed that the Davis place wouldn't be easy to miss, but she was wrong. The brush along Pinewoods Lane grew thicker when you passed the edge of town, the houses more hidden.

She was on her way back, in fact, when she noticed a small black mailbox with "Davis" carefully applied to the side with stencils bought at the hardware store. The driveway was asphalt, and the house was set well back in a yard full of wonderful old shade trees.

The place was kept up diligently, but by somebody without much money or imagination. The house was white, the paint just beginning to age a little. The trim around the windows was glossy black, a recent application. Vinyl siding was probably outside their budget, which was the only reason that the house still displayed its lovely old lapped board sides.

Besides the huge mailbox, another sure sign of a big family was the fact that the driveway was full of cars. There were four vehicles parked alongside the road at various angles. None of them were new.

Sally turned off her engine, but did not get out of the car immediately. Rather, she listened. Members of dysfunctional families are usually loud, so she expected to hear at least some of them. In these families, someone is always yelling, the TV is usually blaring, and there's a general sense of chaos. But this family was so quiet, she wondered at first if anyone was home. Or maybe Houston had been louder than she'd realized.

She mounted the porch on gray, weathered steps and looked into the dimness beyond the screen. An empty living room, the couch covered with a weary-looking green bedspread. She knocked, which eventually brought movement in the shadowy area beyond the living room. She could see a silhouette pause there. When it came forward, it turned into a nondescript, washed-out woman in late middle age, who peered at her through the screen . . . and said not a word.

Then a voice boomed out, "Who is it, Lana?" and soon a large man loomed up behind his silent wife.

When she saw Mr. and Mrs. Davis together, Sally remembered Mrs. Kavitz's gossip about their being first cousins. It was obviously just gossip, because she had never seen two people who looked less alike. He was big, burly, and dark, with curly hair sprouting from his knuckles and the bottom of his neck beneath his white Sunday shirt, while she was tiny and timid, with dishwater-blond hair and eyes that were just a little too quick for comfort. Was he another wife beater? She hoped not. She hated to think that Maryvale would turn out to be a morass of batterers and their victims. Not exactly what she'd hoped to come home to.

Sally introduced herself and explained her mission. "I'm questioning everyone along the road about the recent animal mutilations," she said. "We don't want it to happen again. We think it must be children who are doing this, so I'd like to talk to your whole family, if I may."

An expression of what could only be called amazement slowly reconstructed Lana's face. Her eyebrows went up, her lips opened, and she stared, not saying a word. Clearly, she was going to defer to the squat, red-faced man behind her.

A smile creased Sam Davis's face, tight with irony. "How many tax dollars is this gonna cost, Miss Bureaucrat?" he asked.

"Uh, I—"

"Right! You have no idea." Then he pushed his wife aside and opened the screen door. With an intentionally overdone gesture of welcome, practically a bow, he said, "Come on in, Miss Tax Increase." As she passed him, he closed his eyes and belted out one very powerful holler: "Kids! Get in here, do it NOW!"

The Davis offspring appeared immediately, sitting down in various parts of the living room. They all faced Sally. They ranged from the oldest, who had to be Jeff, to a little boy who looked about ten years old. There were eight children in all—six boys and two girls, both of whom resembled their mother. It looked as if Lana had conceived almost yearly, with only occasional time off. They were clean, nice-looking kids, but they seemed unnaturally obedient. Even the teenagers had responded instantly to their father's call.

Sally got a chair out of the dining room and positioned it so that she could see them all. Speaking in a careful voice, she recited the history of the past six months' fires and animal mutilations. She described the tortured animals vividly, but kept her voice soft so that the younger children would not be terrorized.

As she talked, she made eye contact first with one child and then another. She looked deeply into their eyes. And she kept returning to Jeff. At times, she spoke as if directly to him.

Her eyes swept past a sea of expressionless faces. If any of them had a secret, they weren't giving it away—especially not in front of Dad.

"Okay," Sam Davis said briskly, "that it? That's the whole story?"

"I want to ask if any of you have heard anything—any gossip around school, for example—"

"It's still summer break," Jeff said. He was the first one to speak.

"Well, before, did you hear anything before? The first mutilation was last March."

No more replies from any of them. They were holding something back, and they were good liars, probably from long practice. This was a family that was used to circling the wagons in order to ward off intruders. If there was anything to be learned from them, she would have to talk to each child alone, away from the rest of the family. As long as they were together as a unit, this would not work.

Unfortunately, it was illegal for her to contact a minor without the parents' permission, and she doubted that Sam would consent to her questioning them without him in attendance. But maybe she could risk it once they were back in school, if she could get permission from the school authorities. She would start by asking the school principal why he had referred Jeff to Elizabeth.

"We're done here," Sam said, standing up. "Momma is gonna be dealing with nightmares tonight as it is. No more, lady."

Sally stood and thanked them for their time. Sam promised to contact the sheriff's office if anybody remembered anything.

As she walked back to her car, she reflected that Jeff was puzzling. She had expected to meet a kid with an attitude, maybe even in rebellion. But he was clean-cut and tightly wrapped. He didn't display any of the psychopath's carefully constructed charm, or the lack of emotion. He'd been affected by her descriptions of the animals' suffering, she'd seen it in his eyes.

She was liking this situation less with every hour that passed. Something was not right in Maryvale. As she passed Suzanne's place, she found herself slowing down, then stopping, then turning in. She wanted, and badly, to see if Suzanne had gotten that dog yet.

As she drove up to the house, Suzanne came out onto the porch. Sally had to admit it was good to see someone she could relate to again, after her little American Gothic encounter down the road.

Suzanne wore an old blouse and jeans covered with a thousand different colors of paint.

As Sally got out of her car, she apologized for interrupting Suzanne's painting, which it was obvious she'd done.

"Don't worry, I was looking for an excuse to quit for a while. I really can't concentrate." She sat on the porch steps, put her chin in her hands. "I keep seeing her ghost slinking around the corners the way she used to. I almost called out to her when I saw her in the kitchen this morning."

"I told Hank that you wanted to hire Glynesse. Have you called her yet? She's our key to finding out if Hank's responsible for Suzette. I'm not going to be able to reach her, but there's a chance you can, if you're alone together." Sally didn't tell Suzanne that she was worried Glynesse might no longer be alive.

"She called me, believe it or not."

"She called you?" Sally felt a scream that had been building in her mind go silent. Sweet relief.

"First thing Friday morning. I'm going to pick her up and bring her over here Tuesday at nine." She looked around her immaculate living room. "I have a regular cleaning service, so I'll have to find something for her to do."

"Whatever it is, keep her nearby, so you can question her closely."

"I will."

"And look for signs of abuse. Bruises, eyes swollen from crying, swollen lips. Wife beaters go for the mouth, because it's the voice they can't control."

"Do you suppose I could talk her into letting me take a Polaroid of her naked body? Say I want to paint her? We could put them in a safety deposit box like Nicole Simpson did." Suzanne sighed. "As if that would help. Incidentally, here's something a little weird—when I talked to her, she also suggested the dog thing." Suzanne said "dog thing" in the tone of voice of a true cat person. "She told me a friend of hers has a new batch of bull terrier pups."

"I hope so—that's the kind of dog you need." She could see by the way that Suzanne kept glancing toward her barn-studio that the truth concealed by her southern charm was that she was ready now to get back to work. "One last thing," Sally asked, "what do people usually do around here for fun on weekends?"

"Ummm, I usually paint. Right now I'm getting ready for a show in Houston, but I'm afraid I paint all the time, anyway." Then she said something that really pleased Sally. "Why don't you drop around more often?"

"Why, thank you. That's really sweet."

Suzanne stood up, then, and Sally did, too. As she was leaving, she got a surprise.

The tree where Suzette had been hanged was gone, chopped down, the wood carted away. She wondered if Suzanne had hired Hank to do it.

On the way home, Sally reflected that she hadn't been particularly eager to please a man for a long, long time, but she really wanted Suzanne and Elizabeth to like her. Was she getting to the point where the opinions of girlfriends were more important to her than what men thought of her? And if so, did that mean that she was giving up in some deep way? She hoped that male companionship wasn't going to become part of her past, not to mention sex.

Sally had sworn off men many times. The trouble was, some cute guy always came along and stirred up her hormones again. Maybe her real motive for moving here was to find a place where there were no men who appealed to her, so there was no temptation to fall off the wagon.

Sunday night: fabulous if you liked ABC's lineup. Or had a good book. A thrill of very real terror shuddered through Sally when she realized she only had twenty pages left.

"There's no bookstore in town, is there?"

Elizabeth, half asleep, was staring at the TV. "Gladewater. Barnes and Noble."

Later, when Sally turned out her bedside lamp, moonlight crossed with leafy shadows flooded her room. The breeze sighed, bringing a breath of coolness from the vast pine woods that surrounded the town.

She got up, gazed out the window. A small shape moved slowly down the sidewalk, an old woman out for her nightly walk. The voice of a mockingbird echoed in the tremendous silence.

Despite all the disappointments, she knew, in this moment, why she had returned. She loved Maryvale, and always would. Maryvale in the moonlight.

Monday morning, she made sure to get to the office early, before Ed started out on his neighborhood rounds. Sure enough, he was there with his boots propped up on the desk, draining a mug of coffee.

He knew the name of the high school principal right off the top of his head, of course, but then he knew everyone in Maryvale off the top of his head. "Tom Keener. Nice guy, very dedicated. Actually talks a few of 'em into going to college."

Ed found Keener's number on his bulging Rolodex. When she called to introduce herself, his wife told her he was at the school getting some paperwork done in preparation for the fall semester. "I'll call Tom and tell him you'll be by," she said. "He'll make sure the door's unlocked."

As she left, Ed called after her, "Have a good one."

"For sure," she replied. No more mention of the forms meant the receptionist's desk was left unmanned once again. Fine by her.

There was a little bustle going on in Maryvale this morning, cars and trucks on the main drag. It didn't amount to much though—five cars.

The high school was a rectangular tan brick box, like every other Texas high school built in the sixties. A weathered sign on the dusty front lawn proclaimed it as "Home of the Wildcats." She remembered wishing, as a girl, that she could go here to school. She remembered walking up this very sidewalk and looking through the glass of one of the locked double doors. She'd never been in Maryvale when school had been in session. Once, when she was caught in a wild summer shower, she'd sheltered under the benches out by the football field, and watched the rain blowing in lonely curtains across the empty turf.

The double doors had been olive drab metal then. Now they were blond wood, and one of them was ajar.

She entered, and found a long hallway, hard gray tiles on the floor, walls of lockers, cinder-block construction. It was a fortress built to house students and to resist being totally destroyed by them.

Tom stepped out of an office up ahead. His dark silhouette beckoned to her. "Sally?" he called.

She waved and hurried down the hall. Tom was a tall man with a working paunch and a friendly, flushed face. His hairline was retreating rapidly, and he had the big hands of a guy who had really been born for farm and ranch life, not pencil pushing in a high school.

"So," he asked as he ushered her into his office, "you're the new county social worker." He gestured her to a seat in a gray steel chair in front of his matching steel desk. "The commissioners finally did what they should. That's good. You're gonna have plenty of business around here, lady."

"I'm finding that out." She decided not to mention that she was officially on the books as the sheriff's receptionist. She noticed a shelf full of sports trophies on the wall behind Tom's head, and that his desk was strewn with familiar-looking federal and state forms.

He smiled, twiddled his pen as if he was eager to get back to them. "Now, what can I do for you?"

"I want you to tell me anything you can about Jeff Davis, who graduated last spring," she said.

"May I know why?"

"We're concerned about these animal mutilations."

"I am, too. I don't like the look of it. Looks like it could turn even meaner, you ask me."

"If he's the one who's setting fires and torturing animals, he needs help and I want to get that for him. Did you suspend him because he was destroying school property? Threatening other students?"

Tom leaned back in his chair. "No, nothing like that. He was more sinned against than sinning."

"That could mean a lot of things."

"Jeff was always quiet, did good work, and it was clear to all of us here that he was intelligent. He was secretive, though, to a fault."

"In what sense?"

"When I started trying to get him to fill out some college aps, I just could not get any cooperation. Not that he didn't want to go to college. He didn't want to put any personal information on the forms. His English teacher told me the only assignment he didn't do really well on was when he had to write an autobiography. His was five lines long."

Pathological secretiveness meant something, always. This boy was troubled. "But you didn't suspend him over that?"

"I'm getting there. You know, one thing the legislature requires is a certain amount of phys. ed. For that, you have to get a physical either from us or from a private doctor. Last fall, Jeff was examined and I received a report that he had cigarette burns on his back. Under the law, I was required to get him interviewed by a registered clinician, and report the results to the state police. To make a long story short, he absolutely would not do that interview. I had to suspend him from school before he was willing to do it."

Sally was appalled. "Couldn't you have Ed arrest his parents?"

"I had to move carefully. I wasn't sure it was the parents. Could've been some gang-related thing. I told his folks he was having trouble concentrating in school, and I thought Elizabeth Lerman could help him. She's our resident youth psychologist."

"I'm rooming at her house."

"Okay, so you know her. I hoped she could get him to identify his abusers, but he wouldn't open up. He wouldn't talk even when I threatened to kick him off the

bowling league, which was his pride and joy." He sighed
in frustration.

"But he doesn't have to admit anything in order to get
help. As a school official, you're required to report suspected cases of child abuse, not investigate them or make
any value judgments."

"And I would have done it, too, if he hadn't been about
to graduate. But I decided not to interfere, since I figured he
was about to leave town anyway. I never guessed he would
keep on living at home. I just wish he would go out and get
a life for himself. He's a young man now. I can't see how
they could be doing that sort of thing to him anymore."

"But that house is filled with vulnerable children! Those
parents could be torturing every one of them. You do understand that?"

Tom Keener cast his eyes down. He rubbed his temples.
"I understand that the focus of that kind of thing is often
restricted to one child."

She thought of the Davis household, all those obedient
young boys and girls, their soft, unfinished eyes studying
her. "You can't take that for granted."

"I'm going to check the other kids this fall," Tom as-
sured her. "We've got two of his brothers here in the high
school right now—Sam Junior and Kenny, so I can check
on them personally. You've got to understand, Miss Hopkins, I have to get more evidence against the Davises, if
I'm going to be able to do more than get his dander up and
end up out of a job myself."

"The building code enforcer has that kind of power? I
find that hard to believe. He's a low-level bureaucrat."

"He's also the brother-in-law of a county commis-
sioner and a church deacon and a whole lot of other
things that count around here. And confidentially, he is
not a tolerant man."

"I've noticed." She felt the old familiar sense of frustration and anger rising up in her. Right now, just at this moment, Houston had caught up with her. She was still stuck
in the same web.

She shook hands with Tom Keener and promised to keep him posted on her own investigation of the Davises.

When she arrived back at the office, the forms she'd put away were stacked on the receptionist's desk once more, a not-so-subtle hint. Ed just could not get it through his thick backwoods skull that something horribly dangerous was happening here.

Part of her wanted to walk out on the damned fool. But she could not do that, not now. She was involved. She would not walk out on those hurting kids out there on Pinewoods Lane, and she would not walk out on Suzanne or on poor Glynesse. And, in the end, she would not walk out on Ed.

So she sat down and began to work on the forms again, as the shadows leaned long and the afternoon settled toward evening. She wondered how long they had before the killer who was lurking out there somewhere decided to act. The wall clock hummed, the second hand sweeping relentlessly around its blank, empty face.

Sally was making breakfast the next morning when the phone rang. "I'll get it," she said to Elizabeth, whose head was in the refrigerator. She padded out into the hall in her worn old slippers and picked it up.

"Sally, I just heard! Oh, God, Sally!" A female voice was high and panicked.

"Suzanne?"

"Yes!"

"What's the trouble, Suzanne?"

Elizabeth took her head out of the refrigerator and came into the doorway.

"It's Glynesse. They found her dead! And Hank is missing!"

Sally could not speak. Her mind raced—Hank had done it and she felt sick inside. She should have been more aggressive, she should have been more careful, damn it!

"Sally," Suzanne continued, "do you think Hank killed her to stop her from telling me something? When I went over there to pick her up for work this morning, nobody answered the door. The pickup was gone, too. I've never heard the house so quiet and I was suspicious that something wasn't right.

"I drove back home and called the sheriff's office right away. Ed put me through to Rob Farley, and he went over to their place and broke a window to get in, then he came and told me. He said she looked like she'd been dead for most of the weekend."

Sally concluded the call as quickly as she could without upsetting Suzanne any further, then filled Elizabeth in. Elizabeth literally reeled back into the kitchen and collapsed into a chair. "Believe me, Sally," she said, "nothing like this has happened in Maryvale, not in all the time I've been here."

She knew Ed would be over at the Sunderland house with Rob right now, and she wanted desperately to join them, but she felt that she'd failed them professionally, failed them and failed Glynesse and—well, just totally failed. And a life had been lost. A *life*.

Nothing remotely like this had ever happened in Houston. Truth to tell, the stakes had never been this high. So maybe the problems of little ol' Maryvale were actually out of her league.

She dragged herself to the office and sat listlessly at her receptionist desk. "This crap is all you're good for," she said to herself, staring down at a HUD water quality test report.

She worked for half an hour, dully, mechanically, never looking up, listening for the phone with a frantic and despairing heart. She was hoping it would all turn out to be a horrible mistake, and Suzanne or Ed or Rob would call and tell her that.

The phone did eventually ring, and when it did, Sally snatched it up with the speed of a striking snake. "Sheriff's office," she said.

It was Ed, calling from the Sunderland house. She quickly explained that she knew about the murder. He asked her, "What did Hank say to you, darlin'? Anything about any hunting camp he might have? Where he might be going?"

All she could remember was his lie about going to trim trees.

Ed also pointed out something she hadn't thought of: it was a double murder, since Glynesse had been pregnant. Whoever did this would wind up being given a lethal injection for sure. When it comes to execution, the Texas judicial system doesn't flinch. The legislature had been debating whether or not to extend the death penalty to murderers as young as eleven years old, but since the recent Supreme Court ruling, they'd have to be content with just incarcerating them for the rest of their lives. The harder Texas got on criminals, the faster the crime rate dropped. Or so the state's statisticians made it appear.

The forms swam before her eyes. She couldn't just sit here doing this while a psychopath roamed the town. She had to focus on the case, no matter how badly she felt about her abilities.

No matter how it had looked, Hank must have been the animal torturer, and therefore this had not been a crime of passion but a graduation to a new level of evil. Odds were, his wife was not his last victim, but his first.

She hadn't been smart enough to see through his lies, and had let a serial killer out through her fingers by being too academic about the whole thing.

But what did she know about serial killers, anyway? Nothing more than she'd learned in a few abnormal psychology courses.

She put her head in her hands and wept.

"Sally?" It was Rob's voice. He and Ed were standing at her desk. She hadn't heard them come in. How long had they been watching her? She sniffed and straightened up, then followed them back to Ed's office.

"Thirteen years," Ed said, his voice tired. "And the last one was manslaughter. A guy threw a live chain saw at his best friend during an argument." He thought about that for a moment, his eyes hard and distant. "A hell of a mess," he said quietly.

Sally and Rob waited silently for him to continue.

"My dear Lord, the poor darlin's head was stove in."

"What did he use? What weapon?"

"You're assuming Hank killed her," Rob said.

She was surprised. "Aren't you?"

"I agree it looks that way, but you can't assume something like that without hard evidence, if you're going to be a professional in this business."

Ed looked at Sally, right into her eyes. She saw sadness. Deep. "She was hit in the back of the head with what the coroner thinks might have been an ax handle or maybe a baseball bat. After she was dead, the killer beat her again and again with the same object."

"Ed, I'm so sorry I didn't see this coming."

"You saw it coming. You're the only one who did, matter of fact."

"I let the woman get murdered!"

"We did that by not going over there."

"Could you tell if she'd been beaten before?"

"The coroner says her body shows a long history of battery. There are scars around her eyes, signs of broken ribs, a hairline jaw fracture. There's no evidence of past beatings with a baseball bat, though, and no sign of the bat, either."

"He didn't seem like a killer, although I pegged him for a wife beater."

"Did you see Glynesse?" Rob asked her. "When you interviewed him?"

"He wouldn't let me see her and it made me suspicious. But Suzanne said she talked to her on the phone on Friday, so that reassured me."

"I wonder why she called Suzanne?" Rob mused. "You'd think Hank would have told Glynesse to stay away from her."

"I asked Suzanne to do anything she could to get a look at her. Wife beaters learn how to hit carefully, so the evidence is concealed, or heals up fast. They get to be experts at it. I wanted Suzanne to try to get through to her."

"We need to take this thing piece by piece. Analyze everything."

"We were doing that and a woman died!"

Both men stared at Sally, and she realized she'd been shouting.

"Remember, darlin'," Ed reminded her, "all we have here is a dead body. Hank's a suspect because he's the husband and he's gone. But we do not yet know what happened."

"Sally," Rob said, "answer me a professional question."

That was a laugh. "You still want my professional opinion?"

"Yes I do. Hank or no Hank, do you see anything in this killing that makes you think we're looking at a beginning serial murderer?"

"I do, but I also think that's a question for a criminologist."

"But you're what we have, Sally! Now please answer the question!"

She was amazed. In her whole life, these were the first angry words Ed had ever directed at her. "The head was—how bad?" she asked.

"The head was pulped," Ed snapped.

"Rage that extreme is obviously a bad sign. We could be dealing with a badly deranged man."

"Could he kill again?" Rob asked.

"It's always easier the second time, when that barrier has been broken. It depends on if his rage was only directed at his wife. If he's the psychopath, then his rage is more general and yes, he could and probably will kill again."

"The only way to make sure this doesn't happen is to find him, pronto," Rob snapped. "We've put out a description of Hank and his truck. He'll probably turn up somewhere pretty soon, drunk most likely. These guys aren't usually too smart when they run. Most of the time they end up at their mother's house or in the alley behind a bar."

"Are you having any forensics work done?" She knew that there was no forensics equipment in Maryvale, beyond an old fingerprint kit in the back of one of the supply lockers.

Sally caught Rob and the sheriff exchanging glances while they thought she wasn't looking. "There's something you're not telling me, isn't there?"

Rob cleared his throat. "There are some unusual aspects about this killing, that we'd also like your professional opinion on."

"Such as?"

Both men fell silent again. Ed was beet-red. Rob shuffled. "Well?"

"The position of the body, for one thing. The legs were bent up at the knees and spread wide so that, well you know, so as to reveal her private parts."

"Is that all?"

"That's all, except that her face was beaten so hard, you couldn't even tell she was a human being from the neck up. Concentration on the face."

"Did the killer have sex with her first, then beat her face in afterward?" It was a question Sally wished she could have avoided asking.

Rob cleared his throat. "Forensics found no sperm," he said.

Ed looked like he was ready to turn and run out the door. "She hadn't had sex in recent days," he muttered.

"What kind of forensics was done?"

"The unit came down from Gladewater," Rob said. "They're pretty thorough. They gathered DNA off her body, dusted for prints, vacuumed for traces and hair, pulled the debris from under nails and the mouth, in case she bit her assailant, and they did a penetration analysis, all orifices."

"And the results? Aside from the penetration analysis, which I assume was negative."

"It was negative. And, as of right now, so was everything else."

"The scene was very clean," Ed said.

Sally thought, *An organized psychopath, the worst, most dangerous kind. He can think, plan ahead, play careful.* She said, "The killer is leaving a signal for us here. He wanted to have sex with her, but he couldn't function and he blamed that on her. The sexual failure led to uncontrollable rage. Since Glynesse was pregnant, you'd think this would rule Hank out—but unfortunately, it doesn't."

"Why not?" Rob asked.

"Once a woman is going to have a baby, most men will feel protective toward her. But some men—men like this killer—will be especially angry. Filled with hate. Most men recognize that women play many roles in life, but not all. For these creatures, we're either the mother or the whore, and they usually hate both. There've been a few serial killers who preyed exclusively on pregnant women, but most of them go after the whores."

Ed said, "We need to go out to old Mrs. Sunderland's. Find out what she knows."

Sally did not reveal her shock that they hadn't immediately gone to the mother's house. "He might be there," she said.

"He might," Ed agreed.

"If he isn't, you won't get anything out of her, you know." The famous willingness of mothers to stick with their kids till the end was no old wives' tale.

"Texas gals of Mrs. Sunderland's generation were raised to believe in God, country, and that it's a sin to tell a lie. She might choose to keep her silence, but her face will tell us whether or not she's heard from her son. If we don't think she's telling us the truth, we'll pull her in and drive her slowly past all her friends' houses in the cruiser. She'll tell us the details."

There was a hard side to Ed that he could call on when he had to.

The trip out to Hank's mother's place turned out to be useless. Her house was empty. She'd disappeared as well. At first, this concerned Ed and Rob. But when they checked with her neighbors, they found that she'd driven away on some sort of a vacation.

One member of her bridge club thought it was a spa in New Mexico, another, California. They thought maybe she'd used one of the Houston airports. Rob put a call into Houston and had them check their airport parking lots, and he got some of the other troopers checking travel agencies.

Ed went to Judge Ellis to get a warrant to search her house. He thought that Hank might be there while his mother was away, hiding in the basement.

Sally and Rob went back to the office, where a painful silence fell. "Can I talk to the forensics tech?" Sally asked at last.

Rob regarded her from behind a foam coffee cup. "Why?"

At least he was direct. "For one thing, I want to know exactly how she moved just before she was hit. Was she surprised, or defending, or even trying to run."

"Which will tell you what?"

"Maybe if she knew her killer."

Ed came storming in the office muttering to himself. Judge Ellis had turned down the warrant application because he couldn't present any evidence that Mrs. Sunderland had been party to a crime, or that Hank was in the house.

Pretty strict judge, Sally thought.

She found herself wondering who would be next. This surprised her: on the surface, she wasn't at all sure that that they were dealing with a psychopath. But underneath, obviously, she thought differently.

She could feel him in the wind. He was pacing hungrily, ready to pounce again.

Saturday evening came, and Elizabeth disappeared again without a word. A secret lover, Sally thought, but why? Was he married? Or was it another woman, maybe? Whatever, the existence of Elizabeth's very private social life made Sally even more lonely. She was tempted to escape to Houston in order to hit the club scene, even though it meant shacking up in a cheap motel, because she didn't have the money for the Ritz-Carlton or the Four Seasons. Or the Hilton. Or Motel 6. At least there would be music and men. And if she wanted to take a little of East Texas with her, there were even places to line dance in Houston, where you could watch stockbrokers and insurance agents cavorting around in their western duds like they'd been born with hay in their hair. Sometimes they even switched from white wine to long necks.

She was beginning to seriously consider it when a car pulled up. And, lo and behold, none other than Suzanne the paint lady got out. She wasn't covered with paint now. In fact, she was dressed for line dancing, in a flowery skirt, petticoats, and a fringed western blouse.

"Hey there. Ever been to the Bluebonnet Palace?"

"Never heard of it."

"Get in the car, woman."

The dance hall started as a glow off in the woods, down a long, dark road. You'd never in a million years believe that there was anything out here but scrub and pine. But they rounded a curve and there stood a very large establishment with a huge sign outlined in lights: BLUEBONNET PALACE. From inside, she could hear the wail of fiddles.

There was no cover for ladies, and they got plenty of welcomes from guys whose string ties and Stetsons probably came from Rank's rather than Neiman Marcus. They were loggers, a few farmers, ranchers, and other guys who worked with their hands. There were even some genuine cowboys. Their muscles were the hard kind that came from hard work, not the pumped-up version that comes from exercise machines.

After a few beers, Sally accepted every invitation to dance that was sent her way, and found herself not caring whether or not her partner was interested in a mature, lasting relationship.

She waved when she spotted Tim Harrelson the carpenter across the room, which got them both introduced to his unmarried baby brother, who was instantly smitten by Suzanne. But Sally wasn't jealous—she was having too much fun dancing and laughing for the first time in weeks.

The Bluebonnet Palace wasn't only for dancing. There was a barbecue pit and, of all things, a bull-riding ring. Between dances, you could buy some barbecue and a beer, then go watch the bull riders compete.

The people who had created this knew what they were doing. Dancing and then watching bull-riding is as sexy a combination of activities as you will find, and by ten, couples were pairing off and disappearing into the starlit night, wandering out to their pickup trucks for some good old-fashioned making out.

Sally was tempted by more than one guy, but she kept

imagining Glynesse as she must have looked all beaten up, and didn't feel safe going home with a stranger.

When Suzanne and her new beau finally dropped her off in the early hours of the morning, she worried she might wake up Elizabeth. But as they drove up, she could see that the lights were on in the living room.

"Wassa matter?" Sally asked. "You worried about me being out too late?" She was about to tell Elizabeth how worried she'd been when Elizabeth didn't come home the weekend before, but she shut up fast when she saw the look on her face.

"My God, Elizabeth, what's wrong?"

"Ed called."

"Ed, uh—when?"

"Sally, there's been another murder!"

The world lurched.

"Sally?"

She grabbed the doorjamb, caught her breath. "Who—who—"

"Nobody you've met, I don't think. A young girl by the name of Wanda Ellis, who worked at the Rite Aid."

Sally hit a chair. Rob's friend. "Beautiful young girl," she managed to whisper through bone-dry lips. What if they'd been lovers? Poor Rob! He must be devastated. "Ed . . . does he want me?"

"He said to tell you not to come to the crime scene. He said he'd bring you up to speed at the coroner's meeting in the morning."

Not go to the crime scene? Why not? She was sick of being either ignored or overprotected! She didn't know what to do, but she didn't want to defy Ed. She called Rob at home, but the phone rang and rang. Obviously, he was at the crime scene. The only other way to reach him would be through State Police Dispatch, and she couldn't do that except for official business. She couldn't blame them. A social worker really has no place in a criminal investigation.

She spent the night tossing in sweaty sheets. Hank must

be hiding nearby, and he was clearly on the prowl. He'd gotten a taste for shedding blood, and didn't intend to stop with killing his wife. Sally replayed her conversation with him over and over again in her mind. Should she have recognized the killer inside him?

When the dawn chorus woke her, she thought she'd slept for perhaps an hour. She got up and took an ice-cold shower, threw on her clothes, and rushed over to the office without breakfast.

Rob and Ed were there, back in his office with the door closed. She went to it, started to push it open, then paused. There was a low murmur of voices. "Ed, it's me."

"Just give us a minute," Rob's voice said.

The coroner's meeting must already be under way, which made her almost choke with frustration. She paced the hall, noticed that Ed's morning pot of coffee was already empty, and set about making another one.

The door opened at last, and Ed called her from amid a small group of very tired-looking men. She went in, feeling hesitant as she entered their silence.

"Billy," Ed said, "this is our social worker, Miss Hopkins. Sally, this is Bill Frist, our county coroner, and Tilford Harkins from State Police Forensics."

Neither man smiled. Both stared at her.

"Sally's from Houston," Ed continued. As false a smile as she'd ever seen creased his face. "I'm so glad you did that," he said, heading past her, for the coffee. Rob was there, his eyes red from exhaustion and, Sally suspected, private tears.

"We're borrowing some hounds from the state police canine unit," Ed said. "They're being trucked in now, along with their handlers, and we should be able to take them out this afternoon. We've got to find that son of a bitch fast."

"What we can't figure out is why the heck he killed Wanda," Rob said.

"Was it the same pattern?" Sally asked.

"Well, we've been looking at that," the lanky forensics technician said. He glanced at Ed, who gave him a quick nod, obviously approving his involving Sally. "We have a clear pattern, ma'am. This must be the same killer."

Sally's mind raced. Should she continue? Why not, she'd been let into the damn meeting. The worst they could do would be to ignore her, or tell her to shut up. "I've got some questions," she said.

"Sure," Tilford responded.

"Was it the same weapon?"

"No question. Same bat. It was a Louisville Slugger, pine, size eight and a half, maybe nine."

She thought that was a small bat, made a mental note to find out. "And the blows—how did they land?"

The coroner cleared his throat. "Ed—"

"Tell her. She's the resident brain, maybe she'll be able to help us. A college girl."

"Well, now, the way he works is he comes up from below and behind."

"For the victim, the lights just go right on out." He snapped his fingers, and from the way his small lips twisted, she could see that he was flushed not with embarrassment about anything, but with rage.

"And then, was her face—"

"Six blows delivered this time, five the last," Tilford said.

She knew just what she had to ask. "Light or heavy blows?"

Rob looked at her with sudden interest. "What would you predict?"

"I'd say that they were light, methodically placed, designed to destroy the face very efficiently."

"Now, why is that?"

"He's organized. Intelligent. He knows what he's doing and what he wants to do."

"Well, you called it just right," Tilford said.

Unless he's an old man and lacks strength, she thought. "Once again, no sign of struggle?"

Nobody spoke. Their silence communicated the answer.

Tilford said, "Definitely the same bat."

"And what about the position of the body?"

Ed snapped, "It was arranged in an identical manner."

Sally saw a possibility—remote—that maybe Hank wasn't a psychopath at all. "Could he have been cheating on his pregnant wife by having an affair with Wanda?" she asked. "She was a beautiful young girl."

Rob's jaw set, his neck colored. "I can't believe she'd have anything to do with scum like that."

"Sometimes girls relax their standards when they're lonely," Sally said softly. She was thinking about the handsome auto mechanic she'd been tempted to go home with last night.

"No." Rob was firm. "But she could have refused to go out with him. That might have been what set him off."

"Here's what I think happened," Ed said. He had dropped down into his chair, but he was not leaning back. His feet were not up. "Hank may have realized by now that there's no hope for him. No matter how hard he runs, sooner or later we'll find him. He's got nothing to lose, so he can let all his hatred for women come out and punish any female who ever treated him bad. He may have done his poor old mother in, too. She hasn't turned up yet." He turned toward Sally, raised his eyebrows. He was looking for her thoughts again, and she was beginning to feel, at last, a part of this.

"If this isn't a love triangle that exploded in the guy's face, or was about to, then we are certainly looking at a seriously ill man, who will most certainly kill again. The positioning of the bodies tells me that he comes up behind them, knocks them cold, then tries to have sex with them—"

"No semen," Tilford said.

"Exactly. He fails. Then he gets mad. He destroys the face of his oppressor. What other evidence is there? Anything to identify him?"

Tilford stared straight ahead. "We've got a very good operation."

"He can't find so much as a hair," Bill snarled. "No DNA, no nothing."

It had not seemed odd that Glynesse hadn't defended herself. But this was different, this was not the man's wife. "How about her hands? Any defensive injuries?"

Bill shook his head. "Clean."

"And where was she?"

"Living room. Looked like she'd just let him in the front door, then turned and headed toward the kitchen."

That could not be right. "She opens her door, sees Hank there with a baseball bat in his hands—so she decides to just let him in, then turns her back on him and heads for the kitchen? I don't think so."

"So what do you think?" Rob snapped, his tone telling her that he still didn't have a very high opinion of her ideas.

"What I think is that she would not have done that, even if she knew Hank well. Especially not then. It's all over town that we think Hank killed Glynesse with a baseball bat. So when he turns up at his lover's house with the same bat—it just doesn't work. And if he *doesn't* know her, well, it doesn't work even more."

"Maybe she was out of the loop," Ed said. "Less informed than you think."

Sally considered. Ed was a good policeman, no question. "This should probably be our theory," she said. "So we've got to alert local women, tell them to be careful. Rob, can you send troopers around to distribute leaflets? We need to tell the newspaper to print a story about it. And we need to warn Suzanne right away. He may be after her next. She needs to leave the area right now."

"Good idea, Sally," Ed said. "You take care of getting the flyers printed. Plus, go over to KYNN in Hearne and have them start spreading the word. And see if you can get the TV station in Gladewater to run a story, with Hank's picture. But it's no good asking the Maryvale *Herald* to print a story. It's just your basic small-town pennysaver and this is Wednesday, so it won't be out again until next Tuesday. But they do have a printing press where we can get the leaflets done." He sighed. "This is big city stuff, Sally. We're really gonna be coming up from behind."

"Do we have a picture of Hank?"

He turned to Rob. "When you get a chance, go over there to find a snapshot of ol' Hank. At least we can enter his house."

Rob nodded. "Will do. But, Sally, be careful what you say about Hank. We don't have enough evidence to charge him yet, so we can't print anything that implies he's a criminal at large. It might mess up our case against him. Just say that he's missing and we want to find him and talk to him. Blow up his photo real large, so it looks like an FBI wanted poster. Offer a reward."

"Have we got money in the budget for a reward?"

"Just offer it anyway."

"Good idea," Ed agreed. "The troopers can knock on doors, stick those leaflets in mailboxes, and put them up in store windows and at the post office. We'll paper Maryvale with 'em. And the next time he shows up at some poor soul's door with a baseball bat in his hand, she will not be deceived."

"Even so," Sally said, "I'm worried that this won't be enough. Just saying we want to question Hank makes it seem less dangerous than it is."

"Sally, bless you, you don't understand how things work in a little town. The troopers don't just hand those things around, they give out a personal warning with each one." Ed smiled. "Gossip is our biggest ally. After word gets around that we think Hank killed an innocent young woman, as well as his wife, even his hunting buddies will help us look for him."

"I see—they'll turn him in for killing Wanda, but not for killing poor Glynesse, who was just his wife, his private property to do whatever he wanted with."

"Nobody said that," Rob said.

Ed agreed. "But you've got to understand this: everyone's heard about marriages going sour. But at least once the spouse has been killed, it's over. The guy's either going to run or turn himself in. He's not going to go out and kill someone else."

"But Hank's just proved he's different." Sally started to call Suzanne. Rob put his hand on her shoulder. "She knows," he said. "We informed her late last night. We were waiting for her when she came back from the Palace."

"Where is she now?"

"Packing," Ed said, "she better be."

Rob put a hand on Sally's arm. "Sally, there's something we need to tell you."

"Yes, Rob?"

"What we were talking about when you came in was your own possible level of exposure in this thing. You could be in danger, too, Sally, and we want you to leave here."

"It's best, darlin'. You need to call a halt here and head on back to Houston."

Click went her brain, click. Were they firing her at the moment they had finally accepted her? "No," she said. Her voice came out all shaky. "I think I'm needed right here."

Ed got slowly to his feet. "Sally, I can't have that. I can't risk it."

It was true enough that Hank might remember their little talk and decide the world would be a better place without her.

"I have no place to go in Houston!"

"Suzanne's willing to take you in. She has a lovely home there."

"My job is here, Ed."

"You're to do as I tell you, young woman."

In silence, she shook her head.

Rob said, "You don't want to risk your life over some worthless scumbag like Hank. You're not a cop, you're not paid for that." He sighed. "But it's true that we can use you here."

"Good, because I'm going to stay."

Ed's eyebrows lowered and a crimson flush spread over his face. He opened his mouth and she thought he was going to scream at her. But he whispered, "You'll do as you're told," and stalked out.

Tilford said, "Is he your father?"

"My uncle," she all but snarled.

"You look enough alike." He smiled then, and Sally was surprised to see just how sad his eyes were, locked in the wrinkles of the smile.

Rob hurried off as well, to connect with the dog unit out on the highway.

Sally was left alone with Bill and Tilford.

"Any more questions?" Tilford asked. "Any answers, Miss Hopkins? Thoughts?"

Sally remembered a book she'd read about FBI profiling.

"I can tell you that he'll be neat, well turned out, maybe even with his clothes color-coordinated. He'll obviously be somebody who people do not and cannot even begin to suspect."

"Like a cop," Tilford asked.

"Or a minister or—well, if you think about it, in a little town like this there's nothing to be gained by, for example, isolating all the people both women were familiar with because everybody knows everybody."

"So what do we do?"

"Truthfully, I just don't know. Get the flyers printed would be my guess."

"And not go back to Houston? Like Uncle Ed told you?"

She shook her head tightly and went off to get the flyers printed. But she stopped halfway across town and realized she could do nothing without that picture of Hank. In their hurry to get the dogs working, Ed and Rob wouldn't be able to get it to her right away, so the only solution was to go to Hank's house and get it herself.

As she drove out, she began to have a creepy feeling that Hank might be somewhere nearby, and her imagination started to suggest that he would be so enraged when he saw her that he would attack again.

Ed was right, she knew it. Maryvale had gone from being a refuge for her to a death trap.

But, in the event, the house was festooned with yellow

crime-scene tape and there seemed little chance that Hank
would dare to be within a hundred miles of the place. As
soon as she entered the driveway, there was a trooper car
behind her, its light bar flashing. He'd been hiding, and
very well. She must have passed him on the road and not
seen him. So they, also, thought Hank might return.

She started to get out of her car. "Remain in the vehicle
please," came a sharp, disembodied voice. This trooper
was not from around here. He and his partner got out, guns
at the ready, and came slowly up both sides of her car.

"License and insurance form, ma'am," the one who
came to her window said. She had them ready. "Okay, Miss
Hopkins, you're gonna have to get off this road."

"I'm the sheriff's executive assistant. We need a picture
of Hank Sunderland. For the publicity."

"Please wait here, ma'am."

They went back to their car, and she knew that they'd be
confirming her story with Ed—assuming he could be
found. But, of course, it was different, now. Everything
was totally different. Ed's radio would be on, always, from
now on.

A moment later one of them got out of the car and came
over to her. "A trooper will go in there and look for a picture, while you wait here. Ed says you're to head on over
to Houston as soon as you're finished with the leaflets.
You're to go to Suzanne's home there. She's leaving this
morning."

Sally glanced up the hill, but the brush was too thick to
see the house from here.

While she waited impatiently, one trooper ducked under
the tape and entered the house, while the other stood near
her car with his holster unsnapped and his hand on the butt
of his gun. She realized that she was being guarded, and
knew, then, that her imagination hadn't been so far off. The
police, also, thought that Hank might be around here.

The second trooper came out holding a creased snapshot
of Hank and Glynesse that looked like it had been taken at

the beach. It wasn't great, but she wasn't about to complain. She said thanks and got the hell out of there.

She drove over to the *Herald* offices, through the silent morning streets of Maryvale, trying to somehow anticipate Hank's movements.

Would he come after Suzanne? Maybe. Or her. Yes, he would come after her, Ed was right about that.

She arrived at the *Herald* building, a two-story yellow brick structure with a cement sign above the double doors: "Maryvale Herald, 1924."

They'd built this building back in the heyday, the unimaginable time when little town America was the center of the nation, and a local paper like the *Herald* was the center of the town. There was a rightness about that time, Sally thought. And then she remembered how the Ku Klux Klan had dominated this part of Texas in those days, and how the old lynching tree along the river was still a place notorious for ghosts and memories of a very different era.

She confronted something so obvious that she almost thought she'd lost her mind even to come here. The *Herald* was closed on Sunday, of course. In fact, this building was barely alive. It only opened on Wednesdays, when the little paper was assembled by three people, who wrote it, printed it, and dropped stacks in front of local businesses.

There was nothing to do now but go back to her desk and wait for the inevitable confrontation with Ed.

She was going to defy him. No matter what he said, she was staying in Maryvale. These crimes belonged to her. This criminal, whoever he was, was her criminal, her responsibility. She had known before anybody that he was here, and she was determined to be a part of his capture.

And it hit her again—murder, murder in Eden. She opened her mouth, cracking her jaw. That was tension, iron hard, the razor-sharp terror of the situation.

As soon as she got to the office, she fired up the dispatch radio so she could listen in on calls. She couldn't do anything with it except contact Ed, because all official business was routed through State Police Dispatch in Gladewater. But she could listen, and that's what she did.

She sat listening all day and into the night. In late morning, a couple of troopers came in and stood by the coffeepots chatting in low voices like doctors at a bedside. She listened to increasingly frustrated dispatches about the dogs. They couldn't get a scent except around Hank's place and in one spot along the highway where he'd apparently stopped to take a roadside leak. Heading west, though, that was a clue.

At least, they considered it one. She wasn't so sure. Anyone from this part of Texas would know that dogs would be brought into play. To Sally, that little roadside discovery seemed more like a trap. She suspected that he'd gone east toward Louisiana and the heart of the South beyond, heading toward Mississippi and Alabama, where a man could lose himself for a long time.

She drank coffee and dozed anyway. Then, toward evening, the radio spat an exchange between Rob and the dog handler. The dogs were being called back. They weren't going to find Hank Sunderland.

Sally considered going to a motel, but that meant a thirty-mile drive. She thought maybe that her presence at Elizabeth's would draw Hank. She didn't have a gun, not even some pepper spray. But she had her intelligence and the telephone. If he appeared, she'd use both, and she would defeat him.

Or was that a ridiculous idea?

She spent the evening staring at the TV, not seeing the lineup of shows, listening to the slightest stirring of the house. Elizabeth was still gone, and Sally dearly wished now that she was not.

At ten, she wandered out onto the front porch and stood in the pool of yellow light for a few moments, peering out into the night and, she knew, announcing her presence to Hank.

She wanted the confrontation. Truth was, she wanted the collar.

Toward morning, she slept a little . . . behind locked doors and windows.

On her way to work Monday, she drove past the *Herald* and found the front door ajar. Mal Bridges was inside setting type for some ads. Sally explained what she wanted, and he promised her two thousand leaflets the next morning.

She went to her desk in the virtually abandoned sheriff's office, and waited. Maybe she'd have a confrontation with Ed. Maybe another murder would be discovered.

She chewed Tums and drank coffee, which led to a need for more Tums. Hourly, she expected Ed to storm in and confront her, but that didn't happen. In fact, he wasn't even on dispatch. He could be at home, she thought, but she had no intention of calling him.

Toward four, an elderly lady walked in. She was impeccably dressed in a silk dress and pearl necklace, with stockings on, too, despite the heat. At first, Sally assumed this was another citizen coming in to inquire if they'd caught the culprit yet. "Can I help you?" she asked, plastering on the kind of southern-girl smile that made the locals comfortable.

"I'm a friend of Mrs. Sunderland's. The sheriff was out to my house asking me about her last week."

Sally thought this little old lady was unlikely to be a friend of Glynesse's. Perhaps she was referring to old Mrs. Sunderland, Hank's mother.

"Have you got some information for us?"

"I just wanted to tell you that Luella has returned home. We didn't remember where she'd gone, you see. It turns out she was at a retreat in Austin these past few days, for her health, you know. Her sister in Kerrville heard talk about the murder of Hank's wife and got in touch with Luella, so she cut her stay short and came right home. She's terribly upset and won't say anything to anybody, but I think the sheriff should know."

"Yes, ma'am," Sally said, "you're right about that." Sally heard a tremble in her voice that she struggled to control.

They might be on the verge of catching their man. "Thank you, Mrs. . . ."

"Royal, dear. Nellie Royal."

"Mrs. Sunderland is at home right now?"

"That's what I'm trying to tell you, dear."

"Thank you very much, Mrs. Royal. I'll tell the sheriff at once. We very much want to talk to Mrs. Sunderland about her son."

"You don't think he's been killed too, do you?"

My God, thought Sally, *there's actually someone in Mary-vale who still thinks Hank is innocent.* "We don't know, Mrs. Royal. That's why we're trying so hard to find him."

"Well, that's good. I'll tell Luella the sheriff will be out to see her."

"Oh, no, Mrs. Royal, you don't need to do that!"

"Why not, dear?"

What could she say? That Mrs. Sunderland could be hiding her son and had come home to stock up on provisions? Or that he might actually be in her house? "Well, ah, she might not feel up to talking with us about Hank, and it's very urgent."

"Oh, I'm sure she will. She wants to find him just as much as you do." And with that, she left.

After Mrs. Royal's exit, Sally radioed Ed and Rob. "Well, thank God she's alive, at least," Ed said when she reached him. Then it came: "Where are you?"

"At the office."

Was there a sigh over the radio? "Okay," he said at last. Then, "You have a care, darlin', you're making me gray. I'll corral Rob and we'll head over to her house right away. You want to meet us there?"

So, a change of heart. Strange, but Sally wasn't complaining. She wrote down the directions. She reached Mrs. Sunderland's small white bungalow before the others and parked down the road a distance, where she couldn't be seen from the house. She could see an elderly Cadillac in the driveway, dust caking its powder-blue surface.

Soon Ed and Rob came roaring up to the house in separate cars, both with light bars flashing. Sally met them on the roadside. By the time all three of them were at the front door, Mrs. Sunderland was standing on the porch waiting for them.

"Hello, gentlemen," she said, not seeming to notice Sally. "Come in, please. I just heard about my daughter-in-law's tragic death. I'm very worried about my son. Have you found him yet?" The idea that her son may have done the deed seemed not to have crossed her mind.

They entered the house, a place of dimness and drawn shades, the air-conditioning hissing softly. There were big old antiques everywhere, the kind of massive, dark stuff that was passed down from generation to generation across small-town America, especially across the South. Sally had seen a few similar pieces in Hank's house, but nothing like this. Mrs. Sunderland could have kept an antiques store in business for months.

Hank seemed like a redneck, to be blunt, and his family seemed to be feuding rednecks. But this woman appeared to belong to a lost southern aristocracy. Her manners and her way of life were dying, though. She had not been able to communicate her standards to her kids, for example.

Ed's manners were impeccable. He took off his hat and held it reverently in front of his chest. "We're so sorry for your loss, Luella. So very sorry."

"She was going to have a child," Mrs. Sunderland said in a small voice.

Ed bowed his head at the thought of the suffering she'd been through. "We don't know where Hank is. We thought he might be with you. When, if I may ask, was the last time you saw him?"

Sally held back and let Ed do the talking. He was exquisitely diplomatic, but so careful with his eyes, examining the place with a skill she had not known that he possessed. Rob stood behind him, huge in the small foyer. When Ed had removed his hat, he'd snatched off his own like an edgy schoolboy.

"When I left for Austin last weekend, Hank and Glynesse seemed just fine, as far as I could tell."

"Neither of them seemed worried or upset by anything?"

"If they were, I didn't pick up on it. The last time I spoke to Hank was on the telephone Friday night. I went to Austin Saturday morning, so I was out of touch for a day. When the news about Glynesse's death came out, my friend Eugenia Liverson called my sister Kathleen, who got in touch with me. I came right back as soon as I heard, but of course it took me another day of driving to get here. I've been worried sick about Hank, I can tell you."

"I'm sure you have," Ed murmured. "Can you think of any place he might be? Did your late husband have a hunting lodge or fishing shack? Is there any place Hank talked about wanting to visit, or somewhere special where he's been in the past? Some place where he might go to nurse his grief." Ed's hypocrisy was amazing. He had hidden skills of interrogation.

Mrs. Sunderland's forehead wrinkled, but then she shook her head. "Hank liked to stay close to the comforts of home, if you know what I mean. I can't think of any place he could be."

"If he was too upset to stay in his house, could he have gone to a friend's place?"

"Perhaps. Have you contacted everyone he knows? I can give you some suggestions of people to call."

She went out and returned with a pad and pencil, then carefully made a list. Looking over her shoulder, Sally couldn't spot a single name they hadn't already checked out.

"Mrs. Sunderland, please contact us the moment you hear from him," Ed said. "We're concerned about his welfare."

"Do you think—" She stopped, her eyes scared.

"What, Luella?"

"Ed, I'm just so concerned."

"So are we, Luella. We'll keep you informed."

As they walked back down the light-flooded road, Ed's demeanor changed. He became the hunter again, full of intensity, his voice sharp with deep anger. "God damn, I wish

I had the manpower to put a tail on that old gal. Plus, I need an order to tap her phone." He shook his head. "But it's not gonna be easy to get. Judge Rowell's scared to death to sign off on a thing like that." He brushed a grasshopper off his gray uniform shirt.

Locusts wailed in the fields. Flocks of grackles swept back and forth, feasting on the young corn. God help the local farmers.

"Welcome to the real world, Uncle Ed," Sally said.

Ed lowered his head, shading his eyes under the brim of his Stetson. "The real world moseyed on out here a while back," he said.

"I wonder if Mrs. Sunderland will take any action when she hears about the second murder?" Rob asked.

"I doubt it," said Ed. "She probably won't relate the second killing to her precious little boy. Oh, she might think the same person killed both her daughter-in-law and Wanda, but she'd never for a moment think that person could be Hank."

Rob cleared his throat. "Well, we thought we had a lead but it looks like we're back where we started. I guess Ed and I better drive around and continue our inquiries, and you need to get to the station in case any more information comes in."

Briefly, he touched her shoulder, a gesture that told her he was still worried about her decision to stay on in Maryvale . . . and also that he had accepted her presence here at last.

"Right," she replied.

Sally got in her car and drove back along the narrow county blacktop. On one side, there was adolescent corn, on the other, a pasture full of longhorns, the toy ranch of one of the weekenders. Nobody would eat longhorn meat these days. The only market for that stringy, strong stuff was pet food companies. But they were Texas in its heart, the mean-spirited cattle with their lethal horns, so hearty and so cussed that they'd been able to walk a thousand miles to slaughter, and still feed a nation.

She looked out toward the other field. It was a working farm. The farmer hoped to take a couple of thousand dollars out of that corn.

It was dense, and she wondered if they'd brought the dogs out along this road at all. They certainly should have, because if Hank was anywhere around here, he was near his mother's house, she would bet on it.

The next day death struck Maryvale again. It wasn't a lovely young woman who died this time, but Letitia Vane's beloved Pomeranian, Harry. She found him hanging by one paw from the fine old magnolia that graced her yard with its deep shade. The scented ruins of one of its big white blossoms were scattered across her lawn beneath where the dog dangled.

She came to the office, her makeup trenched with tears. She barged right past Sally, muttering, "Ed better be here." When she stormed into his office, Sally was close behind. "Ed, I swear to you that I'll have you recalled if you don't stop this horrible business. Horrible!" Her red fingernails slashed the air before her, making her seem helpless in her hurt and her rage, and pitiful. Then she saw that Ed's office was empty. "Where is he? Sleeping in on a Monday morning?"

"Mrs. Vane, please," Sally said, taking an elbow.

Letitia shook her off, then turned on her. Her eyes were glittering, sunken dots, her face a white mask of fury. "Don't you touch me, you—who are you, anyway?" she snorted. "Oh, yes," she said, "our new tax burden." Then she stalked out.

Ed came out of the bathroom looking like a whipped schoolkid. He'd actually hidden, it seemed.

"Darlin'," he said, "I got some BC Powders out by the coffee. Could you mix one up for me?"

As Sally made up the old-fashioned headache remedy, she reflected that she was now thoroughly baffled. Once a killer moves from animals to humans, he rarely regresses back to pets again. Thus the animal mutilator and the murderer could well be two separate people.

Sally was still in Ed's office when the phone rang. Since Ed had a cold handkerchief on his forehead, she picked it up. "Sheriff's office."

A whisper. Terrified.

"Can I help you?"

Like a ghost calling from beyond the grave, or the wind wailing past winter eaves, came a voice saying, "He's here . . ."

Claws tore at the inside of Sally's gut. "Stay calm. Tell me your location and we'll have help there immediately."

"This is Suzanne—"

"Suzanne, it's Sally. We're on our way!"

She slammed down the phone and flipped on the dispatch mike. "This is base. We have an emergency. This is—"

"Go on."

It was Rob's voice crackling through the speaker, and that made her almost weak with relief.

"Rob, Suzanne just called. Hank's there."

"I'm rolling."

Ed, who overheard the call, jumped to his feet, grabbed his hat, and headed out the door to his cruiser. "You stay here and man the office," he called over his shoulder.

Sally knew that she was needed here, but she was burning to follow Ed. More than that, she sensed that Suzanne needed her. She made her decision—she fired up her Camry and headed out.

She was roaring up Pinewoods Lane when she realized

that all the police vehicles were at Hank's, not Suzanne's. As she braked, a thousand thoughts raced through her mind. Suzanne was dead and he was cornered in his house. There was a hostage situation in there and Suzanne had a gun to her head.

In fact, Hank was sitting on his porch, rocking fast. Ed sat beside him in a second rocker, while Rob, his notebook open, took a statement. And Suzanne was nowhere to be seen.

It turned out that nothing had been as it seemed. Hank claimed to have left town Thursday afternoon, long before Glynesse's murder. Sally realized he must have been planning his trip when he'd told her he needed to go prune trees. He'd called his mother on Friday from the road.

Rob looked up at Sally and said, "We've been trying to reach you." His voice was curt.

"I thought I'd be needed here, so I came on out."

Rob faced her, his eyes hard. He was curt. "Please make an immediate call to the Starlight Community to confirm that Horace Sunderland has been there since last Thursday at approximately four P.M. Confirm further that they have an alcohol and anger management program and he is enrolled in it, and he attends regular retreats there as part of this program." He turned back to Hank.

Sally's face was blazing and her underarms were swimming as she leaped into her car and drove over to Suzanne's. There was no point in racing back to town—she could use the phone there and comfort Suzanne at the same time.

Suzanne sounded relieved as she buzzed her in the gate. She gave her a big hug when she ran up the steps to the porch. "Don't worry," Sally told her. "It turns out it couldn't have been Hank. He was away at the drunk farm. I've got to call and confirm this."

Suzanne looked baffled, but she nodded toward the phone.

After Sally identified herself, she was put through to the Starlight Community's director, Dr. Al Wilford.

"Sure Hank's a patient. He's been with us for over a

year. He was definitely on the anger management retreat, I conducted it personally."

"Could he have left at any time, say at night?"

"You check your car keys when you check in. That's part of the drill. We do not run away from our problems at Starlight."

"And he couldn't have gotten them?"

"Hank was here," Dr. Wilford repeated firmly. "What's the problem, anyway?"

"It's a police matter," Sally replied. "We're just following routine." She couldn't believe she'd actually said that. But now she knew why cops used the line. It explained everything but said nothing.

She went back to Hank's and confirmed his alibi with Ed and Rob. Hank turned his anger and humiliation on her. "First you come up here and accuse me of killing my neighbor's cat, of all the damn things," he said, his eyes wet and his voice shaking with rage. "Then you accuse me of killing my own wife and unborn child, and if *that* ain't enough, you also think I killed the young girl from the drugstore!" He shook his head in wonder.

Mrs. Sunderland's Cadillac came roaring up the dirt road. She was so tiny, it looked like it was driving itself.

The door burst open, and she ran out. As she got closer, Sally saw that her face was red, her eyes streaked with tears. She threw her arms around Hank as best she could, since the top of her head only reached to the middle of his chest. She wailed, "My poor baby!"

Hank allowed himself to be led off to his bedroom to lie down.

Sally followed Ed and Rob back to the office. Now they'd *really* want her gone. They'd wasted time looking for Hank, and she was at least partly responsible for that. And now, just when her presence at the office had been essential, she'd let them down.

When she got there, Rob and Ed were already in his office. She went to the back, tentatively knocked on the door, then pushed it open.

"We got a real bad situation now," Ed said. "There could be a serial killer on the loose in Maryvale. Now that I'm not worried that you might have Hank after you, I need you to stay on."

"But stick to dispatch," Rob said.

"She needs to do what I tell her to do," Ed snapped.

Sally was amazed. You just did not hear Ed use that tone of voice, not ever. Nor had she expected anything approaching this result—the exact opposite of what she'd been ready to face.

"Let's be careful," she said. "Remember that we also have another dead animal, and that suggests that the animal killer hasn't graduated to people yet."

"So what are we looking at?" Rob asked.

"I think we should see if we can find somebody who maybe dated Glynesse in the past and was dating Wanda now. There might be a motive there somewhere."

Rob gave her a searching sort of a look. Questioning. "But if you're wrong, then we could be wasting more time. Lives could be in the balance, Sally."

"I don't recall anybody much dating Glynesse when she was in high school. And that's a ten-year difference, there." He turned his now careful eyes on Rob. "Do you happen to know if Wanda was dating anybody in the right age group? Someone much older?"

Rob shook his head. "She wasn't dating," he said. "Not to my knowledge."

"Problem is," Ed said at last, "unless the killer flew in here from somewhere far away and started killing strange women, he doesn't exist."

"In what sense?" Sally asked.

"In the sense that we'd all know if Wanda was dating an older man. You don't hide stuff like that in a place like this. You can't."

"So maybe it's something like a salesman, here from time to time?"

"Not enough business for 'em here. Nobody's got

enough cash lyin' around to make it worthwhile going door to door. Even the Bible salesmen avoid Maryvale these days."

"It can't be someone who's prowling around just Pinewoods Lane, either," Rob said, "Wanda's on the other side of town."

"You're certain it's not your serial killer, darlin'?"

Sally shook her head. "I'm not sure of anything." Then she said, "Why is it always us?"

"Us?" Rob asked.

"Women! Why are we always the victims?"

"It comes down to strength, I imagine," Rob said. "A man's generally stronger than a woman, so he can overcome her."

"It's male hormones. You've got some kind of a problem in there. Violence, hate, ages of warfare—all male."

Rob lifted his eyebrows at her. "It's clear to me why you're still a single gal. You don't like men."

A literal electric shock went through her. What had gotten into this taciturn country boy? "My life is none of your damn business! And what about you? I don't see you out and about on Saturday nights."

"Maybe that's not what I'm interested in."

Sally opened her mouth to continue the fight, but was cut off by Ed. "You two better save your energy for solving these crimes. Rob, you need to do more investigation about who Glynesse and Wanda both might have known who could have killed them." He turned to Sally. "As for you, concentrate on those fires and pet killings. We need to know if they're connected with the murders, and we need to know that definitely." He picked up his hat and went out. Then he paused, turned. "Now," he said, "both of you lovebirds." He left.

The silence was thick. Finally, Sally spoke. "I guess maybe investigating cat killings is all I'm good for."

"I don't notice that you've solved any of them yet," Rob said.

"Okay, then maybe I'm not even good for that. But then there's the question of why you can't figure out who the hell killed Glynesse and Wanda."

His face flushed, his eyes grew fixed. "There's very little to go on."

"But you've lived here all your life. You know all the secrets."

"Ed knows all the secrets." He paused, reached toward her, stopped himself. "Look, I'm sorry for what I said. I shouldn't have gotten personal."

Sally was surprised. She could count on the fingers of one hand the number of men who had apologized to her, no matter how badly they'd acted. Of course, there was some truth in what he said, wasn't there? She was angry, very angry, and he'd been astute to pick up on it. "I'm sorry, too," she said. "Let's forget it, please."

Rob asked, "Have you got any leads?"

"I'm planning to go over and talk to that Jeff Davis kid again tomorrow."

"What's this about Davis?"

Sally remembered that she hadn't yet had a chance to tell him about visiting the Davis household or the school principal. She filled him in now.

After she finished, he said, "No matter what this kid has or hasn't done, he needs some help. If he's been hurt as much as you think he has, he at least needs to get up the courage to leave home. Why would a boy who's been treated like that not get out as soon as he could?"

Sally sighed. "Even hell can be a way of life, if it's all you know. I think Glynesse proves that."

"I'll take him in if he needs a place to go. He always seemed like a nice kid."

Sally was amazed at this offer. It would be a real act of kindness. She remembered some of her clients in Houston. "The bullies of this world love to dish it out, and they're always on the lookout for perfect victims. Sometimes they marry 'em, other times they give birth to them. Looks like Sam Davis raised a victim to torment."

"It's enough to make you want to live your whole life alone," said Rob.

"Do you?"

A slight smile crossed his face. "Listen, I want your thoughts on our case, too. I've been going over the coroner's report. The estimated strength of the blows seems strange to me. I mean, I see a guy like this as blasting away in a frenzy of hate. So why all the careful taps?"

"He might be smart, maybe very smart."

"In what sense?"

"In the sense that he's trying to minimize evidence. Look at the forensics production."

"It's lousy."

"Because this is a smart, careful man. He knows that violent blows will spatter more, will pick up splinters from his bat, will spray blood back on him. He's learned how to satisfy his need without giving himself away."

"Tilford strike you as competent?"

"As competent as the rest of you."

Rob looked at her a long time. He shook his head slightly, as if clearing away a really ugly thought.

They separated at that point, each heading toward an empty house. It was now Wednesday night, two days away from the start of another lonely weekend.

Before she left, Sally called the *Herald* and found that the flyers had been distributed—uselessly, as it turned out. She drove over to Flagg's and prowled the aisles, trying to find something to cook for dinner. It was hard, because for some reason tears kept coming, and they made everything look blurry.

She spent the evening thinking. The mutilations and vandalism were the work of somebody under the age of twenty. Probably a boy—inevitably a boy. Maybe as young as nine or ten. Abused, of course. Maybe in an ongoing abusive relationship. Probably, in fact, going out and torturing every time he was tortured himself, poor kid. Give back. Satisfaction. Having power of the kind that was wielded over him.

She slept a restless sleep that night. Elizabeth was there, but not communicative. Fine by Sally. She needed time to think, and not only about the case. There was truth in what Rob had said about her, a lot of it, and she wasn't sure that she liked what she saw down that lonely road—a life of dust and sorrows, as empty as the desert.

The next morning she decided there was actually nothing to gain by going out to the Davis place again. Those kids were too cowed to speak in front of their parents. Somehow she would have to see them separately, away from their own turf, and that would mean waiting until school reopened in a few weeks.

She drove home through the silent streets of a profoundly shocked little town. When the citizens of Maryvale had gotten their leaflets about the search for Hank, they'd all assumed the sheriff and troopers had identified their man, and all they had to do was find him. Now that gossip had gotten around that Hank was innocent, everyone was locking their doors again. Whenever a car or pickup slid past, Sally could see the occupants looking at her, since they knew that she was part of the investigation.

When she parked at Elizabeth's, the sun was gold behind the old trees, and the katydids were joining their voices to those of the cicadas. When she'd been a scared little girl in those nights of long ago, she'd gone to Ed and he'd taken her onto the edge of his bed and said, "Now, darlin', just listen. Katy did, Katy didn't, Katy did, Katy didn't. They just can't decide, can they?" And the mockingbird would sing to the moon, and Ed would sing to her, "Sleep and rest, sleep and rest, little girl, sleep and rest . . ."

She thought to herself, *The world has ended, and we don't even know it.*

The next thing that happened to the case was that it stalled dead in its tracks. The story made the *Gladewater Press-Regent* and the local TV station, and Ed even held a press conference that attracted a reporter from the *Houston Chronicle*.

The national press ignored the story, probably because the lives of the two women proved infuriatingly uninteresting. Wanda had one or two boyfriends from the local high school. She might have trafficked in marijuana a couple of years ago. But Glynesse was in no way whatsoever connected to the local drug scene, which was, in any case, about as laid back and easygoing as a drug scene could be.

No more killings took place, and as August staggered toward September with its promise of cooler weather coming, Maryvale began to heal or, at least, its open wound stopped bleeding.

One benefit of the discovery of Hank's innocence was that Suzanne stayed around. Sally discovered through her that there were quite a few artists living in Maryvale, escapes from high Houston rents. Most of them seemed to feel at home, and mixed fairly well with the old-timers, although Sally doubted any of them could win an election for dogcatcher.

Suzanne introduced her to several couples, and after waiting vainly for a dinner invitation, she realized that she simply needed to pick up the phone on Saturday night and ask if anyone was up for a movie or some Mexican food, or dancing. There were so few choices of things to do, there was no need to plan ahead.

Driving home from one of these get-togethers, where she had been eating enchiladas and arguing about politics, something odd happened to her. She had a flash of memory that was so vivid, so intensely frightening, that she had to stop the car. It was so real, it was almost like traveling to another world. A second later the memory was gone. With it came a hideous sensation of being trapped, of suffocating.

The memory—or was it a waking dream—had involved somebody coming toward her, a dark figure. But that was all. There was no context. Just this—well, this troubling recollection.

She knew why it was troubling. She just didn't want to admit it.

Later, there were other, similar memories, equally obscure, equally accompanied by a pounding heart and a cold sweat. She found them so puzzling that she began to write them down, as disjointed and confused as they were. Her notes were things like "saw shadow, felt elevated heart rate, sweating . . . awoke due to terror."

She began to think that the case might be causing a traumatic stress reaction. She hoped not. She didn't want to turn out to be too sensitive to do investigative work. Frankly, she was hoping to graduate from social worker to deputy sheriff. She considered talking to Elizabeth about the memories. Better to face them head-on than let them get the better of her.

Meanwhile, Ed and Rob, with the help of Tilford and Bill the Dead Body Boy, had gotten exactly nowhere. They had searched the area around both murder scenes, but found no trace of the weapon, even though they knew it had to be a baseball bat. Their latest step was to use the National Crime Database to determine if similar killings had happened anywhere else. The Maryvale murderer could be a psychopath on the move. They didn't like to admit the truth: if the killer was still here, but in order to find him they needed another woman to die.

Sally had done little better with the animal mutilations. No more had taken place, and no more fires. This supported the theory that one killer had done it all and he was on the run and hiding out somewhere. However, Sally had a hard time believing this, so she kept looking.

She had delayed interviewing the Davis kids again before school started, because of the parental permission issue. Now that school was due to start in several days, and she would be able to interview them there as part of her job as a county social worker, all she would need would be the permission of the principal.

She was fairly sure that Jeff had the blood of Suzette the Siamese and Harry the Pomeranian on his hands, and the fires, and the other animals.

But when it came to linking him up with the murders of Glynesse and Wanda, she was full of doubt. If the same person who tortured animals was killing young women, she needed to search for an older recluse who would turn out to be suffering from maturation problems.

She brought the matter up with Ed. "Are there any hermits in the area? Maybe who live alone and are easily provoked, sometimes violent?"

"The only possibility is Jackie Hardcastle. He lives way up on Burnham Road. Used to live with his mother, but she died two years ago. But we talked to him. There was no reason to include him as a suspect."

Sally wondered. She thought she might pay him a visit herself.

"You think he's—what?"

"If he's suffering from retarded maturation—arrested development, they used to call it—he could be responsible for all the crimes, and that needs to be checked out. Although my prime suspect in the mutilations is still the oldest Davis boy."

"The Davis boy? You mean Jeff Davis?" Ed had literally turned white. What was the matter, was *everyone* scared of this Sam Davis character?

She soldiered on. "In my opinion, he's an abused child. It could be familial abuse, where the whole family scapegoats one child and punishes him jointly. It's a devastating form of abuse."

"What's this about? What would the Davises have to do with it? Why them?"

"Ed, I just told you. You're not listening."

"I'm listening to you go off half-cocked again is what I'm listening to. Theories are not evidence, darlin'."

As much as Ed knew about this town, he plainly didn't know a thing about this family. She related what she'd learned from Tom Keener, which was unquestionably hard evidence of abuse. "So we have convincing evidence that Jeff has been abused, and physically abused children often turn out to be sexually abused, as well. And sexual abuse is one of the things that can create a killer."

Ed leaned his chair far back and stared at the ceiling. He uttered a long, groaning sigh. Sally saw that despite all he'd seen, especially recently, the crime of child abuse still had the capacity to shock him. He looked at her through stricken, sad eyes. "What do you want me to do?"

"About the Davises? Nothing, yet. I'll tell you if we need official intervention." She paused. "When is this Mr. Hardcastle likely to be home?"

"All the time, I'd say. He comes into town to buy groceries and gets his mail no more than once a month. He's a real hermit. But he's also a dead-end street. Of that I am sure."

"Why are you sure?"

"Because of the family history. The Hardcastle name is on the Maryvale Founders Role."

"Which means what, exactly?"

"I have never had a Hardcastle in jail. My predecessor, Sheriff Rawson, never had a Hardcastle in jail. In fact, they've been law-abiding citizens of this place since the day Main Street was staked out with pine spikes in 1837."

Sally suddenly saw a picture in her mind of the son out of *Psycho,* tending his dead mother's corpse as if she were still alive. Perhaps he killed animals as some sort of bizarre sacrifice, trying to bring Mama back to life . . . and maybe then moved on to young women?

She shook her head. That was crazy thinking, totally unscientific. She stood up. "I'm going to interview him anyway. I need to form my own impression."

Ed nodded in silence. His eyes were sunken, his expression distant. She could hear his boot tapping on the floor. "By the way, Ed, I'm fixing beef Stroganoff out of one of Elizabeth's cookbooks this weekend. Come over and eat with us. Rob's going to bring a bottle of wine by way of a peace offering, and—"

"What do you mean, 'peace offering'?"

"We had a little disagreement. It's by way of mending fences. I cook, he brings the booze."

"That sounds real nice, darlin'."

"I want you to come, too."

"Oh, heck, honey, you don't want an old codger like me over there."

"Honestly, Ed, you're impossible to pry out of that house of yours."

"I guess maybe I got a little of old Hardcastle in me."

"What if we packed up the dinner and brought it over to your place?"

His face remained blank—carefully blank, she thought, like the face of a poker player who was being just a hair too sly to conceal his bluff.

She watched him fidget, then take a fingernail file out of his pocket, sigh, and put it away.

"What's the trouble?"

A shudder seemed to go through him. When he looked up at her, she was startled. How sad he looked, and how old. "Good night, Ed."

"G'night, darlin'." He didn't even look at her as he pulled his frame up to full height and went out of the room.

She followed him to the parking lot, and watched his car as it moved slowly off into the night. She had just started to stick her key into the ignition of her own car when her mind seemed to leave her body and enter another world.

She was in a dark room, lying in bed. The door opened a crack, letting in just enough light for her to see past a lump of blankets that must have been her feet. Then a large shape covered the crack of light and the room was plunged into darkness again. She felt like she was suffocating. Again, she was aware of that face that she couldn't quite see. For a moment, she felt like she was going to scream, like she was trapped in here, like the daylight would never return.

Then she was gasping, coughing, her hand gripping her car key so tight it was frozen. She hadn't yet put the key into the ignition—it had all taken place that quickly.

She quickly grabbed her purse and fumbled around for her notebook, where she'd begun keeping a record of the incidents. She was breathing hard, her heart was hammering, but she managed to write down the details of the episode. She scrawled the date and time and closed the book. She sat, eyes closed, gathering her strength. Still shaking a little, she opened the notebook again and read back through her notations. The episodes were now coming more often, sometimes as many as two or three a day. When she first bought the notebook, she'd had only two such experiences, and they were weeks apart.

She stared down at her own scrawl, and faced something that she had not wanted to face: these blackouts may have started because of stress connected to the murders, but they weren't *about* the murders. They were about her.

But what? When? There was terrible trauma back in

there somewhere, trauma that was eating at her soul from the inside.

She was not the person she'd thought she was. Somewhere in the story of her past life, there was something so terrible that she dared not remember it.

There was nothing to do about it now, though, except keep on with her plans for the day. She followed her uncle's instructions about getting to the Hardcastle place, and soon found herself in front of a long drive, with a battered mailbox near the entrance. It had two rows of self-stick letters on the side, the kind that glow in the dark. They spelled out "HARD" on the first line and "CSTL" on the second.

On her way up the drive, she passed a small clapboard cottage with a quaint old front porch, complete with swing. The paint was peeling and the yard had gone to weeds, but otherwise, it was an appealing little place.

At the end of the drive, she came upon a log cabin that still looked fairly new. This must be where Hardcastle himself lived. Sally realized that when Ed said he had lived with his mother, he hadn't meant in the same house. The cottage must have been her place before she died.

The door of the cabin opened as soon as she pulled up in front. The man who looked out was dressed in jeans and a T-shirt. He did have a beard but it was a short salt-and-pepper one that did not reach down to his navel. "Howdy," he said, giving the usual Maryvale greeting. To his credit, he didn't seem nervous, or even very curious about her.

"I'm Sally Hopkins, from the sheriff's office." She wished she had some sort of official ID to show him. She'd have to talk to Ed about that.

"Sure, I've heard about you. Come on in." Heard about her? She hesitated before entering.

"Have a seat. Can I get you an iced tea or a Coke?" If he was a psychopath, he was the organized type. She asked for tea and glanced around the room while he was in the kitchen. It seemed to be a combination living room, dining room, and office, and was acceptably clean. The walls were lined with bookshelves that seemed to hold mostly scientific and historical texts. One section appeared to be devoted to the Kennedy assassination.

When he came back with a glass in his hand, she told him, "I'm investigating the animal mutilations that have gone on around here recently. Have you heard anything about them?"

"Yep." He sat quietly, adding nothing.

"Well, I wondered if you had any idea about who might be doing them."

"Why would I know anything about it?"

"We're also questioning people about the murders of two young women, Mrs. Glynesse Sunderland and Miss Wanda Ellis."

He shook his head. "I heard about them, too, but I don't know anything about it." He remained placid.

Sally was stymied. She wasn't going to find out anything if she couldn't get more of a response from him than this.

"Do you live alone out here, Mr. Hardcastle? It must get lonely."

"I've got plenty to keep me busy." He glanced around at his library.

"The sheriff told me your mother died recently. My condolences."

He sighed, finally showing some emotion. "It'll be two years in October."

"Was she ill for a long time? It must have been hard living out here alone with a sick elderly woman."

"I managed."

Sally was intentionally prying, trying to elicit some emotional response from him, but he seemed unperturbed. She added, "I love her little house—I assume that was hers. Would you ever be interested in selling it?"

His brow darkened and he stood up, glowering down at her. "I expect you need to be going, Miss Hopkins."

This was most interesting. He really did not want her in that house. "Have I offended you, Mr. Hardcastle?"

"Look, I don't take well to folks. I'm sorry. And my ma—" He stopped. She saw that he was choking back tears.

"Our mothers are precious to us."

"What do you care? You don't know anything about it! You don't know what she was, who she was."

"I'd like to, Mr. Hardcastle. I'd like to know more about her, and about you."

He sat down across from her. For a long time, he stared at her. She tried to smile slightly, to appear nonthreatening. "Are you for real, lady?"

"I am indeed. I'd like very much to know more."

"Why?"

"Well, I'm a county social worker. I want to get to know folks. And you seem to me to be grieving, Mr. Hardcastle. I can help you with that."

"I am grieving."

Her training told her that this was an invitation. She went for it. "We could set up a meeting, and I can give you some of what are called coping strategies. To help you work toward the place we can all go, where we reconcile ourselves. Not that we get over a loss like yours, but we can learn ways of living with it that honor it."

His eyes literally painted her, looking up and down, pausing in all the usual places. He had not the slightest interest in her ideas. He was mentally stripping her. This man was not normal, not by a very long shot, and Sally thought she might be on to something here.

He was eager to make a date to discuss matters further. She could see an almost animal hunger in his eyes.

"If you want, I can bring some literature on grieving and coping. I've got some material that might really help you."

"I'd like that very much." He spoke in a distracted manner, his eyes still painting her.

She thought quickly. There was an opportunity here. "I can come back later, if you're not busy."

"Lady, I'm not busy." He looked around the room now, almost as if he was suspicious that somebody might be there guarding her.

She stood up. More slowly, he followed her to his feet. She thought, suddenly, that she might need darkness to do what she had just decided to do. "What about eight," she said.

His face seemed to tighten. "What about sooner? Like now."

He was coming on to her. Clearly. "No can do," she said, "got a meeting."

"You people always got a damn meeting."

"Then eight it is." She smiled. "See you then."

As she left, he pumped her hand with both of his in a way that suggested a very different and more normal response to her offer. Specifically, it suggested gratitude.

This man's range of emotional responses was very unfocused, she thought as she got in her car. Not frankly abnormal, at least, not on the surface. But that was the way with these men—they presented a viable appearance, concealing the monster beneath.

As soon as the cabin was out of sight, she slowed down so she could look in the windows of his mother's house as she passed. Jackie's fixation on it had suggested to her that he might be hiding something there, maybe even something to do with the murders.

She got out of the car and walked up to the cottage, her shoes crunching in the dry grass. She went up on the porch, found the place locked. There were still curtains on most of the windows, but she could see that the interior was bare except for what looked like a mattress on the living-room floor. So he'd stripped the place of furniture. It wasn't a shrine, then. So what was it? She looked harder. There was a sheet there, and on the sheet some dark splotches. Blood?

She could see it from outside, so it became a legitimate object of search. Or did it? Yes, she thought so. Now she had the right to enter and collect it as evidence and take it to Tilford Harkins for testing. Or was it "fruit of a forbidden tree," because she'd had to trespass to see it? She'd read the rules of evidence just once, and they were complicated and subtle and she just wasn't sure where she stood.

The best thing to do would be to get a warrant, but she did know this: in the absence of stronger evidence, that wasn't going to happen.

When she got back to the office, there was nobody there. Ed had not returned, but that wasn't unusual, it was already past six. Except for Rob, the troopers rarely showed up here. She went in, turned on the dispatch radio, and called him, getting nothing in return but static. Ed was off the air, too.

Which was maybe just as well. It might be a mistake to tell them that she had just decided to use her meeting with Jackie to enter Mrs. Hardcastle's cottage, and to hell with the law. Officially, she'd be breaking and entering. That would be a big deal for Rob. In his usual stiff-backed way, he would translate it as a breach of the peace. Maybe he'd even charge her.

But Jackie was just too defensive about that house. She had to see more of what was in there.

Back at home, she ate a Lean Cuisine at the kitchen table while Elizabeth sat drinking herb tea.

"You're in a hurry," Elizabeth said.

"I have a meeting."

"On the case?"

"In a way. I'm going to do a grief counseling with Jackie Hardcastle."

A blast of tea came out of Elizabeth's mouth. Her eyes widened, then narrowed. "You're not serious?"

"Why not? The man's grieving is in need of intervention. Two years is too long for a maternal passage."

Elizabeth was not deceived. She said, "I wish you wouldn't do this."

"There's something wrong out there. You can feel it, like it's coming out of his pores. He's way too affectless to be real—except when it comes to his mommy's cottage. Then he's downright threatening. Plus, he's got the library of a paranoid."

Wham. It was dark. The door was opening, a shadow filling it . . .

"Sally? Hey, Sally!"

Sally was staring straight ahead, still as a statue. She shook herself slightly. "I'm sorry, I was going to tell you. It's these visions I've been having lately."

"Visions?"

"Like memories, except I don't know when or where they took place. They only last a second or two, but when they come, they're so real, it's as if they were happening right here and now." She reached for her purse and dug out her notebook. "I've been writing them down."

"Spill it, girl."

"Well, here's the first one. It starts with a strong smell of frying food, for some reason. I'm alone in the dark, then I smell that smell and a dim light comes into the room. My bedroom. Suddenly there's someone with me, but I can't see who it is. I'm afraid of him, and my heart starts pounding and I feel suffocated, like I can't breathe." She was getting sweaty just thinking about it.

"If we sit down and talk about it calmly, you may be able to coax out a little more, enough to identify what it is you're remembering."

"I need to get out to the Hardcastle place," Sally said.

Elizabeth took her arm and steered her firmly into the living room. "That can wait. Put everything else out of your mind. We're going to explore the past." She sat them down opposite each other.

"Are you going to hypnotize me?"

"Since you've got the basic memories already, a nice, calm conversation should help you expand on them."

She consulted the notebook, which she'd taken from Sally. "There's a certain sameness to these memories. Let's work on the most recent one first, since it's freshest in your mind."

Sally shivered. "It was like all the others, basically. I was in the dark, then there's a dim light, a dark shape, a feeling of suffocation, then it's over. Do you think someone tried to kill me when I was a child? I know I was in the way, but could my family have hated me that much?"

"Let's not draw any conclusions just yet. First, let's try to see if you can remember a little bit more. What do you mean by suffocation? Is there a hand over your mouth or nose? A pillow coming toward your face?"

Sally thought about it. "That doesn't ring a bell." She tried to relive her memory of a few minutes ago. "It's like there's a weight on my chest, so I can't breathe. My heart starts beating faster and faster, like I'm about to be crushed to death. My eyes are screwed up tight. I can't see, I'm just waiting to die." She noticed her chest heaving, just from describing it.

"The part about your eyes being closed, and the weight on your chest, that's new. You've remembered more. Can you go on?"

Sally was shaking her head back and forth, unable to find any words.

"I think you know what you're remembering."

"No!"

"Sally, you're a grown woman, a master of social work. I don't need to interpret these images for you. What would you think if I described something like this?"

It became clear to her then, as if someone had torn blinders from her eyes. She was remembering someone sneaking into her bedroom to have sex with her, feeling his weight on her chest. She was, herself, a victim of child abuse.

Elizabeth could tell just by looking at her face that Sally knew what her memories meant. "Who do you think it was?"

Sally found it hard to speak. "It must have been Dad." She stared at Elizabeth with sudden comprehension. "Do you think that's why my mother killed herself, because she knew?"

"I can't answer that, but we can explore it."

"But if she knew, why wasn't she strong enough to take me away? Why did she leave me with that horrible man!" Another idea dawned. "Do you think my stepmother hated me because she was jealous, because my father . . ."

"Maybe. It could have been unconscious, something she never thought about in an organized way."

"Do you think he was, you know, doing it to me after they were married? Or only after my mother killed herself, but before he met her?" Sally was whispering. "But he must have been doing it before, or else why would my mother . . ."

"Enough for now, dear one. You'll wear yourself out. We need to take this all very slowly."

"I'm going to call him on the phone and confront him. I'm going to do it tonight."

"I think you should wait a few more days," Elizabeth told her. "Wait until you've calmed down and thought it out. You need to be very sure of yourself, because he's going to deny it. He may not even remember it. It may be hidden from his memory by traumatic amnesia."

"But that's not fair! He can't get away with it by forgetting it ever happened!" She was crying now, and Elizabeth moved over to her chair to comfort her.

"Shh, forget it for now. You have my official permission to think about other things until—how about tomorrow afternoon? You don't have to think about it again until then, when the day is ending, and you're feeling relaxed and need to take another look. And then only think about it for fifteen minutes, OK?"

Sally nodded. "It's a deal." She looked at her watch, then out the window. "It's time to get ready to go."

"You're still going out there to break into that house, aren't you? You really are something, Sally Hopkins."

"I'm not going to break into the house."

"Don't make me laugh, of course you are."

"I have to find out what he's hiding, Elizabeth!"

"You have to stop obsessing."

"Women are dead! And it's not over, I swear, it's not over!"

She ran out to her car, and thus didn't see Elizabeth's face cloud into a worried frown.

16

Sally drove back out to Burnham Road and parked by the Hardcastle mailbox. She had fifteen minutes before she was due to meet Jackie. It was easily enough time to take a quick look through the cottage; then, if she found nothing, go up to the meeting and really do a grief counseling, which the poor guy certainly needed. If she found anything at all, however, that seemed odd or out of the ordinary, she would not go to that meeting. A highly organized sequential murderer was going to present an excellent face, then strike suddenly.

She could well imagine both victims letting Jackie into their homes. They would not have been suspicious of somebody they'd probably known all their lives. She had no intention of walking into a trap.

She went into her trunk, where she kept a small box of car-related tools. A screwdriver with a nice, thick handle was all she really needed. She put one in her pocket and set out into the roadside brush.

Was this dangerous? Elizabeth had thought so. It didn't feel dangerous, though. In fact, she could see the cottage not far ahead, and Jackie's place was a good five hundred feet behind it, separated by deep brush and a thick stand of pine.

She could easily enter the cottage, even use her light—which made her stop. She went back to the car, took the flashlight out of the glove compartment, stuffed it into the pocket with the screwdriver.

As she returned, the last of the sun left, and the shadowy outline of the cottage became her only guide in the blackness of the rapidly falling night. She walked up to it, sensing its presence as she got closer, feeling what she thought was a sullen malevolence, as if the house itself was watching her, and did not like what it saw.

Of course, that was all imagination. She was a social scientist, not some sort of parapsychologist or whatever they were called. The house saw nothing. However, it was not inaccurate to say that her intuition was telegraphing danger, and perhaps she should heed it.

So, she would. She'd make this very quick, just a fast look around and then off to her meeting.

By shining her light in the small window at the top of the front door, she could see into the front parlor. And there was that mattress again. She had to ask herself, why would it be there? She shone her light on it. Weren't there black stains on it, and something next to it—what was that?

She could make out a black stub of a handle, a clutch of straps.

That was a whip.

As she pressed her nose against the glass, Sally's imagination began to take over. Unable to get laid any other way, Jackie might be abducting young women and bringing them out here to rape and torture. Too guilty to use his mother's bedroom, he'd slung her mattress out onto the living-room floor. Afterward, he killed them and buried them in the woods.

She stopped herself. That didn't make sense, because the bodies of Glynesse and Wanda were found in their homes, not out here. No bodies had ever been found in these woods.

This was a torture chamber, though, there was no question at all about that. So maybe Jackie had started here at home with prostitutes he got from Houston. Nobody would notice if they turned up missing. When tormenting "bad" women was no longer enough for him, he went after more upright ladies. When they rebuffed him, he killed them in a rage with his baseball bat and arranged their bodies in sexually explicit positions. That bat might even be in there somewhere.

She had to enter. She went to a back window, took out the screwdriver, and held the base of it against the glass. She tapped it once hard. The glass didn't even crack. She did it again—and the whole window shattered, broken glass cascading down with what seemed like a deafening roar.

She backed off into the woods and watched the road and the brush. Made herself stay there for five full minutes.

All remained quiet, so she returned to the cottage. Once inside, she shone her light into every corner of the parlor. She ran quickly through the rest of the house, making a cursory examination of the two small bedrooms and old-fashioned bath. There was some sort of root cellar underneath a door set into the kitchen floor, but she was no fool and she had no intention of going down there.

Finally, she approached the mattress. It exuded a musty, sour stench of old sweat. The whip was cracked and looked like something from the horse and buggy days. Jackie must have found it lying around. He was probably too shy to order sex toys from catalogs.

Or was he? She bent down and spotted a set of handcuffs peeking out from underneath the bunched-up pillow. She knew not to touch them or otherwise disturb the crime scene. She decided to search for the bat. The room was dark and dusty, and she kept running into cobwebs. She was afraid she would smudge some incriminating fingerprints if she opened any cupboard doors. She almost tripped over a pile of clothespins on the floor.

Then she heard something. Distinct, a crunching sound, outside.

It was the crunch of tires: a car was in the driveway. She raced to the back window and dove out, sprinting through the brush and out to the road.

Her own car stood silent and dark on the roadside. She opened the door on the passenger side and slipped in, wincing when the overhead light came on. She crouched down on the seat so she couldn't be seen, and reached over to engage the door locks. She was afraid to start up the car, lest she alert Jackie, who appeared to have stopped next to the cottage. Even if she got a head start, she didn't know if she could outdrive him.

She crouched there in her dark car, trembling and drenched in sweat, as the minutes moved with excruciating slowness, three, five . . . ten. Now she thought she heard movement in the nearby brush. But how could she, with her windows rolled up?

Total silence, now. She sat up. Not a sign of anybody, no car, no movement. She rolled down her window. The night air, summer dry and still hot, surrounded her. Not a sound, though, not a single sound.

She clambered over to the driver's seat, cursing the jerks who invented the center console. Fumbling for her keys, she had a moment of panic when she thought she'd dropped them somewhere on the road, but she eventually found they'd fallen out onto the passenger seat.

She stuck the key into the ignition, after missing a couple of times in the dark. She flinched when the engine roared out into the quiet night. Looking nervously up the drive to her right, she put the car into neutral and eased her foot off the brake. She tried to coast for as long as possible, but the road was too flat. She was going to have to put her foot on the gas pedal and when she did, she might as well floor it and get the hell out of there as fast as possible.

She was no stunt driver, and the car skidded in the roadside gravel as she started off. A tree shot toward her. Just in time, she managed to veer away. As it sped past the window at a distance of three feet, she turned on her lights. She drove the car hard, concentrating on not losing her way on the twisty dirt road.

It might have been her imagination, but she thought she saw a pair of headlights behind her, gaining steadily.

She considered stopping at Suzanne's or at the Kravitz house, but she was lost on the tangled back roads, and wasn't sure she could find them. Her best bet was to keep aiming for the highway, where she might find an open gas station with a phone she could use to call Rob or Ed. At least there would be other drivers around, maybe even some truckers, who could ward off whoever was back there. She went around a couple of curves too fast, almost losing control.

When she looked in her mirror, she could still see those headlights. The roads out here were basically old ranch trails, some dirt, some blacktopped. She needed a state road, anything that would lead to the highway. But there was nothing and there seemed to be no way to get out of here.

Of course, *he* would know these roads perfectly. *He* would be able to anticipate her moves, would be able to—to catch her. The truth was, she might not be able to get away.

An image of the filthy mattress floated into her mind, and the whip, black, coiled, waiting.

She went around a too-steep curve, almost lost the car in a dry creek, then sped up the far bank so fast it felt as if her wheels left the ground when she mounted the crest. At first she didn't think her old car would make it, and she hammered the wheel, smashed the gas pedal to the floor. The car groaned and bolted forward with all the enthusiasm of a spent horse. She could picture what would happen next: *Wham*—a bumper would smash into hers! *Wham! Wham!* She started honking, trying to somehow get some attention.

A glow ahead—flickering in the trees. Was it the highway? She got her speed up to eighty, praying for a trooper to be out looking for tickets. Nine-thirty on a Friday night was an ideal time. The weekenders would be racing to reach their ranches.

When her tires finally hit the pavement, the car swerved

wildly. Her prayer was answered: a light bar soon started flashing in her rearview mirror.

Clifford Collins got out and came up to her window. When he saw who it was, he frowned, bewildered.

"Miss Hopkins, are you all right?" He must be thinking she was drunk or having an epileptic fit to be driving that way. His red hair and freckles took on a green cast in the light of his flashers.

Sally was breathing hard. "I was being followed, maybe by a murderer. Let me use your radio to call Rob."

"Is this an official call?"

Damn the cell phone companies for leaving Maryvale without a tower. She thought quickly. What should she say? An official call had to be logged. Maybe she wasn't even allowed to make one. She hated to call it an emergency. With all the trouble in the county, the press was going to come out for any emergency involving a woman. "Personal," she said.

Cliff and Sally both knew that the rules mandated that he keep his channel clear except for required communications, but Sally's obvious fear convinced him to let her make her call.

She got out and got into his car. It felt so safe in here, with the sawed-off shotgun glowing in the dash lights.

It took four attempts, but Rob finally answered. Troopers kept radios in their homes around here, thank God. There were too few of them, and communications were too poor, for it to be any other way.

Breathlessly, trying to force a calm she did not feel, she told him what she'd found in Jackie Hardcastle's cottage, and what had happened next. "You've got to get here quick, Rob," she said, cutting through his protests. "He could be destroying evidence. He could be out there somewhere, waiting for me to try to go home."

Rob and Cliff agreed that Cliff would escort her to the exit for Burnham, the next town, and wait with her until Rob arrived.

In about twenty minutes another cruiser pulled up and

Rob leaned out the window and waved to her to follow him. It was the first time she'd seen him with mussed hair and facial stubble. Cliff pulled away and the two of them were left to themselves on the nearly empty highway.

Rob led her quickly to Burnham, then across back roads. To her amazement, they were soon back at the Hardcastle place. She'd have to get a really good map of the county to figure out how these roads worked. She could not take a risk like this again, not with the kind of danger that was present here.

Rob kept going past the mailbox until both of their cars were well out of sight. He parked and walked back to her car. "OK, let's talk," he said. "What's really going on?"

She explained her suspicions, and detailed what happened. She told him frankly about her break-in.

"Just remember this," Rob said. "If you're caught entering a civilian's house without a warrant, your job is going to be terminated. I'm only here because you reported you were being threatened. I didn't hear anything about this break-in, okay?"

"Thank you, Rob."

"Come on," he said, his voice stern.

He walked back to his car and drove it to the foot of the drive, with Sally following close behind. Tramping up the drive, their boots made loud scrunching sounds that Sally was sure could be heard all the way up to the cabin. When the cottage came into view, Rob signaled her to stay back, then crept up closer. A dim, flickering light was now coming through the window, as if from candles or an oil lamp.

Sally could swear she heard grunting noises from inside, maybe even stifled screams. My God, they were going to catch him in the act. She realized what it meant when people said their blood ran cold. It literally felt like that, a cloying, awful coldness growing in her body.

She forced herself to move closer. Rob appeared to be holding back, trying to peer through the window without getting too close.

She heard a *ssst!* sound, then a stifled gobble of a cry, as if somebody were screaming from behind a gag. Then again, louder, *SSST!* And the cry, a frantic gabble this time.

He was using the whip on his victim. And Rob was just standing there.

"Rob," she whispered, "my God—"

SST! SST! SST!

Sally went past him up to the house. She put her hand on the doorknob.

"Sally!"

Somebody was being tortured to death and he must be crazy not to intervene. She turned the knob.

"Sally, don't do this!"

The door was unlocked this time, so she pushed her way in.

She saw a shape on the mattress—huge, a pile of flesh. Then she understood that it was Lillie Rank, the proprietress of Rank's Emporium, all three hundred plus pounds of her. She was spread-eagled on the mattress, her cuffed wrists and ankles attached to spikes in the floor. Her mouth was tightly gagged, with soft screams coming out from behind it. There was a clothespin on each of her nipples and more clasped tightly to her genitals. Sally shuddered. At least they'd reached her in time.

Jackie was a dark, hulking shadow, standing above her with the whip in his hand. Although the light was dim, Sally could tell he was naked. He was hairless and white, like some sort of gigantic newt, and his features were distorted so that he looked like a gargoyle in the flickering light. She tried to stop her eyes from traveling to below his waist. He opened his mouth and roared something incoherent.

"Rob!" She expected Rob to jump him, overcome him, grab the whip from his hand, and press a pistol to his temple. Then she could comfort the woman, reassure her that the monster was captured, remove her impediments, and wrap the poor soul in her warm jacket.

But Rob ran straight to Jackie instead. He put his arm around his shoulder and walked him to the back of the room, out of the candlelight. On the way, he picked up

Jackie's discarded clothes from the floor and helped him into them. He had clearly decided that Jackie was the kind of madman who could be easily subdued. Sally wanted to warn him that psychopaths didn't give up that easily.

Meanwhile, Lillie was shaking her head back and forth, screaming as loud as she could beneath her gag. Sally bent to pull it out of her mouth, but it was tied tightly and would have to be cut. The noises she heard when she leaned in close sounded like cussing worse than anything she had heard before in her life, even in Houston. She removed the clothespins from Miz Rank's breasts, but was afraid to touch the ones on her vulva, because she was heaving and bucking so hard.

"Rob, help me. Give me your pocketknife." And Rob was there when needed, as usual, cutting away Miz Rank's gag and listening to her spew forth curses that would have impressed the kids in a ghetto school.

"Get these godfk'n handcuffs off me!" she screamed. Rob was already working on it, having been handed a set of keys by a now tame and shame-faced Jackie.

"Who is this cunt?" screamed Lillie, pointing to Sally. Jackie was now down on one knee beside her, trying to comfort her. Sally couldn't understand why he wasn't in handcuffs himself—and then, quite suddenly, everything became clear to her.

She almost choked on her own stupidity and turned and ran from the house. She was about to jump in her car and take off when she heard Rob shouting her name. She'd caused him so much trouble already, she didn't dare disobey orders again. She sat in the driver's seat and waited, with her eyes shut tight, all her energy drained away.

She sensed Rob standing there long before he said anything. She waited to take her punishment. Then it dawned on her. "You bastard, you knew the truth all the time, didn't you?"

"I knew Jackie was humping old Miz R., sure," he replied, with uncharacteristic bluntness. "Everybody did. I just didn't know what kind of games they were playing. I'd heard rumors, of course. But, Sally, you're like a bull in a china shop around here, girl. These folks have been shamed tonight, and they're gonna hurt from it for a long time. That's not fair to them."

Sally didn't know whether to feel angry or ashamed, but if she'd ever felt like a good-for-nothing, it was now. "Ed's right, I should go back to Houston," she said, not daring to look at him.

His reply surprised her. "Hell, no, Sally. Things were too tame around here before you came along. You actually had me believing for a moment that ol' Jackie might be a killer. We need you to keep things interesting for us." She could see his grin, despite the dark night.

"Besides, we've got a real serious crime to solve here, and you're contributing. You'll get to know the town better, in time. Know who to suspect and who not."

"Maryvale has even more secrets?"

Rob just smiled as she started her car for the long drive back home. She wondered if he would tell Ed about her fiasco. For once in her life, she hoped Elizabeth would be in bed when she got home, because she'd done all the explaining she was up to for one night.

Monday morning found Sally sitting glumly at her desk after a lonely and miserable weekend. She was sure that gossip about what had happened at the Hardcastle place was all over Maryvale by now, and she expected to be fired any minute. Jackie was humiliated and Miz Rank was furious.

Sally had gone back to completing forms and working on the animal cases, while waiting for the ax to fall.

But before it did, she intended to achieve one thing, which was the closing of the animal-mutilation case.

This was the first day of school, so she could now interview the Davis children with only their supervisor's consent. If she worked fast, she might be able to get some useful information out of them before their father found out and raised hell, as he would certainly do.

She was sure that the Davis family was the solution to the mutilation cases. Which made her wonder—she'd been sure about Hank being his wife's killer. That had been wrong. Then she'd been sure that Jackie Hardcastle was a serial killer. That had *really* been wrong.

So why would she be right now?

God knew. Probably she was going down another path that would lead to all hell breaking loose . . . and more trouble for Ed.

She hadn't seen him yet, and she wasn't looking forward to it. He was always early, too, so his lateness troubled her even further. Was he agonizing about firing her?

It was pushing ten before she heard his boots coming up the hallway from the back, where he'd parked his car.

He came straight up to her desk. "Well, darlin', sounds like we had us quite a little adventure."

She started to give him the speech she'd rehearsed, about how she'd been confused, how it was logical to think the worst. But all that came out was a muttered, "Yeah, I guess I did."

He said nothing.

"I'm real sorry, Ed. I hope it doesn't cause you any trouble."

"Well, I hope so too, Sally. But you were right about one thing: there sure was something odd going on over there. Trouble is, it's not against the law." He chuckled to himself.

She couldn't believe his tolerance. She cried out, "I never expected to see anything like that here! I thought small-town folks had old-fashioned values."

"Good Lord, Sally, they do. Just—well—they shape them a little bit to fit their needs."

"But how could those two ever do those kinds of things together? She's so much older than him, and so much . . . larger."

"There's no accounting for tastes, sweetheart. The important thing is, they didn't break the law. You can't raise a hand to an errant child these days without finding yourself in jail, but you can beat somebody black and blue if they ask you to."

"I know that, Ed. I spent half of my life in Houston trying to get battered women to complain. But Jackie and Miz Rank—I mean, that was an advanced S and M scene. Something off the Internet. It's not—assault? Could it be assault, Ed?"

He cleared his throat. "She wants it. Or says she does. Until that changes—well, it's their business. Anyway, I need you for other things. Urgent business, darlin'. As you know."

She let that sink in, realized what it meant: she wasn't going to be fired.

He looked down at her, his eyes full of what she could see was a great pain. The murders had changed Ed, had changed his attitude about the town, too. The sadness in those eyes went very deep.

"There's something beyond the current crisis, Sally. Something I want you to think about very, very carefully."

"Okay, Ed. Sure." She waited, looking into those miserable eyes.

"Darlin', I'm gonna retire. Soon as the case is closed."

"Retire? Oh, Ed, no!"

"I'm getting old, Sally, and what's worse, I'm out-of-date. It's time for someone new to step in. It's two years to the next election, so the county commissioners will make an appointment to fill in the rest of my term. They'll take my recommendation, and that person will have a good chance of getting elected when the time comes."

"Will Rob want it?" As far as she could see, he was the only choice.

Ed laughed. "Sally, you really need to learn how things work around here. Rob's got a state job. He's not gonna expose himself to the electorate every few years. Who needs that? Plus, this darned job hardly pays spit."

Sally was baffled. "So, who then?"

He went on. "I'm out of step with the ways things are now. Come down to it, I'm just another man with a gun, and the troopers provide all the guns we need. No, what we need is somebody who understands people—their psychology, why they do what they do—so maybe that person can get down in the cracks with them and come to understand them, and head off trouble like the kind we're having now." He paused. "Someone like you."

Oh, God, he was offering her his job. Not firing her,

telling her she ought to become sheriff. "After what I did? You want to appoint *me*?"

"You made a mistake, but you can learn from that. And you came at the Hardcastle situation from the right direction. He did indeed torture women, and finding him was a very good piece of detective work." He smiled. "By the way he asks—you know—that you—well—"

"I won't reveal their secrets."

"Well, that's fine, darlin'. That's real fine. Sounds like you're gonna make a good sheriff, for sure."

For once in her life, she was too surprised to respond.

"You'll have to make sure to get acquainted with everyone in town. Make it your business to do that. Lots of folks won't like the idea of a woman sheriff, let alone you." He stopped. "Make 'em realize you're good, darlin', and you'll be sheriffin' around here for a while. Tell you what to do—solve those mutilations. That'll give folks reason to believe you can do the job. So what do you say—do you want it?"

Sally's mind was telling her, *You'd be crazy to accept, you know nothing about law enforcement, you'll only screw up again,* but the only word that came out of her mouth was, "Yes."

"Well, that's just fine. Real fine. We'll celebrate at Cantor's. They always have cherry pie today—it's still your favorite, isn't it?"

They had lunch together, and toasted with their iced tea glasses. She ate the cherry pie afterward. No cow slobbers, though.

After lunch, her mind still reeling from Ed's surprise offer, she headed over to the Maryvale Middle School to start her interrogation of the Davis brood.

She drove up to another squat, flat-roofed tan brick building, straight out of a 1968 architecture textbook. *What got into people then,* she wondered, *to make them want to build such eyesores? And now the builders are dead and gone and the rest of us have to live with this awful stuff.*

She walked through the double metal doors and looked for the principal's office.

Middle school was one of the worst experiences in most people's lives. It certainly had been in Sally's. Belton was so miserable that the teachers beat the students out the doors when the bell rang. Parents never went near the place. It was a drop zone, a warehouse. She'd been teased mercilessly, known as "Long Nose," because that's what Grace Carruthers called her, despite the fact that her nose was perfectly normal. But Grace Carruthers ruled. Now, she ruled a nail parlor in a dreary strip mall, a bottle blonde with a past to be forgotten and no future. Sally had done better, damn it, and if by some miracle she actually ended up as a sheriff, she'd do a whole lot better. Grace's moment in the sun had been seventh grade, and Sally could not be more glad.

This place was no Belton, she saw that right away. The walls were graffiti-free; the lockers were all neatly closed and locked. The classrooms were quiet, with the voices of teachers echoing faintly up and down the hall.

She reached the principal's office and found a beefy-looking lady named Wallace Reed. She had brown hair, wore a pin-striped suit, and could easily have been raised army. In fact, she could have been a drill sergeant. The Maryvale County School Board had known what it was doing when they chose their middle school principal.

At first she refused to allow Sally to interview any of the Davis children. "I can't allow my students to be taken out of class without a written request on Social Services letterhead," she said firmly. "And I'm not at all sure you're right about this business of not needing parental consent. I'll need to review the regs."

"Miss Reed—"

"If you could come back tomorrow, Miss Hopkins, that would be just fine." She went back to her own forms. Dismissed.

Sally could not come back tomorrow, because by tomorrow Wallace Reed would have found some regulation that enabled her to do what she wanted, which was to get Sally out of her school and keep her away from her kids. Wallace might be stern, but she was also a bureaucrat, and she did not want trouble.

"Miss Reed—Wallace, if I may—"

Wallace looked up from her paperwork.

"I know the older boy has been beaten," she said. "Tom Keener told me he was sure about this. We have reason to believe that he's been subjected to torture."

"But why drag his siblings into it?"

Wallace Reed dropped a notch in Sally's estimation. The school board had hired a disciplinarian, that was all. She was not well trained.

"If one child is abused," Sally said, "studies tell us it's possible that they're all being abused. We need to determine if this family needs intervention, or if fostering is mandated, which it will be if there's a finding of parental incompetence with endangerment of a minor child. And I don't propose to be prevented from making this determination."

Ms. Reed sighed. "There are troubled families all over this county," she said. "As long the kids are doing well in school—getting decent grades, not acting out—I don't ask too many questions about their home lives. I've got too many kids who are obviously failing to worry about the ones who aren't. The Davis children do very well, and they're model behavers."

"Let me do the determining, Miss Reed," Sally said. "I will follow procedures and I will follow the law. But I also *will* interview these children, and I propose to start right now."

Wallace Reed looked up at her. Slowly, she stood. "Very well," she said in a low, changed voice. She marched over to her file cabinet and began to rifle through the drawers. "I've got four of the Davis children here at the moment," she said. "Ashley, who's thirteen; Bobby, twelve; and Bixley, who's eleven. Also Veronica, who's fourteen but was held back a few years ago, so now she's in classes with her sister."

Sally remembered the two blond girls she'd seen at the Davis home, standing in the midst of all their brothers.

"Can I talk to Ashley first?" she asked. Wallace Reed checked her file cabinet again, then looked at her watch. "She's in Domestic Lifestyles right now," she said. Was this the new name for Home Economics? "I'll send a runner to fetch her." She walked to an adjacent room, where a boy sat sulking over a book at a desk that was much too small for him. Sally guessed he was working off some kind of punishment. She gave him a scribbled note and he was off.

"All the students, both boys and girls, have to take one semester each of Domestic Lifestyles and Industrial Lifestyles," she informed Sally with pride. The last one, Sally thought, must be the new politically correct term for Basic Auto Repair. "We want our students to begin their adult lives as well-rounded individuals."

Sally decided she'd love to visit a Domestic Lifestyles session, just to see some of the tough guys trying to learn how to make Jell-O.

Pretty soon a small, white face peered around the door. "Hello, Ashley," said Ms. Reed, her voice booming with enthusiasm, "there's someone here who wants to talk to you."

The small face began to look very worried indeed, so Sally decided to be straight with her. "I'm Sally Hopkins, from County Services," she said, extending her hand. The girl just looked at it, baffled, so Sally withdrew it and continued. "We're just doing some more interviews about the animal mutilations. You remember I stopped by your house?"

Ashley nodded.

Sally thought she might be able to get somewhere with the girl if she could just get Drill Sergeant Reed out of the room. "Perhaps I could speak to Ashley alone," she suggested. For a moment it looked like Ms. Reed might protest, but then she clearly thought better of it and left.

"Now, Ashley, how do you like school?"

"Fine, ma'am."

"And your brothers and sisters?"

"Fine, ma'am."

"And at home. Would you say everything's good at home?"

"Yes, ma'am."

"But you get punished."

She nodded.

"Does it hurt too much, do you think?"

"I get sent to my room."

Did her eyes grow wary? Sally couldn't be sure. If she looked at this girl's back, would she find scarring? She thought that this frightened little slip of a thing might be a very crafty liar.

After fifteen minutes more of this useless sparring, Ms. Reed came bustling back in.

"I'd like to talk to one of the boys now," she informed her.

Soon a sulky child appeared, a boy called Bobby Davis. He was as neat as a pin, this child. Too neat for a twelve-year-old, she thought.

This time she was careful not to start off with questions. Ashley had been very concealing, and she thought this child would display precisely the same behavior. So she talked about family anger in general, and the way it can get out of hand and turn into violence. She stressed that this is never the child's fault, so any child who experiences this should not hesitate to report it to a sympathetic teacher or the school social worker, so that he can get help. "I'm the school social worker," she said.

But she couldn't elicit any response other than the expected yes, ma'am, no, ma'am.

The other boy, Bixley, was no more forthcoming than his brother had been, not even when Sally spoke directly about Jeff. "Jeff got a spankin' once," the boy said.

"You're certain of that?"

A look of absolute horror crossed his face. "No! No, I ain't. Not. I'm not. It was just—they were joking. Him an' Dad, they joke around like that, you know."

"No, I don't know, Bixley."

"I guess it was okay. Yeah, it was."

"What was?"

"The joking around. It was like this." He demonstrated paddling somebody who lay over his lap. "But they were laughing, you know."

"Do you get spanked?"

"Oh, no, ma'am. None of us do."

"There's no law against it, Bixley, unless it's too rough. Would you say you get spanked so hard you can't sit?"

He stared at her, silent. Finally, he said, "We got a very nice house. You've seen our house."

"Yes, I have, and I agree with you."

"So what's this all about, lady?"

And that was the end of that. She realized that this one, for certain, was going to inform his father about this interview. There would be hell to pay, she was sure.

Veronica, the last Davis sibling at the school, turned out to be a slightly more sophisticated version of her sister, and even more careful.

Too careful. They were all way too careful.

As Sally left, the bell announced lunch. Classroom doors suddenly slammed open and students spilled out into the hall. Sally was borne toward the door on a tide of shrill preteens. It felt almost as if she was being pushed out of the school by some sort of unspoken consensus.

Over the din of talking students, she could barely hear the classroom intercoms crackling away. She wondered why would anyone bother to make announcements when the kids where all milling around in the hall, headed for the lunchroom.

Then she listened more carefully and realized they were broadcasting the Lord's Prayer. It dawned on her that this must be the mandated daily prayer period that had recently been passed by the state legislature. It was unconstitutional, of course, but it would remain a part of the curriculum until the Supreme Court said no, which would give it at least two or three years.

Sally's next stop was the high school. She thought that there might be a somewhat better chance with the older boys. They'd be more free of their father's domination, and if the household was as dysfunctional as she thought, they could be very, very angry.

She had called ahead that morning and spoken to Tom Keener, so she knew she was welcome at the high school. She figured Sam and Kenny, who were seventeen and fifteen, would be the siblings who were closest to Jeff. They would look up to him as the oldest brother. They'd have likely seen his punishments, or even participated. And they might, themselves, be victims.

The sign in front of the high school now proclaimed, "Wildcats beat Jackrabbits." Sally wondered if that meant they'd already beaten them or were hoping to do so in the near future. She made her way down the now familiar hallway to Tom's office. He'd told her he wouldn't be in, but said that his assistant Amelia would accommodate her.

She arrived at the office to discover Amelia looking worried and embarrassed. "The Davis boys are in the conference room," she said in a low voice, after they had introduced themselves. "I'm sorry—I couldn't separate them. They insisted on staying together."

So they planned to present a united front, meaning that Daddy had anticipated this meeting and coached them. This family was working hard to hide something, that was now certain.

Both boys looked clean-cut and athletic. Jeff had been unwilling to meet her gaze when she'd observed him in the home setting, but these two betrayed no hint of uneasiness.

Sally had considered asking them to lift their shirts so she could see if there were any scars underneath. Legally, she could not force them to do anything. But now that seemed out of the question. The last thing she wanted was for the father to hear that she'd wanted to see areas where they might bear scars. Truth to tell, she doubted that she'd be able to get any information out of them at all.

"Hi, I'm Sam Davis Junior," the oldest one said as soon as she entered the room. "And this is my brother, Kenny. He's fifteen and I'm seventeen. I'm a senior," he added.

They listened solemnly as she described the crimes she was investigating.

"You told us this at the house," Sam reminded her.

"I'm telling you again. Because I need all the help I can get. People are suffering, boys. Not to mention the poor animals."

Kenny asked, "So, you're interviewing every kid in town?"

"No, I'm not. Just the ones who live on Pinewoods Lane. Most of the crimes have taken place in your neighborhood."

"Not Wanda," Kenny said.

Sally was very interested in this statement. She hadn't been talking about the murders. Why had he assumed this?

Sam was quick to correct his brother. "She's on the cat killings, dummy."

"Oh."

"Boys, if either of you have anything to tell us about those poor women—"

"We don't," Sam said. "The state police have already questioned everybody in the neighborhood and the little kids are all having nightmares. And we don't know anything about the cats, either."

She had no choice now. It was time to put it all out on the table. Now or never. "Principal Keener has evidence that your brother Jeff was being beaten and disfigured with burns over a long period of time. The only place this could have happened was at home. Now I want you to tell me what you know about it."

Sam looked straight at her, eyebrows raised as if in question. Kenny squirmed—but he'd been squirming since she entered the room, so that wasn't an indication of anything.

She was determined to wait for them to respond, no matter how long it took.

Finally, she heard a throat being cleared. It was Sam Junior, the spokesman. "I hope you can understand this, ma'am. Jeff was in trouble. A lot of trouble."

"Yeah," piped in his brother. "Dad was trying to help him."

Sam slid his eyes around to Kenny, as if telling him to shut up. Kenny got the message. Sam Junior continued. "If anything like that ever happened to Jeff, and I don't know that it did, then I expect it was only done to rescue him, and I expect he's grateful for it now." Kenny nodded in agreement.

Sally was flabbergasted. How did Sam Davis Senior ever manage to brainwash his kids so effectively?

She leaned over toward the boys, causing them to lean back a little, to get away from her hot breath. "Burning a child's skin with cigarettes," she pronounced, slowly and clearly, "is not discipline. It's torture and what's more, it's illegal."

"Oh, no, m'am, that couldn't be."

"That's right," added Kenny, earnestly. "Neither of our parents smoke."

Sally wanted to reach over and wring their cowardly necks. They must have sensed this, because they leaned back even farther.

She went to her feet and slapped her palms down hard on the table, causing the boys to jump up from their chairs. "You haven't seen the last of me," she declared. "I'm going to talk to you boys again—separately—and if I find out either one of you is lying, I'm gonna arrest you as accessories. Your father has committed a crime and there is going to be state intervention."

Kenny had a smile on his face, as if he thought she was joking, but Sam had gone pale.

"You can go back to your classes."

There was one child left, the youngest, still in elementary school. She'd have to save him until tomorrow. Hopefully, she'd still be able to conduct the interview, despite the fact that the parents would now know what she was doing. She remembered the child was smallish and shy, hiding behind his siblings.

The odds were against a small child offering any useful input, especially after what would undoubtedly happen tonight, which would be a strict parental instruction to tell the lady nothing. But you never knew, did you, not in this crazy business of hers.

It was just pushing one, so she thought she might try for a meeting with Tilford Harkins. Having Ed propose her as sheriff was one thing, and solving the mutilation case was another, but the county commissioners were bound to want to know what she proposed to do about the murders.

She drove over to the office. Ed sat in his usual place, sipping coffee. She dropped down in the chair opposite him. "I want to talk to Mr. Harkins," she said. "I'm assuming that I'll go before the county commissioners for approval."

"Well, they're gonna—you know—I mean—"

Ed was too modest to say that they were going to automatically approve her, but that was probably his expectation. "My assumption is that they'll want my ideas about the murders, also."

"Yeah, that's good. That makes sense."

"What have you gotten from Tilford?"

"The usual stuff." He went in his desk, pulled out a forensics report. "Nothing very creative, if that's what you mean."

She looked down a list of findings. There was nothing

that stood out, no positive DNA evidence, no specifics about the clothing the perp had been wearing or anything really useful. She looked up at Ed. "Is Tilford any good? I mean, what's he doing out here in the sticks instead of, say, Dallas?"

"He's always been top drawer in my book. I gotta admit, though, I haven't used him a lot. No need." He went silent, staring off into some middle distance. What was on his mind? There were reasons here, she felt, that were not being stated.

"It says here the perp wore Carhartt jeans. That's something."

"Narrows it down to every man in the county and most of the women. Helped us a lot."

"Washed in Delft. Delft can't be the only detergent in town."

"Unfortunately, it's the only one you can get out of the vending machine at Fluffies." That was what everybody called the Fluff 'n' Dry Laundromat at the far end of Main.

"One thing we should do is get them to change it. If we have another murder and we get another thread that's been washed in the new detergent, we'll know he uses the Laundromat."

He sat there as still as a mummy, his hands folded before his face, his eyes closed. Then the eyebrows rose. The eyes opened. "Definitely mention that idea to the commissioners."

She felt herself literally flushing with pleasure and was ashamed for it. Sure, the strategy was a good one, but if it mattered at all, it would be because somebody else had suffered and died.

She called Tilford's number and had no trouble arranging a meeting for three. She drove up to Gladewater on the quiet country highway that connected the larger community with Maryvale. On the way, she saw the ghosts of ancient roadside signs painted on the sides of gray old barns, and cattle lolling under trees, and houses buried in groves of oak and pine.

She stopped the car on a long rise, and looked out across an empty valley. Down in its depths, the pines were tall and dark green, following the line of a river. From somewhere far away, there was a steady pounding, perhaps a rock quarry in operation. Closer, bugs hummed in the Queen Anne's lace that hugged the roadside, and the air was perfumed with the hard, fresh scent of wildflowers, Indian paintbrush, black-eyed Susans, and tiny white flowers that clung to the line of soil between the shoulder and the tarmac as if it were the last open space in the world.

She was surprised to find that Tilford's "office" was a ranch house on a suburban street. It was nondescript, its garden tumbledown, its grass dry. There was an air of abandonment about it, almost. Just the sort of place where a madman would live with his memories, she thought. And then she thought: it would be the supreme irony if Tilford was the killer. It would also, however, explain the perp's apparent expert knowledge of forensics procedures.

Before she could ring the bell, Tilford opened the door. The first thing she saw was the most elaborate radio-controlled airplane she had ever encountered.

"It's a B-24 Liberator Bomber," Tilford said. "Scaled to fly with the same characteristics as the original."

"It's—boy, is that thing ever detailed."

"The pilot is my dad. The plane is the 'Swell Susan,' his plane. He died in her."

Tilford must be a World War II orphan. He looked not a day over forty, but he had to be pushing sixty.

"Come on back," he added, "to my lair."

The forensics lab consisted of a workbench in the garage, and about half the floor space.

"It's no big deal," he said, more than slightly understating the case. "Vegas CSI works out of a garage, too."

"They have a huge lab."

"The TV show has a huge lab. The actual unit works out of a garage not a lot bigger than this. I know, I've been to a forensics convention in Vegas and got a tour of their facility." He chuckled. "The reality of forensics is that we're the second-class citizens of criminology. It's the detectives who get all the cash."

His lab, which ran along one wall of the garage, smelled faintly of some chemical, perhaps ether or formaldehyde. She wondered if the black Chevy Malibu that filled the rest of the garage smelled the same.

She decided to start right in. "The jeans interest me. Can you tell me how old they were? Or the size?"

"The threads were aged probably thirty washings. They were consistent with the Carhartt brand. As far as size, no can do, no information."

"Now, what does thirty washings mean? Old jeans? New?"

"Maybe three months old. Average."

So the jeans were basically a dead end. "What would you say is the most important piece of forensics evidence you've gathered so far?"

He took a deep breath, remained silent for a moment. "You know, I think it's actually not something we found, but something we didn't. Normally, people in these cases—rage cases—they literally just drip evidence."

"Such as?"

"DNA from flying spit, hair, bits of blood and skin, finger and skin prints and oils, lint from inside cuffs that can later be matched to the pants—the list is long."

"But not in this case. In either attack. Why would that be?"

"I've come to the conclusion that these people were killed by somebody they were certain would not attack them. They went down like sacks of potatoes tossed off a truck. Absolutely no warning at all."

"And the reason for the blows being so light?"

"In my opinion?"

"Sure. We've already got the coroner's opinion."

"I noted that the bat—"

"You're certain it was a bat?"

"Oh, yes. Louisville Slugger. We got a little varnish off Glynesse. Which, incidentally, tells me that the bat hadn't been used much before. With blows that light, you're not going to dislodge varnish unless it's a pretty new bat."

She made a mental note to find out about baseball and the Davises.

"So what did you note about the bat—"

"Well, about the blows, actually. The first one, in each case, impacted the anterior inferior cerebellum, which sent a shock wave up through the tissue of the brain and into the temporal lobe, which bounced against the skull, causing instant loss of consciousness." He looked at her. "Somebody who knew the sweet spot could knock you totally unconscious with a blow there from the heel of the hand. It's that sensitive."

"So, the killer knows anatomy?"

"Probably. Of course, luck could play a part. The first one was so easy, he decided to keep on that way."

"And the blows to the faces? They were light, too."

"Delivered with surprising care, even finesse."

"Any footprints?"

He shook his head. "Been too damn dry. And the dogs were no good, either. Same reason." He sighed, shook his head. "I'm just afraid we're not finished."

"In what sense?"

"You feel it like you feel a tornado in the night. You can hear it out there, you know that it's going to touch down, but you don't know where."

She could not agree with him more. As she drove home through the softly rising night, with the moon fat and low on the eastern horizon and the evening star gleaming in the west, she thought she might know why Ed was calling it quits. He couldn't stand the truth: they were going to have to wait for another crime, and hope he slipped up somehow and left crucial evidence behind.

In other words, for this to come out right, somebody else had to die.

She went home and found she couldn't eat, then went up to her room and tried to read the *Houston Chronicle*. She stared sightlessly at the pages.

Elizabeth appeared and tried to help her with her black-outs, but it was no good. She was too tired, too afraid, too agitated to do anything except feel sick about them.

The next morning she came in to find that Ed had deputized her and issued her a gun.

She spent two hours at the state police shooting range at the Burnham barracks qualifying on the weapon. It was an involved process, that included an examination in the legal uses of her firearm, and thorough training on it. Ed had taught her to shoot when she was a girl, so she did well.

Many people she knew in Houston had carried guns without bothering to qualify under the state's concealed weapons law. Some of her girlfriends kept guns in their glove compartments or night-table drawers. You could even buy a handbag from the NRA with a special hidden gun pocket. You didn't have to remove your gun in order to fire it, you just aimed your purse at the perpetrator, and if you fired a hole in the leather, the NRA would replace the purse for free.

After a quick lunch at her desk, she headed out for the elementary school. She'd received a temporary badge, so now she was able to act officially in her new capacity as a deputy sheriff. She wasn't ready to make arrests, not until Ed and the county attorney had briefed her in procedures, but at least she could reinforce her demands for answers if necessary. She was probably lucky that she hadn't had a badge and gun when she'd approached Jackie. That was one lesson she didn't plan to forget.

The new elementary school had replaced the beautiful old Maryvale Central School that Sally had longed to go to as a child. It had been a tall, red brick and granite Victorian, probably a firetrap, but during the summers when she walked past, she'd heard the band practicing in the basement, tunes that would unexpectedly touch her heart when she chanced to hear them on TV—the Colonel Bogey March, for example, and others whose names she didn't know.

The elementary school was smaller than the other two,

made of yellow brick, so squat and low with its flat roofs that it could have been some sort of bomb shelter.

She pushed through the double doors into an echoing hallway. She'd arrived at lunchtime, and although the classrooms were empty, she could hear a muffled din coming from below. She followed the sound down to the basement, and entered the roaring cafeteria.

The place was literally teeming with kids. Some were unpacking sack lunches, while others stood in line with their trays, waiting to be dealt what looked like an all-carbohydrate lunch of macaroni and cheese, creamed corn and biscuits. There were apples in a big bowl at the end of the line, but nobody took one. The strong scent of peanut butter wafted through the room.

She saw shy kids sitting alone, with their shoulders hunched over their lunches. Popular kids took over huge trestle tables, laughing and elbowing each other, while the lonely kids watched them with dull, slightly confused eyes. It made Sally feel kind of sick to see that the school pecking order was still in place. It took her back to her own lonely kid days. *Children are cruel, it's the way of the world.*

The lunchroom was being managed—sort of—by teachers, most of whom looked ready to tear their hair out. They rushed around, mopping up spilled milk in one corner, settling a dispute in another, comforting a crying child who had forgotten his lunch. Sally wondered when they got around to eating their own lunches, and how they could digest them when the time came.

She went up to one of them. "Excuse me," she said, "I'm looking for Winchell Davis. He's in the fifth grade." The teacher gestured toward a row of tables, then resumed cleaning up a little girl who'd had corn thrown in her hair. Sally realized she was going to be able to walk right over and conduct her interview without any staff formalities at all. Of course, his family must have warned him that she'd be along.

She found him in a corner alone, picking at a bologna

sandwich. Lana was obviously strict about food. There were no candy wrappers or empty Frito bags, and he had milk rather than a soda.

"Hello, Winchell," she said brightly, sitting down across from him. "I'm Sally Hopkins. I came out to your house the other day, remember?"

He nodded, looking up at her with melting big brown eyes that were framed by long lashes. There was something vulnerable about him that made Sally want to take him in her lap and give him a hug. She hadn't warmed at all to any of the other Davis children.

"I'm called Waddy," he said.

Sally cleared her throat, wondering how to begin. She was painfully aware that her previous attempts to engage the Davis children in conversation had failed. She knew that this one had been expecting her. But she also knew that he was ten, and she'd trained in how to interview children. She adopted a conspiratorial manner. "I need to find someone who can talk to me about your big brother Jeff," she said, "and when I saw you out at your house, I thought you might be the one who could help me." She smiled in what she hoped was an unthreatening way.

Waddy gave her a long look. His big eyes were innocent, not like the shadowed, furtive eyes of his older siblings. "Sure," he said, "I can tell you all about Jeff. Him and me are good friends. I don't see him too much 'cause, you know, I'm the littlest, but we get to talking sometimes." He gave her a beguiling smile, and Sally hoped she was finally going to get some information.

"Waddy, do you think Jeff is afraid about anything, or angry, maybe?"

Waddy thought it over carefully. "He's got a lot of secrets," he admitted, finally. "He keeps to himself." He looked up at her earnestly. "All the other kids say he used to be tough on them, but he's always been real nice to me. He takes me down to the creek to fish and he tells real good ghost stories."

This little boy showed no obvious evidence of concealing his own abuse, and it was a rare child that could hide
such problems from a professional at this age, so Sally returned to the theory that Jeff might be the only victim. Jeff
was probably the kind of bright kid who hadn't yet realized
he had brains. His light would shine only a little bit, and
would only be noticed by people who knew how to look for
it, like Tom Keener. If his less-bright parents saw it at all,
they would see him as arrogant.

"I'm worried about him, Waddy," she said. "I think he
should go to college and find a good life for himself. What
do you think?"

"I think so too, Sally." Unlike most kids his age in Maryvale, he didn't hesitate to call her by her first name. "He
don't do much, right now, mostly just sits at home during
the day. He sleeps late 'cause he waits to take a shower till
the rest of us are through in the bathroom. He only goes out
at night."

"Does he have a girlfriend?"

"I never seen one." He smiled up at her. "Maybe he
don't like girls. I don't!"

"Have you ever seen your brother be, ah, mean to animals?"

Waddy looked puzzled. "You mean like goin' fishing?"

"No, no. It's just that, children who are, well, worried
about things sometimes take their troubles out on animals,
when what they really want to do is hurt the people who
have been hurting them."

The boy nodded. "'Cause they're too scared to fight
back?"

This kid had good insights—Jeff was not the only smar-
tie in the Davis clan. "That's right, they're afraid to fight
back, but they also don't think they deserve to. They think
there must be something bad about them, or else other people wouldn't be hurting them all the time. And someone
like that won't think he's good enough to go to college or
get a job or have a girlfriend."

Waddy was thoughtful. "The way Jeff sits around all the time makes our father mad, but he don't say much to him anymore. I guess he gave up."

Depression, Sally thought, *anger turned against oneself. Another classic sign of abuse.* And violent acting out often went along with it. Explosive rages, the total transformation of the person. Not often, but it happened that a depressive would suddenly turn his anger outward. Such people could be lethargic one moment, like werewolves the next.

No matter what he had—or had not—done, he obviously needed help. Unfortunately, though, she needed a lot more evidence to effect a legal intervention. But they were so clannish, except for this little guy, that she doubted that she could gather it.

A loud buzzer made her jump. The lunch period was officially over. "Let's talk again, Waddy. I'd really like to help your brother."

The boy stood up and began to collect his trash. "Me too," he said. He gave her that heartbreaking smile again. This boy must surely be his parents' favorite. "I got to go back to class now. See you later." And he was gone.

Her next step must be to confront Jeff. Problem was, she could be getting in real deep, if he'd gone further than killing pets and burning down barns. If he was the murderer, this was all going to be very, very dangerous. Next time, it wouldn't be the kind of mix-up that Rob could save her from.

Two frustrating, miserable days later, Sally realized that the case had hit a brick wall. First, Ed dropped off the face of the earth. Then Sam Davis's lawyer sent a letter of complaint about her to the county commissioners and another to the superintendent of schools. Both threatened suit, both threatened criminal charges against her.

She didn't think that any criminal charges would come out of it, but the district attorney soon called her to tell her that Davis had made good on his threat and was seeking to prosecute her for talking to a child without a parent present, both serious charges that he was obligated by law to examine, and which might well go to the grand jury.

She was terrified, of course, but also thought that the case was beginning to focus. Then, another setback: her projected perp was now the oldest Davis child, Jeff, and he was sticking close to home. Absent a warrant, he probably realized that she would not dare to show her face there.

She had pursued her theory about anatomy studies, but there were no books or records in any of the local libraries that would suggest that anybody had been studying these matters. Of course, why would there be? They could do it on the Internet without there being any chance of detection at all.

First two days passed, then five, then ten, and even as she began to settle surprisingly comfortably into the routine of being a country sheriff, an inner disquiet began to build. It was clear now: if she was going to get any further, there was going to have to be another murder.

It was horrible, waiting, knowing that because of your incompetence, somebody out there was going to die a miserable, unfair, and cruel death.

Night after night, she woke up hearing screams that were not there. As September drifted into October, the nights grew restless with storms and she waited, feeling helpless, sick with fear, knowing that the next murder was getting closer with every passing minute.

She determined where Louisville Slugger bats were sold in the area, and went to Gladewater to Target, Jay Sport, and Wal-Mart, and to Kaybee Toys in the Burnham Mall, asking each manager for records of bat purchases for the past four months.

The problem was, the bat might have been bought for cash. If so, there would be no record. As it was, she ended up with a pepper spattering of bat purchases in the five-county area. Exactly three of the credit card purchases had involved Maryvale residents.

Irony of ironies, one of them was Glynesse. She questioned Hank, but he did not remember seeing the bat. When she searched the house, though, she found nothing—that is until Rob reached into the bed's innerspring and, lo and behold, there it was.

As fresh as a baby's bottom, too. This bat had never been used to hit anything. Tilford's analysis quickly confirmed two things: none of the fingerprints on it belonged to Hank, and the most recent set did belong to Glynesse.

"I wonder if she'd been planning to kill him," Sally had asked Rob.

"Anything's possible. Most likely, though, it was because she was after rats."

"Rats?"

"Sure. A sweet little bat's just like a flyswatter for the bastards. Use one myself."

Sally was still not sure that she was going to get used to country living or country folks.

And it wasn't too clear that they were going to get used to her, either. She patrolled in her own car with Ed's taped-together town bible on the seat beside her. This was an in-car Rolodex full of names, addresses, and cryptic little notations that told Ed everything he needed to know about each citizen. But it didn't speak quite as eloquently to her. She couldn't decipher his henscratch, the little multicol-ored symbols that had come, over the years, to effectively replace his handwriting. He'd created his own code, and didn't even realize it.

Ed pulled back not only from the job, but from Sally as well. It felt to her that he was ashamed of his failure to catch the killer. It was understandable: he was well past seventy when circumstances dropped this particular load of bricks on him, and not in any way equipped to handle it. Still, it was hard when she called him and he would barely speak to her, and the chili Saturdays were gone with the wind.

She didn't exactly get opposition from people about being sheriff, at least not active opposition. What she got was apathy. People were polite but distant. In East Texas, that amounts to hostility.

Sally decided to take a cue from Ed. Maybe it would help to gain acceptance from her constituents if she dressed the part. It sounded simple, but this was a situation where clothes counted. Unfortunately, though, she hadn't been issued a uniform. In fact, there was no uniform. Ed had made up his own and Sally decided to do the same.

She started out by making a trip to Rank's. After the aw-ful confrontation at Jackie Hardcastle's place, she'd thought that perhaps she would never show her face in the store again. But it turned out not to be a problem, because the gossip that had begun to spread about the night of "upset" at the Hardcastle place had caused Miz Rank to abandon her own store to a couple of bored, gum-cracking kids.

There was a rumor floating around that she and Jackie were planning a move to Florida—normally the last place an East Texan would retire to, it being full of New Yorkers and Democrats. But then again, they could be all but certain of never encountering anybody from around here, not in Boca Raton or Tampa. Sally wondered what Miz Rank would look like in a swimsuit.

There was no place like Rank's for authentic western wear. Even the best outfitters in Houston couldn't come close to this level of authenticity. This was the genuine stuff, the kind of clothes that would survive a real roundup on a real ranch.

The jeans were Carhartt and Workwear, as well as a few bradded Levi's from the days when it was still a work brand. Nothing stylish or intentionally torn or faded around here—life did the weathering for the folks in Maryvale. The reason Miz Rank's had twenty-year-old Levi's was because once she put something on the shelf, she never took it off again until it was sold. Some of the dungarees Sally looked at could have been there since she was a girl.

She prowled around in the corners of the store, ignoring years of accumulated dust kittens, waving off the begrudging "Let me know if I can help you find anything" voices echoing from the front.

Then she found what she wanted: old-fashioned cowgirl jeans with plenty of room for the kind of hips that filled a saddle. The Levi's label looked like it was from about 1970. She'd look good in these. She gathered up a stack and headed for the droopy curtain in the corner that served as a dressing room.

When she finally emerged from Rank's, Sally felt East Texas approved. She was wearing a pair of not-too-blue jeans and had two more pairs just like them in a bag. She also wore a white shirt, yoked in back and tucked into a tooled brown belt. Her boots were simple but well made, with toes that weren't too pointed to do any work in. She already had the Stetson she'd purchased when she'd come here with Rob, in innocent times that seemed like years ago.

Her swearing in was almost a non-event. The chief surprise was that Ed didn't attend. The County Commission office was located on the main floor of the courthouse, a small conference room behind a tall oak door with a frosted glass window in it. The commissioners weren't there. She was sworn by Katie Blanchard, the commission's ancient recording secretary. Sally dared not ask her age, although she was fascinated. Could Katie Blanchard be over a hundred? If not, then she was aging too fast.

She was sworn on the county's official Bible, a worn little book that dated from 1876, and had the name of every sheriff recorded in it. Between 1876 and 1912, five of them had been shot. Since then, only two.

They'd made the official change without making an official announcement. Ed had said when he offered her the job that the time to make the announcement was when she had earned the goodwill of the citizenry, and this could best be done by catching whoever needed catching.

She wondered how she would handle driving around in the official cruiser with "Maryvale Sheriff's Department" stenciled on the sides . . . and how the rest of Maryvale would handle it. But it turned out not to be a problem, since Ed was keeping the cruiser for the time being. He probably wasn't ready to buy a new car.

But she could wait, because Ed had a point. If she ended Maryvale's crime wave, folks would likely be tickled to see her cruising around in the black-and-white. Before that, every time they saw her, they'd judge her, and it wouldn't be a good judgment.

Actually, Sally couldn't see how much of anything had changed. Ed still drove around town in the cruiser regularly, like a ghost, Sally thought, because she never heard from him or saw him at the office.

Rob was distressed by this, because he respected Ed's abilities, and knew that if they didn't make some headway soon, state police headquarters would jack up the pressure. The first thing that would happen would be that they'd look for similar crimes in some other state, and then demand FBI help. Then the Texas Rangers would come to town. No matter who turned up, it would be an admission of defeat for the county's trooper detachment, and especially its commander.

Sally knew one thing—they had to break new ground, and soon, or she'd call in the cavalry herself. Another woman must not be sacrificed.

Rob had always been a bastion of calm and good sense, but now she could hear the panic in his voice, a choppy edge that had never been there before, a tendency not to listen when he needed to and to rush off after leads that were obviously going to go nowhere.

She decided that the only way to calm him down enough to make him listen to her theories was to feed him. She needed man food. She prowled through Flagg's on her way home for some decent steaks. Then she dropped by the Evans vegetable stand to see what they had left. The season was winding down, but there were some nice homegrown tomatoes for sale, with those flaws that prove they're the genuine article.

When Elizabeth heard about the dinner meeting, she insisted on eating out. "I've got work to do at the office," she said, with a knowing smile. This annoyed Sally a good deal more than she knew it should.

"This is not a date, goddamn it," she told her. "I'm the sheriff now, and I've got to act like one. If I can't catch the kid who is torturing pets around here, not to mention the murderer of two women, I may as well crawl into Ed's hole with him, or head back to Houston."

"I'm sorry, hon." Elizabeth was contrite. "But I do think I'll make myself scarce this evening. It might help Rob to realize that this is not just a social occasion. He's such a gentleman, and he really likes women—unlike many I've met—but his gallantry can get in the way of giving us gals equal credit for having brains. He wants to protect us, to shelter our tender sensibilities from the harsh realities of life. Plus, he's shy."

Sally let that last line drop. He could be as shy as he wanted. Her purpose here was to get past the friction between them. They needed to work together. "When I first came here, I couldn't decide if Rob was for me or against me. Now I'm beginning to think the problem is that he has a gentlemanly need to treat me like a glass doll. I find out about all the little crimes that go on around here, because they all get reported directly to the sheriff. But Rob hears about other things, tough stuff, that he shared with Ed but will not share with me. I never get to hear about any of it, because it might be too hard on my delicate ears, and that has got to end."

"He sees it as man talk," Elizabeth agreed. "That's going to be your greatest impediment when it comes to doing your job. You've got to go up against what their mommas have raised them to believe, that a woman should be insulated from the ugly." She eyed Sally's new clothes. "I'm not sure that outfit helps."

"What am I supposed to do? I can't run around here in a tweed suit looking like Margaret Thatcher."

"She did all right for herself."

Their conversation was cut short by the sound of truck tires in the driveway. Elizabeth grabbed her briefcase and made for the back door. "Bye, hon," she said. "Don't worry about me. I'll grab a pizza out on the highway. It's better than your cooking, anyway."

That reminded her. "I've got to unpack the groceries!" She started for the kitchen, then turned toward the front door when she heard Rob's knock.

She led him over to the dining table where she'd laid out pencils and pads. "I want to have a serious talk. We need to communicate, Rob. I have to be included in what's going on in this town."

He looked at her so seriously that it was almost funny.

What was going through his mind—how to tell a woman all the terrible things he knew . . . or how to avoid doing so?

"Want a beer?"

"That would be great."

She went to the kitchen. "Damn! The beer's not cold. I forgot to put it in the refrigerator."

Rob went in. "You ought to put those steaks in there, too," he said. He helped her empty the shopping bags, then rooted around in the icebox for something cold. He came up with a diet Dr Pepper, which he proceeded to pour down his throat.

Sally washed the tomatoes, then fired up the broiler in the oven. "Wow, meat!" he exclaimed. When she looked at him confused, he laughed. "I come from a big family and I didn't see a solid piece of meat like that very often when I was growing up. Usually it was ground up and hidden underneath plenty of potatoes and peas—if it was there at all."

She smiled wryly. It was rare for Rob to reveal any personal details about himself. "Now they tell us this is the way we're supposed to eat."

He went over to help her. "Uh, you might want to think about adjusting the oven rack one notch higher. You want to broil 'em, not bake 'em."

Sally wondered if that's why her steaks always turned out vaguely gray in the middle.

"Have you got any Parmesan? You can cut the tomatoes into thick slices, then sprinkle cheese on them and broil them right along with the steak."

He looked appalled when she took a green cardboard can of grated cheese from the cupboard.

"Even Flagg's sells Parmesan in blocks," he said.

Before she knew it, he had taken over cooking their dinner. "I'll set the table," she said. She gathered up plates, napkins, and cutlery and headed for the dining room. There was just enough room for elegant dining, as long as no more than two people were being gracious at the same time.

Her resentment disappeared when she cut into a perfect steak. It was just pink enough inside, and nice and done on the surface. "How did you ever do this?" she asked.

"It's an old bachelor trick. You take the meat out before it's done, because it always cooks a little more afterward."

"I never used to cook steak in Houston," she said, around a jawful of meat. "Too messy. I used to stop by the Flame Steak House once a week for my fix, the way you guys stop at the whorehouse." She stopped, but too late. She'd offended him, she was sure.

But he threw back his head and laughed. "Sally, you used to shock and scandalize me," he said. "But then I figured, where's the harm in the truth? I've got to admire someone who's not afraid to say what they think."

"You really mean that?"

"Absolutely. Except I don't stop at whorehouses."

"It was meant as a metaphor."

"I see."

"Then how about this: I'm supposed to be the sheriff, but I don't know a damn thing about what's happening on the murder case because you troopers aren't telling me."

He took this more calmly than she'd expected. "You're right, Sally. I've been thinking about that myself." He stood up. "The beer's cold by now."

She heard him open the freezer, where he'd put it so it would chill fast. "You know what you can get down Burnham way is Indio. It's sold only around Monterey, but Hector Rivas brings it in. Sells it to a few friends."

He came back carrying one of the Heinekens she'd bought.

"And Indio's the best, right?"

"Best in this hemisphere. But this will do fine for now." He toasted her with his bottle. "Thanks, Sal."

"Rob, I don't know quite how to put this. I guess it's best to just be blunt. This investigation looks stalled. I think it was outrageous of Ed to wash his hands of it, but that's another conversation. What I do want to talk about is effective liaison between me and the state police. And I'm not getting it."

"Sally, there are channels and we have to use those channels."

"You and Ed cruising together, working the case side by side—THAT'S the kind of channel I'm talking about."

"There's a reg set on liaison procedures, I think. I can probably—"

"Another woman is going to die! That's the bottom line, unless we catch this piece of filth, and do it NOW!"

As the cutlery jangled, she was shocked to realize that she'd slammed her open hand down on the table.

Without missing a beat, Rob said, "I've been wondering how I can get you more involved."

"So let's get that set up right now."

"With Ed, it was just spontaneous. Informal."

"I'm as informal as they get."

"Problem is, the guys are going to clam up in front of a woman."

And so are you, she thought.

"But that's only because they don't know you yet, Sally."

"You know me! I've been working in the sheriff's office for a over a month."

"But you haven't been part of the police process. Now, suddenly, we're told you're the sheriff. And Ed stops hanging with us. The guys just need to get to know you, and, frankly, they need to respect you, too. They need a reason to believe that you can do this job."

"I don't see your troopers pulling in any serial killers," she retorted.

"That's true enough. And I don't see you making any headway on your theories about the killings being connected to the animal mutilations, either. Theories are dangerous if they don't lead somewhere."

Sally had to admit there was truth in what he said. She needed arrests. Jeff would do for starters. She resolved to get that done.

"I'll do informal liaison for you. Make sure you get briefed on where we are."

"How will that work?"

"Let's meet every day," he said. "Cantor's. Lunch. We'll

share information and let the town see, let my men see us doing it."

And the townsfolk, she thought. Not so bad. When Sally put on coffee, Rob gently persuaded her to add an extra spoonful to the pot, which made the smell drifting in from the kitchen irresistible.

"We could have our first meeting right now," she suggested. She got a pad and pencil out of the small desk in the sitting room and took it with her to the living room. They sat down on the couch, side by side. She could smell his aftershave. Old Spice, the same kind her dad had used. And Ed. Of course, what else?

She wondered, suddenly, what kind of aftershave the killer wore. The thought made her cringe inside, as if some part of her wanted to escape this place, Maryvale in the gathering dark.

Many hours and cups of coffee later, after reviewing the case in microscopic detail, they came up with two critical need lists. One assumed the pet and people killings were not related, and suggested various routes of investigation. Another assumed everything was being done by one person, and had another set of plans.

"If the pet killings are separate, the pets are being done by a group of people, probably kids," Rob said. "It's probably local juvies who need to be sentenced to a long bout of community service."

She thought it was a waste of time to consider this, but she humored him. "Do we have any neo-Nazis around here?"

"None I've seen."

"Drug issues?"

"We have a crystal meth problem. Growing." He brought up the question of Jeff Davis. "Have you made any headway on that?"

"I've talked to everyone except the boy himself." She

gave him the history of her interrogations. "Actually, it occurs to me that I could use your help."

"Why me?"

"I think you can put more pressure on the boy. A big, no-nonsense state trooper like you is going to get a whole lot more of his attention than a girl sheriff."

"I can't arrest him."

"You can ask him to come in for questioning."

"And the line is?"

"Alibi dates. Where was he when each fire, each mutilation, occurred."

"We don't know exactly when they occurred, except for Harry the Pomeranian and Suzette."

"He doesn't know that. Make up dates for the others. And throw in the murder dates, too."

"Is he really of interest?"

"He is of interest, Rob. He is of great interest."

"And you didn't utter a peep when I said I'd take him in if he needed a place to go. Would that be good, for a state cop to be unwittingly harboring the killer?"

She realized that she could have wrecked his career. The media would've eaten him alive.

He said quietly that it would probably be most productive to send Cliff Collins out to the Davis place to question Jeff about his activities on the nights in question. And only use the hard dates. If he was their man, he'd know the dates they had were wrong. If the alibis for what hard dates they had were weak, Rob would then have the legal authority to bring him in for questioning.

Sally agreed to this plan. They also decided that all local law officers should look for kids wearing gang insignia, even though Ed had said there were no gangs in Maryvale. Ed could simply be behind the times. Sally would personally ask Tom Keener and Wallace Reed about this, no matter how much they wanted to avoid her. It would be her job to question any gang members they found about the animal killings. She felt confident she could get more information from a garden-variety juvie than she had from the Davis kids. She was used to encountering hostility—it was all that damned Davis niceness she couldn't deal with.

Rob left, and she watched him go, a big, surprisingly graceful figure disappearing into the dark. As he drove off, she stepped out into the front yard. Lightning bugs drifted just above the grass, and the Milky Way stretched across the vastness of the sky. Katydids argued in the trees, and the soft murmuring of bull bats stirred the near air. Somewhere down the street, children shouted as they chased lightning bugs. Across the way, a TV laughed and chattered, sounding like a madman in a cathedral.

As she went back in, she locked the front door, then patrolled the house making certain that everything was tight.

It was a sweaty, difficult night for her. Once again, storms muttered in the late night, and dry lightning flickered continuously, as if somewhere in the sky, in among the canyons of the clouds, madness reigned.

Over breakfast, Elizabeth reminded her that they should have a "session" soon. Elizabeth had been conducting them for some weeks now, and they were both aware of what the blackouts were about—her dad had obviously abused her. And they knew that if she left this alone, the blackouts would get worse, and her ability to function, to live, would decline. They both knew that Sally's mind was begging for help, and that's what the blackouts were: cries for help.

She wanted to push them aside. She wanted to forget them. She wanted to somehow cut the memories out of her head and have done with it.

The next day she made it her business to drive to every crime scene, going from one to the other in the same order that the crimes had been committed. She included the murders. But if there was anything to be learned, she didn't find it. She finished the day with a little paperwork. Unlike Ed, she did not let her "forms" defeat her. She was efficient, and she knew what she was doing when it came to processing things like state-mandated police action statistics and budgetary compliance reports for the county audit bureau.

Elizabeth had the lights down low when Sally came in, and she'd transformed the living room into a makeshift analyst's space. They'd discussed doing this in her office, but this setting was far more congenial.

The last session had made it clear to Sally that she was dealing with memories of sexual abuse. The perpetrator was still a black shadow, meaning that he was too terrifying for her to face. That was what they would work on tonight.

She wasn't sure if she was looking at repeat events, or a single attack. She didn't know if it had started before her mother killed herself or afterward, when she and her father lived alone together. If the abuse had started before and was the reason her mother took her own life, then, in Sally's eyes, her father was a murderer, and that was going to be very hard to face.

Which was undoubtedly why she only saw the Dark Figure in her flashbacks. It was as if he was painted out, like he was a jigsaw puzzle piece that had been removed. When she finally saw him, she would begin to heal. . . .

She would have put her dad in jail if she could, and that made her feel ashamed, and the fact that it did made her mad.

She let Elizabeth hypnotize her. Memory recovery was supposed to be a controversial process. But the founders of the so-called False Memory Syndrome Foundation, who had spread this canard, had been accused of abusing their own daughter, a prominent research psychologist. According to her, they not only abused her, they allowed admitted pedophiles onto their founding board. In cases like this, the fact was that hypnosis worked.

She lay back listening to Elizabeth's soft breathing, her gentle voice urging her deeper . . . and then she heard something new—a whisper. Instantly, she knew this was important: her first audible memory. Her desperate inner self was gaining confidence that releasing these memories would not mean annihilation. The sound was so clear, she turned her head to see who was talking to her. She asked Elizabeth if her father might have whispered in her ear in order to wake her up without startling her.

"Definitely. He couldn't risk having you make a lot of noise, in case you woke up anyone else. If you screamed, you might even have alerted the neighbors."

Sally hadn't thought about that before. "Why *didn't* I scream?" she asked. "Someone might have heard me, or at least I might have scared him off. I wasn't shy about expressing myself when I was a child, so why didn't I scream bloody murder?"

Elizabeth laughed a little. "You know all this, girl."

"Yes, but . . ."

"You need the doctor to reassure you, I know. That's the magic of the clinical relationship. So, listen to your doctor, lady. Since it was Daddy who was doing it, it *couldn't* be wrong, even though you didn't want it to happen. But kids have to do so many things they don't want to do, from eating spinach to cleaning up their rooms, so you thought you had to obey him."

"So I thought it couldn't be wrong, if Daddy told me it was OK. But I *felt* it was wrong. Why didn't I just accept it?" She shook her head, baffled. "Or maybe I did accept it. But if I did, why did I repress it, and why am I having these visions?"

"Does it make you feel bad about yourself?"

"I can't imagine doing it. The whole idea makes me feel . . . unclean. And yet I let it go on for so long, without telling anyone. What's wrong with me, anyway?"

"That's the way the perp wants you to think. Nothing's wrong with you. Is or was." She paused. *"Even if you enjoyed it."*

Sally felt a horrible, constricting nausea come gagging up from her gut.

"Maybe it was the only affection you ever received, so it didn't seem all bad, not at the time, anyway. But believe me, you never wanted sexual attention. Your instincts fought against it, even if your mind, and probably your heart, full of love for Daddy, said yes."

"So I felt like I could only get his love by giving away something I didn't want to give. I couldn't be loved just for being myself."

"Girl, you are a quick study! Did you hear what you just said? Now, what does that tell you about your more recent adult relationships?"

Suddenly a whole lot about herself that she'd never understood became clear. The reason she was attracted to any man who came on to her, whether she really *liked* them or not. The reason she pushed away sincere attention. Plus her tendency to enter into sexual relationships too soon, and then feel dirty afterward. "I'm one sick kitten," she sighed.

"No, sweetie, you're a normal young woman who became desperately confused through no fault of her own. We all want love. It's natural, what else is there to live for?"

Sally noticed a certain wistful tone in Elizabeth's voice and looked at her hard. "You seem to do all right alone—or do you?"

Elizabeth's face became a blank wall. "We're not talking about me."

"We're talking about miserable dames everywhere. Come on, what's your story? It's time for *you* to come clean. What are you doing out here in the sticks all by yourself? I know loneliness when I see it."

"You're no longer hypnotized."

That was true.

Elizabeth grinned weakly. "Plus, you've figured me out, but then you would, Sally Hopkins. You're one sharp customer."

"So it's your turn to dish out some dirt. You already know all the bad stuff about me."

"You're not bad, Sally. It wasn't your fault."

"I know that, or at least I'm gonna make myself know it. Quit changing the subject! Tell me about you."

Elizabeth leaned back and closed her eyes. "I was a wife once, and a mother. I *am* a mother."

"A mother!" Sally remembered the photograph of the little boy she had seen upstairs in Elizabeth's bedroom. "Is he all grown-up now? Do you still see him?"

"No, he's not grown-up, and no, I don't see him. He's ten years old. I lost custody of him five years ago."

Sally could not have been more surprised. For a mother to lose custody—a mother—in Texas, that was next to impossible. "But, Elizabeth, you'd make a perfect mother!"

"The judge didn't think so. Oh, my, Sally, I might as well tell you, there was a lot of booze and a lot of drug abuse. You talk about a sick kitty, welcome to the club. The judge could've handled one or the other, but with two DWIs and mandatory drug rehab on my record, I was finished as a mom."

"You—an addict and an alcoholic? I don't believe it."

"Oh, I've cleaned up my act some since then. The drug rehab was effective. My experience inspired me to get my psychology degree so I could help others."

"If you're rehabilitated now, you ought to be able to regain custody. Heck, mothers get back custody all the time, even when they shouldn't. Kids are dragged away from foster parents who brought them up from infancy, just because Mom has a certificate saying she's gone off junk. You're miles better than that."

"Maybe, Sally. Maybe not." Elizabeth began to weep. Sally leaped out of her chair and ran to embrace her friend, who had once seemed so strong but was now revealed to be entirely and tragically human.

"Do you want to see your little boy again? What's his name?"

"J-Joshua. Josh."

"I'll help you, dear. You've helped me so very much."

"No, Sally, we've just started! You've got a long way to go."

"Shhh, it's my turn to take care of you now." But she remembered the Dark Figure and shuddered.

They sat on the couch together for what seemed like hours, wrapped in each other's arms, each weeping privately. Sally was the first to break away and dry her eyes.

"Enough therapy for one night. We're the weeping sisterhood. How about I rustle us up something to eat?" At Elizabeth's look, she laughed. "OK, I know I'm a lousy cook, but I'm learning some new techniques from Rob."

"Are you sure you're just learning cooking techniques?"

Sally flared up. "Look, I may not have a social life in this hayseed town, but that doesn't mean I have to fall for a hick like Rob Farley!"

"Tell you what," Elizabeth said, "why don't I cook tonight, and you can do the dishes. I've got some canned goods in the kitchen that I can find a way to be creative with."

Sally agreed to this arrangement with great relief.

As they ate, she thought about that whisper. As soon as she heard it, she'd come right out of hypnosis and deftly turned the conversation away from herself and toward Elizabeth.

Now, as the night wind sighed in the big old live oak that shaded the house, she wished her inner self had let her hear the words. She listened for them in the wind, but the wind kept its secrets.

Dawn had not yet come when the phone started ringing. Sally rolled over, picked it up.

"Hey, Sally."

Elizabeth came in. "Sally—"

"It's okay, it's for me." She returned to the phone. "Rob?"

"Sally, you need to roll."

She felt the slow release of her breath, and then gurgling nausea, followed by the hammering of her heart, and helpless, choking rage. "Tell me," she managed to say.

"It's Mrs. Bragg. She was a fourth-grade teacher over at the local elementary school. She taught there, it seems like, forever."

Sally took a deep breath, another. She was not going to faint, of all the fool things, no way. Still, the room turned, it reeled—and then a horrible, choking sadness twisted within her. It had happened, another woman had died!

"Sally?"

"Yes . . . yes, okay."

Elizabeth, God bless her, showed up with some water.

Sally drank, took a breath, forced her mind to work. "Okay. When was she killed? Did the killer use his bat again, if that's what the weapon is? Was her body arranged in the usual way?"

"Yep, our killer is consistent, all right. She taught class Tuesday, same as always, but when she didn't turn up yesterday, folks at the school got worried. That's unheard of for Edna Bragg. When she didn't answer her phone, they sent the school secretary out to investigate."

"She found her dead?"

"She didn't see the body. She found the house locked up tight, which is unusual for Mrs. Bragg. She went home and worried about it, then phoned several more times, and still got no answer. She finally decided to call us about seven P.M. last evening.

"By that time the station was closed, so the call went through to Cliff Collins, who was the on-duty. It'd been a busy night, what with kids driving around shooting paint-balls at folks' cattle, all kinds of junk . . . and the call wasn't any kind of priority." He paused. "Sally, fact is, he didn't check it out until about an hour ago."

"An old woman, living alone? Rob, how can that be?"

"He was busy chasing down some kids who were driving Daddy's Beamer through Joe Ed Coleman's unharvested corn, then a truck lost a cargo of heifers out on the Interstate . . . the long and the short of it is that he was busy most of the night. When he finally got to the house, there appeared to be no sign of life, so he forced his way in."

While he talked, Sally made a mental list of questions to ask, but then she heard sounds in the phone that could only be sobs. "Rob?"

"I'm sorry, Sally," he said. "It's just that Mrs. Bragg was my teacher too—hell, she taught everybody around here. I was what they now call dyslexic, but nobody knew what that was then. All they knew was I did 'mirror writing,' and couldn't learn how to read."

He cleared his throat, managed to continue. "She sat me on her lap every day and held my hand, practicing writing letters. She was so patient—she wouldn't give up, even though she had to skip her own breaks to do it. If it hadn't been for her, I don't know where I'd be."

A thought entered Sally's head. "Rob, how old was Mrs. Bragg?"

"Hell, I don't know, she'd never tell anybody. She was eighty if she was a day, I guess. It was so disrespectful, the way she was arranged on that kitchen floor, with her panties pulled off and her legs spread apart and . . ." Rob's voice had dropped low, and Sally knew that he was coping not only with sadness, but great and abiding rage.

"This murder breaks the killer's pattern of targeting young women."

"A second killer? Copycat?"

"Or else a more complex motive than we thought. This man's problem isn't related to impotence, but he's one smart cookie, smart enough to create the appearance that it is, to throw us off."

"Then what? What are we looking for?"

"That's the question. Answer it, and we've got our man."

"We need you here."

"On my way." As she dressed, she told Elizabeth what she could, being careful to follow police protocol and not include any details.

Driving to the crime scene, Sally reflected that Rob had come a long way in the six weeks since she'd arrived here. He not only wanted to include her, he understood that he needed her. Good. With her along, she felt sure, they had a better chance of solving this crime.

State police forensics were all over the scene. She hurried up to Tilford, who was vacuuming the pitiful corpse of a very old woman with a Dustbuster that made a peculiar, shrill noise. "Get in whites, Sheriff, or stay back three feet, please, ma'am."

She stepped out into the carefully kept little living room that looked like something from another age . . . except for the books in the shelves, which lined one whole wall. Here were the great masters of literature as well as the latest important authors, and a recent set of science texts. This teacher might be old, but she was by no means lost in the past.

"Where's Rob?" She asked nobody in particular.

The coroner blustered in from the kitchen, his face red and sweaty. He was going through a packet of Polaroids. "Pulled out ten minutes ago," he said.

"Hey, Billy."

"This is sick, Sheriff, this is so damn *sick* it's just gonna turn your stomach right inside out."

"Have you got the sequence of blows, Billy?"

"Back of the head, then—well, you can see."

Her face was a swollen mass, recognizable as human only by the one lifeless eye that was still visible.

Sally went into the kitchen and found something interesting: here, the fridge was open. Wanda had been headed toward her kitchen. Glynesse had been found in the door between the kitchen and the dining room. Now, this one had opened her refrigerator.

It looked as if somebody was coming in, asking these women for something from the kitchen, and when they went to get it, giving them a killing blow.

Who in the world would people let in like that, given what was happening in this town?

Had Miz Bragg gone into the kitchen, opened the fridge, then returned empty-handed, but with the fridge still open? Had she realized something was amiss and hurried back to the living room—and taken her blow then? Must have.

He'd called her back and surprised her as she came through the door.

"Tilford, could you dust both walls beside the kitchen door? Vacuum and dust?"

"Sure thing. May I know why?"

"I think he stood in front of one of them, maybe pressed against it. Probably."

"Consider it done."

She used her radio to call Dispatch, and found that Rob

was at her office. When she got there, she got a surprise: He was crying. Bitterly and frankly, his head down on Ed's desk, he cried and cried. Finally, he raised his head.

"Whoever this is, he's breaking the heart of this poor little town."

Sally tried to comfort him, but he pulled away from her.

"I'm a jerk, Sally. I sit down making stupid lists of hairs and possible fingerprints and whose alibi holds water and whose doesn't, while this scumbag—this BASTARD—he makes his own list, doesn't he?"

Suddenly he got up and walked quickly out of the room without another word. By the time she reached the door, he was already in his car, driving away. He'd clearly been humiliated by his show of weakness. She wondered if he would ever let her get that close to him again.

Watching him go, she decided that it was time for her to assert her full authority as sheriff. Ed had pulled out, Rob was losing it, and this case needed leadership. She contacted each of the troopers by radio and told them to meet with her here at four this afternoon to coordinate the investigation. She called Ed at home, but there was no answer.

He was probably in there hiding out. He'd know about the crime, of course. The news would have reached him somehow or another. *What the hell's going on, here?* she wondered. Ed wasn't the type to run away and Rob wasn't the type to break down.

Sally went over every note she or Ed or any of the troopers had made about the other murder scenes. She reread Tilford's and Billy's reports. She also rechecked the Gladewater and Houston papers, and watched tape of the news stories on the murders. There hadn't been a single leak about the sexual position of the corpses. So this was unlikely to be a copycat.

The troopers came in just before four—all of them, she noticed, even the off-duties. They were finally beginning to take her seriously, it seemed. In any case, she knew how to win at least a little approval from them. She'd stopped for a big box of donuts on the way back, and had a huge pot of coffee ready.

While they munched away, she looked into each pair of eyes in turn. "Listen, guys," she said, "I know I can't tell you what to do, and I don't want to. You've got years of experience taking care of business around here, and I trust you'll continue doing this investigation the right way. But we cannot let this man kill again."

There were affirmative noises all around the table, but no suggestions, so Sally gave them an idea of her own. "We may have to face the fact that we aren't able to solve these murders by ourselves. As much as we all hate the idea of getting the FBI involved, I feel we need to call them in. I have the authority to do it, but I want you guys to know, from me, that I think you're doing a hell of a job."

"Except for the fact that we got us another victim," Ed Calhoun drawled.

"Maybe the killer's struck in other states before and just now moved on to Texas," Sally said. "The FBI can tell us that. Certainly, there's nobody who's committed similar crimes in Texas recently."

"I've checked the National Crime Database," Rob said. "There are a few somewhat similar murders, but they're old and they're singletons."

"There could be information that's not in the database," Sally said. "That's the sort of thing the FBI can tell us. We need to start saving lives, and we aren't doing that now."

Her words hung in the tense air. They were an accusation. She had failed, but these men had also failed.

"Sally, this is an excellent idea," Rob said. "I wouldn't have agreed to it a week ago. When we only had the two killings, I was sure they were related and that we were going to find an angry ex-boyfriend hiding in the woods. But hard as it is, we all have to admit that so far we've made no progress."

The rest of the troopers nodded, and Sally thought they looked relieved.

"I'll call the Gladewater FBI detail before I leave today," Sally told them. She knew that the FBI wouldn't officially accept an all-local case like this, but there was a lot of help they could give.

As the meeting was breaking up, Sally asked Cliff Collins if he'd gotten a shot at Jeff.

"The kid's never at home. Hard to track down."

"Where does he go?" asked Sally.

"Well, last night when I went over there, he was just gone. And nobody could seem to remember a thing."

"Let's put a tail on him, okay?"

There was a silence. Shocked, she thought.

Had she snapped at them? Yes, she had.

Rob said, "Consider it done."

It marked the first time that Sally had gotten real cooperation from her law enforcement colleagues. A milestone, in a way.

As they were leaving, he hung back. "Hey," he said, "want to catch a bite at Cantor's?"

She'd forgotten all about supper—but she would have remembered once she got home and peered in the empty refrigerator.

Before meeting Rob for dinner, she went out to Suzanne's, intending to suggest that she once again consider leaving town. As she drove up, the new dog announced her arrival in a very satisfying way indeed. And then she got another surprise: Hank Sunderland came out of the house. What in the world was he doing here?

"The lady is out in the barn painting," he said.

"And, uh, she—you—"

"I'm just checking to see that everything's OK." He drew back his jacket, revealing the butt of a revolver sticking out of an old-fashioned gunbelt.

Suzanne waved from the barn door, then trotted over and put her hand on his shoulder. "I've got great protection," she said, "between Hank here and Toby." She smiled a little. "He does a lot of barking."

"I do a little, too," Hank added.

"Just as long as nobody gets bitten," Sally said. She thought she'd seen it all, in terms of human relationships. But here was this crazy artist transforming a recently widowed redneck wife-beater into what appeared to be a pretty decent sort of a guy.

Ed used to say, "You go along and it all makes sense, and you decide you've got it down. Then something comes along that just beats all, and you realize you gotta go back to square one. It ain't easy to understand folks, darlin'. Folks are hard."

The next morning was spent on the phone, while thinking fondly of last night's dinner. She and Rob had agreed not to talk shop for once, and neither one of them had much to say, but it was a relief to Sally just to eat in companionable silence. And it was companionable, too, she could feel it. Rob had accepted her as a colleague.

She'd finished up all of a huge pile of mashed potatoes slathered in gravy, even though she'd meant to take only a bite. After cleaning her plate, she looked up and could have sworn Rob was trying not to laugh at her.

She drove into the office thinking more about Rob than she'd expected to. She found herself wondering what he did for dates. Or was he mourning Wanda?

She buckled down to work and tried again and again to reach the FBI and was put on hold each time, as if she were some crazed citizen who wanted to report a UFO. She finally gave up and took a break. She was placing a tea bag in her mug when Rob came in. "Cliff picked up Jeff Davis last night," he said.

Sally was excited. "Where did he take him? He didn't bring him here."

Rob smiled wanly. "He didn't need to. Turns out Jeff's big secret is that he's just discovered he's a homosexual. He's been sneaking out of the house and cutting through the woods to the Interstate. Friends pick him up and they go to that Blue Boy Lounge out toward Burnham. He says his friends there will give him an alibi for all the nights in question."

"But that doesn't rule him out. I mean, what if they make false statements?"

"They could, of course. What I want to know from you is, does this change anything? Is he less or more likely to be our killer?"

"Probably less. There are gay serial killers. John Wayne Gacey comes to mind. But they go after males. No, if he's gay, I'd be surprised if women were his victims. And what about his dad? Does Sam know he's gay?"

Rob shrugged. "If he does, telling Dad was one of the great pleasures of Jeff's life. Sam Davis is not gonna like that, no way whatsoever. My guess is that Dad is not gonna want this to come out in public, not at all. For the first time in his life, Jeff probably rules the roost over there, if he's smart enough to keep things hanging over Daddy's head."

He paused. "Oh, by the way, I got in touch with a friend of mine at the Gladewater FBI named Clive Dames." So much for Sally's hours on the phone. "He's not into serial killers, but he's going to talk to some of the agents who work in that area. He promised to run our data through their system to see if anything similar turns up. I e-mailed it to him."

Since Rob had the FBI thing under control, she decided to finally have her talk with Jeff Davis, to see what he had to say for himself. He might not kill women, but he could still slaughter animals. She'd try to catch him before he hit the Blue Boy for the evening. Maybe she'd even go with him and question his friends personally.

She drove out to the Davis house, waving to Florence Kravitz as she passed. Flo was transplanting something from one corner of the yard to another, surrounded by adoring cats.

The Davis house was trim and neat, as usual. All four cars were there, on the drive, so she assumed Jeff must still be at home. She went to the door and knocked. There was a long pause, then the door opened a few inches and Lana's wary face poked out. "Can I help you?"

"Hello, Lana," said Sally effusively as she pushed her way in. No longer did she care about Sam and his threats. Let him threaten, lives were being lost.

She noted that Lana was wearing one of those ruffly little aprons that were in all those sixties sitcoms she'd grown up with. She strode into the living room. "Where's Jeff?"

"He's in his room. Shall I get him?"

"Which room?"

"Uh, upstairs, second door, down the hall. But I'll—"

Sally pushed past her. She hadn't been told to leave, so if she was quick, she could get a perfectly legal look at that room. She raced up the stairs and knocked on the door. "Jeff? It's Sally Hopkins from the sheriff's office. Can I talk to you a minute?"

The door was opened to reveal a handsome boy, with thick, dark eyebrows and black, slicked-back hair. "Hello, Sally Hopkins. I remember you. You took your time buzzarding back into my life. Trooper Collins got there first." He smiled a not-so-nice smile.

A shiver coursed down her spine. She looked around the room. Just as neat as the rest of the house, nothing on the walls, the bed messy but made. It revealed nothing.

"Can we get out of here, Jeff? Let's go somewhere in my car and get a cup of coffee." This house gave her the uneasy feeling that great anger had been stuffed under the rugs. But it was still there, in the air, the very breath of the place.

"I'd love to get out," Jeff said. He grabbed his jacket, a two-year-old Wildcats windbreaker in glossy purple.

As they walked out to her car, she asked him, "Shouldn't you let your mother know you might be home late for supper?"

"Naw, she'll warm up my dinner for me if I'm not home in time. I usually eat in my room anyway."

"Why don't you eat with the rest of the family?"

"No elbows on the table, sit up straight. All food must be cut into pieces no larger than a dime and the left hand must remain in the lap at all times, unless needed." He lapsed into a singsong tone. "The iced tea spoon must not clink against the glass. Both feet must remain flat on the floor, of course, and no talking with food in your mouth. And no interrupting, especially not if the king is making a speech about his politics or his religion."

Hate snapped in his voice, which Sally thought was natural, under the circumstances. He certainly seemed more normal than his repressed siblings. But she reminded herself that he could be the animal killer. No matter her theories, he could also be the serial killer.

She could be going to coffee with an extremely dangerous human being, who might transform at any moment into a monster.

They went out through the silent, watching house and got into Sally's car. A curtain flickered at the window. She could feel eyes on them.

As they drove away, Jeff went on talking about mealtime at the Davis household. "Everyone must take turns talking about their day, but only about something pleasant or enlightening. Dissension is bad for the digestion and besides, no one ever disagrees with Dad.

"If anything needs to be fetched at any time, Mom will get up and get it. If someone drops a spoon, Mom will run and get them another one. And she does it without being asked, just by noticing what's needed."

He paused. Sally could feel the anger radiating off him.

They arrived at the Dunkin' Donuts. Sally put the car in park and decided to challenge Jeff. "Jeff, why in hell do you stay at home, if you hate it so much? Why don't you get an apartment with a friend? I even know a place where you can stay until you get on your feet. Why don't you get out of this town to a place where there are more people like . . . like you."

He smiled. "Like me, huh? What did good ol' Trooper Collins tell you about me?"

"That you're gay. But that isn't what this is about."

"Oh, really? I thought being gay was a crime out here in the boonies."

"Come off it, Jeff, I know what your father did to you. Tom Keener told me about the scars on your back."

The hate in Jeff's glare made her skin crawl. He silently got out of the passenger seat and slammed the door, leaving Sally no choice but to follow him. She was just as glad, frankly. Better to be in a public place with this guy. After she took a seat opposite him in the booth, they both ordered coffee and crullers. Sally hoped she could keep him talking.

"Tell me this, Jeff. Did your dad torture the other kids too? What's going on in your family? Is he too strict? Maybe way too strict?"

The waitress delivered their order and Jeff waited for her to leave before replying. "Not really. Though he wasn't ever what you might call lenient." His face had changed, become sad, the eyes far away. "He liked to whip the little ones with a branch cut from a young sapling. That could really sting. You had to go pick it out yourself, too, and he'd reject all specimens until you brought him just the right one."

He took a gulp of coffee. "His specialty was canceling birthday parties at the last minute. Then you had to be the one to call all your friends and tell them not to come. I stopped wanting to have any more parties after a while."

"You must hate him."

"Of course I hate him, anyone would. That's why I'm going to survive. It's the others—and my mother—that I worry about, the ones who are too scared to admit how much they hate him. They're going to fall apart eventually, because it's eating them up inside."

Sally had to agree with that. But would this guy survive? Maybe, unless he'd already drowned.

Jeff continued. "I know why he picked on me so much. It was because he suspected my . . . tendencies, even before I did. I don't know if he even allowed himself to realize what it was about me that drove him crazy. He just knew I was filled with Satan." He paused. "So he decided to burn it out of me."

Sally's coffee turned to acid in her gut. "The scars?"

He smiled, wryly. "You should see the bottoms of my feet. I guess he picked up that technique in the military."

"You didn't have anyone you could tell?"

"I didn't want to, because I was afraid they'd find out why he was doing it. For a long time I thought he was justified in doing what he did. I even hoped it would work. I wanted those longings burned away." He chuckled. "And they say homosexuality is a *choice.*"

Sally wanted to scream, "Did you torture those pets? *Did you kill those women?*" He was a volcano of hate. He could be capable of anything.

With a conscious, careful effort, she sipped some coffee and tried to paint a look of sympathy on her face. After all, he deserved it, the poor kid. But what if he'd gone beyond sympathy? She needed to keep him talking.

"Jeff," she said, "you're so intelligent . . ."

"Oh, yeah?"

"You know you are. I can tell by your vocabulary, for one thing."

He smiled and shrugged. "So now I'm *really* out of the closet."

"Why don't you go to college? Get out of here, start your own life. Why are you still hanging around?"

Now he really did smile. "Because it drives him crazy, having me around—that's why." So Rob was right. "I've convinced him I'm in league with Satan, so he'd better not mess with me anymore."

"I'm not sure I believe that."

"Seriously, I'm planning to get away, just like you said.

But I've got to have money to go to school. I'm working at
the Blue Boy for free in exchange for bartending lessons.
A bartender can always get a job, especially a gay bartender. Since I'm not making any money right now, I have
to live at home."

It made sense—just. "I've got a friend," she said,
"Trooper Robert Farley. You can live with him. He doesn't
care whether or not you're gay. He won't charge you any
rent, or if you want to, you can pay him back later."

She waited. As she expected, he remained silent.

"There's another reason you're staying at home, isn't
there?"

"Yeah. It's just a feeling, I can't prove anything. But I
think Dad's starting to get worked up about one of my
brothers the same way he did about me."

"One of your brothers is gay too?" Sally asked, thinking,
Karma has hit Sam Davis hard.

"No, at least I hope not. I wouldn't want anyone else in
my family to have to go through what I have. Anyway, he's
too young to know, his hormones haven't kicked in yet. But
I can see Dad looking at him funny. Gazing the way he
does."

"Bobby? Bixley?" She remembered the duo she interviewed at the middle school, the ones who seemed joined
at the hip.

"No, it's the youngest."

"Waddy? He didn't seem at all conflicted to me. He wor-
ships you, incidentally."

He eyed her sharply. "You really have been talking to
my family."

"I was concerned about you. But what about Waddy? Do
you think I should try to have him placed in foster care?"

Jeff shook his head. "You can't, that's the trouble. Dad
hasn't started hitting on him yet. No more than the usual
stuff, anyway, and that's considered normal around here."
He looked at her earnestly. "See, that's why I'm afraid to
leave. I think he'll start in on Waddy after I'm gone, but he
won't dare do it while I'm still around. But what can I do?

I can't live at home for another ten years, until Waddy's grown up." His face took on an expression of raw human desperation, eyes wide, lips twisted. Tears had formed at the corners of those eyes. And then she knew: it wasn't only physical abuse he was afraid of. Jeff Davis had been sexually abused, too, and he was afraid the same thing was happening—or about to happen—to his little brother.

He bowed his head. Poor, brave guy, he was staying on in hell to protect his brother. But what did he do in the late night? Did he walk the streets full of hate? "That isn't all there is to it, is it, Jeff? He didn't just whip you and burn you. He did more than that, didn't he?"

Jeff's head came up, and tears were streaming down his cheeks. "You bitch!" he roared. "You goddamn, nosy *bitch!*"

The entire restaurant came to a halt and all eyes looked their way, but Sally didn't care. However, Jeff did. He leaped up and ran out the door. Sally threw five dollars down on the table, and ran out after him, calling "Jeff!"

Jeff was walking quickly away from the restaurant, but when he reached the highway, he acknowledged that he had to rely on Sally for a ride. He whirled to face her. "How'd you guess, bitch?"

"Don't use that word with me."

Jeff's shoulders slumped. He suddenly seemed very young.

"Come with me, Jeff," Sally said. She put her arm around his shoulders and led him back to the car.

She turned to face him. "Tell me, Jeff, what he did. Or no, you don't need to. I'll tell you." She leaned toward him. "He had sex with you. He raped you."

"Oh, God, oh, God. He made me what I am, Miss Hopkins, he created me!"

"No, he didn't, Jeff. Listen to me: homosexuals are born that way. Nobody can turn a heterosexual into a homosexual or vice versa. People have tried, psychologists have studied this, and nobody's been able to do it."

"I hate what I am!"

She reached toward him. "You were born the way you are. If Waddy's gay, he was born that way too. There's nothing to hate about yourself, Jeff."

Jeff shook his head. That strange distance had returned to his eyes. "He could be doing it already. Waddy used to be so honest with me, used to tell me everything. But now he clams up." His eyes swam. "I'm scared."

His feelings for his brother revealed deep and abiding compassion. Sally began to think that maybe he couldn't be a killer, or even an animal torturer.

Don't deceive yourself, girl. Be careful, don't quit watching this one.

"I'll talk to Waddy, Jeff. I'll get him to tell me what's going on, then I'll have him removed from the setting. What your dad is doing is illegal, don't forget that."

"Is my family better off that way?"

"You cannot let the abuse continue, Jeff. There will be a hearing and your father will be there. You'll have to testify. You'll have to show your scars."

He looked sick. "A hearing? In a courtroom?"

"No, it's not public, not until your father is charged with a crime. If he is. Even then, the identities of the minor victims remain anonymous."

"Can you tell me something?"

"What?"

"If he hates queers so much, why did he make me into one?"

She started to interrupt him, but he kept on talking.

"OK, I know it's just my nature and I should be content with it and all that crap, but how could he stand to, you know, do it that way? If it was an abomination of Satan or whatever the hell it is."

"You want my professional opinion, as a psychologist?"

"Yes."

"Because he thinks he's a homosexual himself."

Jeff guffawed. "God damn, Ms. Hopkins, he's the father of eight kids!"

"He's a pedophile, and he equates that with homosexuality, even though they aren't related. He hates homosexuals because he hates his compulsion to have sex with children."

"But why hate me? I was his lover-boy."

Sally reflected. "Because if you went along with it—"

"I didn't!"

Sally held up her palm. "But he could convince himself that you did, because you didn't know any better. All you knew was that you had to obey your dad."

"I'm not following."

"You represented an ultimate evil to him, an evil he really wanted to burn out of himself. Don't you see, he projected his sexual sickness onto you, and then tried to root it out."

"If he could cleanse me of it, he would finally be clean himself."

"That's it."

Jeff's expression changed. Sally saw a flicker of amusement pass through those lovely Davis eyes. "So it must really mess him up, me working at a gay bar."

Sally agreed. "But I'm afraid that's why he may have turned to Waddy."

"So it's my fault, after all!"

"No, Jeff, no. You have to live with what happened to you. With the scars of that. But we have a chance to rescue your brother. I promise you that."

Jeff grabbed her hands. "I'm going to hold you to that promise. You've got to save him. You're the only person I've ever met in this godforsaken town who understands what's really going on with my dad. Most of 'em wouldn't even listen."

Great, but how in hell was she going to get that kid away from his family, from a father who not only tormented his children, but seemed to terrify the entire town? Still, she told him again, "I promise."

She drove Jeff home so he could eat dinner and get to his

job on time. As she watched him going up the driveway, she wondered what she was really looking at. Did a shadow shaped like Jeff steal down this drive late at night, slip down the moonlit roads . . . carrying a baseball bat?

On the way home, she thought back over the interview. She hadn't asked him about the pet killings, much less the murders. And she should have. She considered getting the troopers to stake out the house twenty-four hours a day. But was he really a suspect?

Maybe she was being foolish. Probably she was. She could well imagine him killing his father, however, especially if he sneaked home early and caught him with his younger brother. But the three women?

She wished she didn't even have to worry about it, but she did. She must. One thing was certain, the only way to insure that Sam Davis stayed alive was to get both boys out of that house. As sheriff, she was charged with the prevention of crime as well as pursuing criminals, so she might be able to get around the slowness of family court. If she could get a complaint out of Jeff, she could arrest the father.

When she got home, Elizabeth suggested another session. But Sally did not feel up to it. She went to bed early, and lay wondering if there was such a thing as an abuse magnet. Here she was, abused herself by her father, now plunged into a horrific abuse case.

Her sleep, such as it was, was thick with nightmares. Every time she closed her eyes, the Dark Figure loomed down at her. Again and again, she would see the sliver of light that appeared as the door opened, and feel the fear and revulsion wash over her. Then the Dark Figure would block out the light and her mind would go maddeningly blank.

If only she could recall that whisper, just one word of it. Or the tone of voice—yes, that would be enough to release the memories, she felt certain. She needed to see him, needed to come to terms with his face looming down.

Dawn came to Maryvale, tentative, clogged by gray, rushing clouds.

Sally drove like a ghost through the awakening streets, past the humble houses and shops, flooded, suddenly, with innocent early sun. As she drove along, she practiced developing her sheriff's eye, looking automatically for signs of anything amiss in this deceptive little town. As she parked, she considered the first step toward getting Waddy out of that awful house.

She suspected that Jeff would not press charges. But maybe Waddy would talk. She could videotape his statement and take it to the district attorney. Under the law, he'd have no choice but to charge Sam Davis, and she could arrest him and maybe they could get a high enough bail set to keep him away from the kids until family court could foster the whole lot of them. Or better, maybe, leave them in the custody of the mother if she was not a conspirator, and send the bastard to Huntsville for fifteen years or so—at least, until they were all grown.

She felt what she thought must be pangs of mothering protectiveness when she thought about Waddy's sweet little face in the school cafeteria. Along with all her other problems, her biological clock was ticking fast. She'd begun to face the fact that she'd probably be essentially alone for the rest of her life. Maybe she could foster Waddy herself. He was a real little doll—sweet and cute, but all boy.

What a laugh. She was an unmarried, unattached career woman, living with a friend who had lost custody of her own child due to drink and drugs. She could forget the fostering program.

After thinking it over, she'd become fairly well convinced that Jeff could well be responsible for the pet tortures, but she felt sure that if she kept her promise to rescue Waddy, his frustrations would cease and his crimes would too. He was no murderer. That was another crime. She had a call from the FBI waiting in her office when she arrived at eight. The agency was sending two men, and they would be here at three. Sally immediately began planning a briefing for them. She informed Rob, then called Ed.

She was determined to get him back into this investigation, and she hoped that the arrival of the FBI would encourage him.

His long familiarity with Maryvale was essential, if the agents were going to get a grip on what was going on here. Her own brief experience was just not enough.

Once again, he did not answer his damn phone.

Okay, that was it. She decided to drive over there and confront him. She hung the "Will Return in Half an Hour, Call State Police in Emergencies" sign on the front door of the office, then headed back out to her car. And another thing: she needed that cruiser. The hell with playing cat and mouse with the citizens. She was the sheriff and they might as well know it.

She drove hard, the Camry rattling and wheezing, but considering her hundred seventy thousand miles, still going down the road like a good car should.

She rounded the last bend, turned into Ed's drive, and saw his car still parked in front of the house. Damn him anyway, not to bother to answer his damn telephone during a time like this.

She knocked on his door. "Uncle Ed! Uncle Ed, are you there?"

There was no reply, but the door was unlocked—unlike most of the others in Maryvale these days. The new era of locked doors would now stay that way forever, another example of innocence lost. She supposed that the pistol Ed kept in his bedside drawer was still a good deterrent. But was he a light sleeper?

She walked into the kitchen and noticed a strong smell of fried chicken, no doubt left over from last night's supper. It made her feel oddly queasy. Then she heard the water running upstairs, and hoped to hell that he wasn't answering his phone because he'd fallen in the tub. He was old enough for that kind of an accident, for sure.

She started up the stairs. When she reached the landing, the bathroom door banged open, sending a puff of steam into the hallway. Ed stepped out buck naked. She could tell he couldn't see her through all the steam. She couldn't help noticing his bony old hips and scrawny shoulders. Suddenly she felt dizzy and ill, like she had when she was in the kitchen. Her head began to feel as if it were splitting apart, and she fell to her knees, onto the steps, and had to grab the banister to keep from falling.

Ed saw her then, and reached into the bathroom to grab a towel. He wrapped it around his waist and rushed to her, calling, "Sally, I didn't know you were here! Are you all right, darlin'?"

And then the ground trembled; she heard the words of the whisper: "Are you all right, darlin'?" She tried to open her eyes, but somehow everything stayed dark. Had she suddenly been struck blind? "Don't call me that!" she heard herself scream. "Don't ever call me that again!"

"But, darlin' . . ."

"Shut up!" She crawled across the landing, then pulled herself together enough to limp down the stairs, one at a time, holding on to the carved wooden banister. She staggered through the kitchen, almost vomiting when she smelled the chicken again, then pushed open the screen door and ran for her car.

Ed had pulled on his pants by then and started after her. As she drove away, she could see him standing on the porch, looking baffled. Thank God her eyes were working again, because she needed to get the hell out of here as fast as was humanly possible.

As she drove, she was blinded again, this time by tears. She could hear herself groaning, "Oh, God, no!" Then a scream burst out of her and she couldn't make herself stop and it was terrifying. And yet, all the time this was going on, a calm voice deep inside was telling her not to run her car off the road.

She didn't know how she made it back to Elizabeth's little house, but somehow she did. She rushed inside, calling out for her, hoping to God she was still here. She sprinted up the stairs, crying, "Elizabeth! I've remembered!"

Elizabeth's bedroom door was shut tight, which was odd, since it was morning. Other times, Sally would have respected her privacy and tiptoed back downstairs so as not to disturb her, but she was in too much pain right now.

She pushed open Elizabeth's door and saw she'd gone back to bed. But no, she was on top of the bed, fully dressed. Had Elizabeth had a stroke? Then she noticed the smell. It was bourbon—the smell was unmistakable—and it permeated the room. Elizabeth was passed out drunk?

Sally fought back her tears, her rage, her bitterness. She had remembered, she needed Elizabeth desperately now, because it was Ed, oh, God, it was *Ed*.

The framed photo of Josh was lying on the bedspread next to her, along with a couple of open photo albums Sally had never seen before, filled with baby pictures. There was a Halloween mask on the bed, a cap gun, an open box full of other treasures from her lost life with her son.

"Oh, you poor creature," Sally whispered as she tried to pull her up into a sitting position. She was as limp as a rag doll. No amount of shaking or cajoling could wake her up.

In fact, she seemed more than drunk, her sleep was deeper even than that. Had she taken pills along with the booze? Was this intended to be a suicide? Oh, God, not that again! Sally raced into the bathroom, but found no empty bottles.

She went back and listened to her breathing. It was steady enough, but that said nothing.

It would be hard on Elizabeth's reputation if Sally had her taken away in an ambulance, so maybe she should let her sleep it off in secret, but Sally was no MD and maybe Elizabeth wasn't going to wake up.

She decided she had no choice but to call Rob.

She tried his house first and found he was just leaving for late duty. He was headed out to the highway to "pick up some small change," as he put it.

In other words, the man was going to spend a couple of hours writing traffic tickets. What did it take to wake these people up?

"Rob, listen," she said, "you've got to come to Elizabeth's house right away. *Right away.*"

"It's a police emergency?"

"Not exactly. But I need you, Rob."

"I'll be there in five minutes," he said and clicked off. While she waited, she renewed her efforts to get Elizabeth into a sitting position. Then she put away the albums and the toys in order to spare her extra embarrassment.

She soon heard Rob's screeching tires. He ran into the house without bothering to ring the bell. "I'm up here," Sally called.

When he saw Elizabeth, he gasped.

"I didn't know if you knew she drank," Sally said, by way of explanation. "She hid it pretty well."

"I knew she spent a lot of nights with the bottle," he admitted.

"Rob, should we take her to a hospital?"

He hefted her up into his arms and carried her down the stairs. Sally noticed that her head was lolling, and her breathing now seemed labored. "Please God," Sally whispered, "don't let her die, just please don't let her die."

"I know a better place to take her than the hospital," Rob said. "Remember where Hank disappeared to?"

"Starlight."

"It's a rehab setup—a drug and drunk farm, basically. There's an excellent program there. It's one of the reasons we've got our little community of Houston expats here. They like to be close to the place."

There was another illusion shattered: Suzanne, Flo and Joe Kravitz—they'd probably settled here not because of the peace and quiet, but because they were addicts or alcoholics or both—probably both.

Rob was positioning Elizabeth in the passenger seat. "You know how to make an emergency incoming call?"

"I—no. No, I haven't gotten to that yet."

He put a seat belt around Elizabeth, hurried back into the house, and grabbed the phone.

"This is Trooper Farley, ID is 3325, I'm incoming with a possible d and p, do not send assistance in the interest of time. The patient is female, early forties, appears in profound stupor."

"Rob, what are you saying?"

"Probably an alcoholic stupor, Sally. But if she's taken pills, there's no time to waste."

With that, he jumped in his car, hit his light bar, and roared off down the street. *D and p,* Sally thought, *drunk and on pills.* Rob thought Elizabeth had attempted suicide.

She sank down into a chair with her head in her hands.

The phone rang. She looked at it. If it was Ed, what was she going to do? To say? It rang again and she snatched it up. "Yes?"

It was the FBI. They were coming in early. In fact, they'd been trying to reach her. "We had an emergency," she said. "I just dispatched the victim to the hospital with a trooper."

"Right. Listen, we'll be there in ten minutes, we're just dropping out of cell phone range."

And into one very dark little corner of the world, gentlemen. Welcome to Maryvale, y'all.

She very much doubted if Ed would be coming anywhere near her, let alone his office, and Rob obviously
wouldn't be back in time, either. So she was on her own, a
wet-behind-the-ears sheriff who didn't even know 10-
codes, let alone the legal niceties of doing liaison with the
FBI. Worse, she was still in shock over what had happened
at Ed's, then Elizabeth—her mind was reeling. She considered pulling over and just going into the fetal position in
the backseat . . . for a little while.

But no, she would go on. She drove slowly and carefully,
aware that, in her state of mind, she didn't even belong on
the road. All the time she kept repeating to herself, "It was
Ed, I don't believe it, it was *Ed!*"

In coming to Maryvale, she hadn't been running away.
She had come back here to rescue herself from a past that
was secretly eating her soul from the inside out.

Maddeningly, the two agents were driving up as she arrived. She wouldn't even have time to check messages.

She sat them down in her office and offered to make
them coffee. Both men were stiff and formal and clearly
didn't expect to hear any information that would be valu-
able to them from the girlie sheriff of a two-bit place like
Maryvale.

"This started with a series of fires and animal
mutilation-killings. We were unable to identify a perp."

They looked at her silently. So, what was she supposed
to do, dance on her desk? She continued on, and they
turned out to be very interested in hearing about the back-
grounds of the three women who had been killed.

Sally told them all she knew.

Their plan was to immediately begin interviewing
everyone who had known the women, going over the whole
case from the beginning. Their assumption was clear: nothing done by the locals would be of any use to them.

They declined a late lunch at Cantor's, without bothering to be too polite about it. They wanted to get back to
their motel on the highway for a strategy session, and said
they'd order pizza. Sally was relieved, because she was too

upset to eat. When they were gone, she looked at her watch and found that the meeting had lasted over two hours. It had seemed like ten minutes.

All her energy suddenly drained away, and she hardly had the strength to put on her jacket. She called Starlight and found out that Elizabeth was in intensive care. There was no use telling them that she was the sheriff and she needed details, they wouldn't release any details over the phone.

She never knew how she found the strength to drive home, but somehow she did. Elizabeth, whom she had hoped would be her shelter in time of need, wouldn't be waiting there to guide her along the road she so desperately needed to travel, the hard road of facing all that Ed had done to her.

She cursed herself for not being more sensitive. Sally hadn't really considered how fragile Elizabeth might be. Now, she could die. Instead of caring about Elizabeth's problems, she'd only been interested in using her to help her with her own past.

And despite all her hard work, she still didn't know who had killed three innocent women. She couldn't even figure out who the hell was killing the local pets!

No wonder Ed had been so glad to see her every summer. Then it hit her: what kind of family had her mother had that could breed a monster like Ed? Maybe she'd been abused too. No wonder she had killed herself.

She considered whether anyone in Maryvale had known the truth about herself and Ed. They all seemed to know everything that went on; they just never *did* anything about it. No wonder they'd been looking at her like she was some kind of a madwoman. No wonder they wanted nothing to do with her.

Meanwhile, night was falling and the killer could be walking the shadows again.

She raced to the phone, snatched it up, called the troopers' back line, and got patched through to Rob.

"Hey, Sally," he said, his voice so calm that she almost screamed with frustration.

"Rob, I need you guys to put a car on the Davis place, and stay with Jeff if he leaves. When he does, I think we have a reasonably good bet there."

"I need a supervisor on this one."

"You are a supervisor."

"Not high enough." There was the slightest of pauses. "Now that we've got the FBI involved." His tone was filled with reproach, or so she thought.

She didn't even have the strength to turn on the lights, much less go to the kitchen to find something to eat. She sat in the living room, staring straight ahead, letting her thoughts and recriminations wash over her. She barely heard Rob when he knocked softly, then came in.

"Sally?"

She looked up when he switched on a lamp. "Why are you sitting here in the dark?"

"Is Elizabeth going to be all right?"

Rob sat down on the couch beside her. "She's been moved out of intensive care. Dr. Wilford will take good care of her. He's an ex-alcoholic himself, you know. They all are—you can't be employed there unless you've been addicted to booze or drugs and kicked it."

"What's going to happen to her?"

"They'll stabilize her medically while she gets the stuff out of her system." He winced. "I'm not sure what all she'd ingested, but it was plenty of something."

"Jack Daniel's."

He smiled at her. "Don't worry, this was really the best thing that could have happened. She had to confront what she was doing to herself, so she could have a chance to get well."

"Can I visit her?"

"She can have visitors in a week. I'd like to go out with you if I may."

"Of course you can, Rob. She might not be alive if it wasn't for you."

"No, it's you who saved her, Sally." He looked away. "I'm ashamed to say that I heard rumors from the court clerks over in Burnham that she was acting erratically, falling asleep in court, that sort of thing. I should have intervened a week ago. Instead, you meddled at just the right moment."

"I guess I'm a meddler by nature."

"We need that around here, Sally. We don't want to admit we've got problems, so we don't do anything about them."

"All I seem to do is stir up a bunch of ants' nests."

"Sometimes people who need help the most don't know it. Maybe after this, Elizabeth will have the courage to try to see her boy again."

Sally's head jerked up. "You knew about that too? Is there anything that goes on around here that you don't know?"

"It wasn't a secret."

"I've got a secret," she said suddenly. She began to pace back and forth. "I came home early, because I wanted to share it with Elizabeth."

"Go on," Rob said calmly.

"My secret is going to blow you right out of the water! You'll never see this sweet little town the same way again!"

Rob remained calm. "I wouldn't have called Maryvale sweet, even before the murders."

She didn't know how to say it.

"Sally?" He was looking at her, one eyebrow slightly raised, concern touching his eyes.

"Rob—it's Ed . . . sheriff Ed, my uncle."

"Something's happened to Ed?" He started to get up.

"No! He abused me when I was a child. He was having sex with me when I came to visit. I loved him so much, because I didn't have anyone else to love, and that's why I couldn't remember it until now."

There was a silence. "This happened when you were a minor?"

"When I was eleven through—oh, I guess—early teenage years. Fourteen, fifteen."

"And you . . . when did you realize this?"

"It's been over—oh, the past few weeks. There were these blackouts, then the memories finally came . . ."

She stopped suddenly. Everybody in Maryvale knew everything. "But you all knew it, didn't you? *Didn't you?*"

Rob looked her hard in the eyes. "No, Sally, I didn't know it. I always thought there was something a little funny about Ed, but I didn't know what it was."

She started crying then, and sank down on the couch next to him, sobbing on his shoulder.

"I might have killed him if I had."

That set off another wave of emotion. Rob reached for the box of tissues on the side table, then handed them to her. "Blow," he commanded. She acquiesced with a tremendous honk, which embarrassed her. Then Rob took her face in his hands and kissed her. She closed her eyes and let her surprise turn warm as the kiss lingered. She imagined them on a little ship in a great storm, as the katydids of the evening began their clatter, and the high larks sang.

He drew away. "I'm sorry, Sally. I, uh . . ."

"Don't stop!" She pulled him toward her and kissed him hard on the lips, then suddenly they were both laughing. Then she put her head in his lap and began to weep furiously once more. He held her as best he could, until she had wept and wailed herself out and lay there exhausted.

"Sally?" he whispered softly.

She sat up and wiped her eyes. She even managed a small smile. "I think I've had what my professors used to call a catharsis."

"Does that mean you're all cried out for now?" He spoke kindly, as if weeping was sometimes the only logical thing to do.

She nodded. What came out of her mouth next surprised her. "I'm starving."

Rob smiled at her. "That's a good sign. Cantor's doesn't close for half an hour. I don't propose looking for something to eat in your cupboards."

She glanced again at the gathering darkness. "There's somebody covering Jeff, isn't there?"

"He's covered, and I want you to let it go for now." He stood up.

"Rob, I want you to know it's really true. I remember Ed doing it."

He lifted her to her feet, hugged her. "Your word is all the proof I need, Sally. You wouldn't say a thing like that if it wasn't true."

"No, I wouldn't. I wanted the Maryvale of my day-dreams. Not this."

"The real question we have now is, what do we do about Ed? What he did to you was not only a sin, it's against the law. But unless you have concrete evidence, it's going to be your word against his before a Maryvale County jury. I wouldn't want to be there, girl."

Sally hadn't even considered that part of it. "I'm not sure I could handle the agony of a trial, Rob. Or seeing an old man in jail. It has a taste of revenge about it."

"Revenge is ugly, Sally, but remember also that the vengeance of the people is a sacred thing, and it's our duty to offer the state the chance to let them decide, guilty or innocent."

"I'm not sure how I feel about that. Let me think about it before you do anything, OK?"

"I'll give you a little time to think about it, but not too long. You're the one who always says these guys don't quit with just one. What if he's abused other children too? What if he's still doing it?"

The room reeled. Sally had to gasp for breath. Of course, why not? He'd gotten away with it, so he'd keep on, they always did. Here she was a professional, and she was acting like the classic victim. Her mind had already gotten busy excusing her abuser.

"Oh, Rob, I've been so dumb."

"We all have, Sally. That's what makes us human." He retrieved her jacket and they went out to his cruiser.

She had to get some things straight in her mind. "Tell me," she asked him, "if this world is as ugly as it seems, this place as much of a mess as we both know it is, then why are we here?"

"I was born here. You loved this place, even though you got some scars here. That's what home is, the place where you find your joy and get your scars."

"But Maryvale is just a little problem. The world is a sea of problems. Why are we even alive?"

"I honestly don't know, Sally, but we're here, so we might as well make the best of it. We won't be here that long, anyway." He grinned at her and she found herself grinning back.

"I haven't really lived yet, Rob," she said, "I've been skating across the surface of my own life. Ever since I was a little girl, I felt like, I don't know, an outsider. A stranger everywhere I went. But not here, this moment, here with you. I'm not a stranger anymore."

He reached for her hand across the sawed-off shotgun that he kept tucked between the seats as a backup. They held hands in silence, driving slowly through the empty streets.

"It hurts too much to love," she heard herself say.

"Let me tell you a little secret: it's worth it." He looked at her, and in that glance, she saw something she did not expect to see. He continued. "The secret is, don't push it. Let it happen. What's good in life will come to you, in time."

She looked over at him. "I believe that," she said, feeling as if she'd finally understood something terribly important. The value to be found in the ordinary world had revealed itself in a good man's loving glance.

They drove the rest of the way to Cantor's in silence. Sally's head was filled with competing words and images. First there was the humiliating meeting with the FBI agents, then the image of her poor friend Elizabeth, who by now must be enduring the agony of alcohol withdrawal. And then, of course, there were the three bodies lying in the morgue or in their graves, and somewhere out there was the essential evil of the murderer, his heart beating harder as darkness fell, his eyes guided by their own pale light.

In the midst of all this turmoil, images of her childhood summers began to flood in, scene after scene, until there was no doubt in her mind about what her uncle had done to her. She wasn't sure how long it had gone on, but she was sure it had happened. Even though it was a horrible thing to acknowledge, it gave her great relief to do so. It takes work to be in denial. Repeating that *no no no* inside is exhausting. But her past was no longer a secret she was keeping from herself.

Rob wasn't the type to try and make unnecessary conversation, so her silence didn't seem to bother him. As they picked up their menus, it hit her: Rob hadn't kissed her casually.

He'd probably cared for her for a long time, but she hadn't noticed. Instead, she'd scorned his seemingly unsophisticated seriousness about his little town policeman job. But this dependable hick—the dedicated, true blue, toe-the-line guy—had decided she was worth loving. She felt herself trotting out her timeworn "I'm not ready to get serious yet" speech, but the words were stuck somewhere inside and wouldn't come out.

Meanwhile, Rob calmly ordered iced tea and perused his plastic-coated menu, ignoring the smear of catsup on the corner. She wished to hell Cantor's served booze, but then remembered that nobody else in town did either; like ten or twelve other Texas counties, Maryvale had stayed with prohibition. You had to drive out to a place on the highway if you wanted to get a buzz on, and the nearest liquor store was a county away in Burnham.

Rob smiled at her, his eyes crinkling. "I'm having chicken and dumplings," he said. "I'm guessing it's the only thing they've got left at this hour of the night. How about you?"

"I'm too tired to think. I'll have that too," Sally said. She folded her hands on the table. She cleared her throat. "Well, what next?"

"You mean what should we do about Ed?"

"No—I mean what should we do about us?"

Rob placed his big callused hand on top of hers. "We can go on just as we have been, for now," he said. "We're friends—and nothing's more precious than that."

He couldn't have surprised her more if he'd confessed he liked to wear women's clothes on weekends. He'd made the speech *she* was going to make, and that made her mad. He'd better not be rejecting her.

Rob looked up as their waitress reappeared and set two steaming plates down with a disinterested clank. "Anythin' else?"

"I'm happy for now," Rob said, and tucked in.

"Me too," said Sally. At least she guessed she was. Now she was afraid that she might have misinterpreted Rob's kiss. Was it just a sign of friendship? At that moment, two men entered Cantor's and walked straight to their table. "Agent Parker, Agent Howe," Sally whispered as they came over.

They pulled up chairs and got right to the point. "We don't see a pattern in these crimes," said Agent Parker, who was bald and smiled far too much.

"Meaning?" Rob asked. His face had clouded when they appeared. He was probably still frustrated that he hadn't been able to find the culprit himself.

"We're not real sure these murders were all done by the same individual. Could be the first one was committed by a deranged individual, then the others were used to settle scores, copycats taking advantage of an opportunity."

"We haven't released all the details," Rob said carefully. "How would a copycat know how to arrange the body or what weapon to use?"

The two agents looked right through him. "We're proceeding on the theory that there are two, possibly three, murderers. We're going to spend tomorrow reviewing your forensics production, such as it is. In there somewhere we are going to find confirmation of this theory." Agent Parker again. Agent Howe apparently did not talk. Maybe they'd taken a cue from Penn and Teller.

They stayed only a short time after that, saying that they'd eaten "out on the highway." Why anyone would scarf down fast food when they could come to Cantor's was beyond Sally's imagining.

As they were leaving, Agent Howe decided to experiment with his vocal chords. "We're going to keep our investigation closed," he said, "in view of the fact that crucial information has already leaked out to the public."

"You know that?" Rob asked.

"Well, not directly, but since these are copycats, it must have." So he blamed them for Wanda's and Mrs. Bragg's deaths. He smiled then, a smile that communicated contempt so cold that it made Sally kind of sick inside. "This means we're going to be operating on our own. Do not try to partner, do not try to parallel. Just go about your business and let us go about ours."

Rob leaned forward. "You're saying that you don't want the state police or the sheriff's department on the case at all, in any way?"

"You're catching on," he snapped.

Rob said nothing.

Sally broke in, "If there's another murder—"

"What makes you think there'll be another murder, Sheriff?" He spoke the last word with an ironic edge.

Sally swallowed her dry mouth. "Because you're dead wrong about the case. You won't solve it in time, and another woman will be killed. And then more, until whoever is doing it either quits or moves on."

Dead silence. Agent Parker rose to his feet. Agent Howe followed. They both looked down at Sally. "Unless this town is chock-full of people who hate each other, there will be no more murders," Agent Howe said. Then he smiled again. Agent Parker smiled, too.

"You have our cell numbers, Trooper," Agent Parker said to Rob.

Cells don't work around here, Sally thought. "But—"

Rob interrupted her. "I have them," he said.

They said their good-byes—barely—and went banging out through the door.

"Cells don't work around here," Sally said.

Rob smiled sadly. "We'd better redouble our efforts. Because we've likely got another murder coming at us like a runaway train."

"Do they have any legal right to prevent us?" Sally asked.

"You could ask the county attorney if you're concerned, but I don't think so."

She decided to bring Rob up to speed on the Davis situation. He did not yet know about Jeff's background with his father.

"I always knew that Sam Davis was a no-good son of a bitch," he responded, after she'd told him about the history of sexual abuse in the family. "Do you think that little Davis boy has been torturing the pets?"

"Awfully young for it. They're usually pretty passive until after puberty. I've been thinking about Jeff."

"Well, what if he's doing the killings and one of his brothers is doing the mutilations? That would look like a single person to us. It would really throw us off."

That was something Sally hadn't thought of. Maybe it was a good theory and would help them solve the case. But not now, after sunset, when she was this tired.

Rob took her home to her dark, silent house. He came in with her, going through the house without apology, turning on lights. "Maybe you oughta move in with me," he said, his voice deceptively casual. So much for being "just friends."

She hugged him around the waist and rested her head on his big, hard chest. He kissed her and he tasted like heaven. Chicken and dumplings and heaven.

She walked him to the door.

"You keep your doors and windows locked, girl, and keep that gun handy," he said as he retreated.

"Done deal, boss."

He went out onto the porch. Moths swarmed in the yellow porch light. Far to the north, lightning flickered.

She fought that dry mouth of hers, fought it hard. He hesitated on the step. Distantly, the dispatch radio in his car crackled as the night patrol called in locations and movements. He glanced toward the car. "Gotta get rolling," he said.

"Rob!" It had burst right out of her, without warning. He stopped as if frozen. What had she been going to say? That she loved him and wanted to be with him too? "Uh, thanks for everything."

A smile filled his face. "I was afraid I'd stepped out of place in there. Well, duty calls. I need to be sure our FBI boyfriends didn't pull my tail off Jeff." He waved as he got into his cruiser.

Sally watched his lights until they disappeared around the corner. She went inside then, and locked the doors and the downstairs windows. The house wasn't air-conditioned, so she had to leave the upstairs windows open.

She was on her way up when somebody began hammering on the door. She froze. Turned. She could see a male head through the diamond window in the door, but couldn't make out any details.

Automatically, she moved toward the door. "Who is it?" There was an answer, but she couldn't hear.

"Rob?" Had he returned? She put her hand on the doorknob, started to turn it. And stopped. She stepped back, drew her gun, then reached forward and unlocked the door. "It's unlocked," she said, "come on in."

The door flew open and Tilford Harkins stumbled in out of what had suddenly become a rainy night. He stomped a couple of times, then ran his fingers through his wet, thinning hair.

"That dang northern came in like a bat outta hell," he said. He looked up at her, and she saw hollow, glassy eyes. He smiled, his thin lips rising across a row of small gray teeth. "Boy, you got a little something, Sheriff? Normally, I wouldn't ask, but—man."

She had holstered her gun, but she couldn't go to the living-room sideboard where they kept the few bottles of liquor they had without turning her back on him, and she had no intention of doing that.

"What do you want, Tilford?"

"Want? Oh, hell, I want to stomp those two FBIs. They might as well have raided my lab like it was some kinda speakeasy or something."

"They took your evidence."

"They took my reports. Just showed a fed seizure letter and took 'em all. No feedback offered. But I got something for you, Sally. Something new." He fumbled in his pocket, brought out a small plastic bag that appeared to be empty. He held it up. "That is a hair, and it is not Mrs. Bragg's hair."

"Human?"

"Human, probably male. Contains no minoxidil, no propecia, not coated with any oil. Can't tell its age, but it feels young. Pliant, supple. Teenager, maybe."

Jeff, or maybe one of the other boys. Nobody would expect anything if one of the Davis boys showed up at their door.

"We'll get hairs from all the Davis kids."

He sighed. "You're stuck on this one group?"

"For good reason. They live on Pinewoods Lane, where the bulk of the animal mutilations have taken place. They are the only family with children on that road. And the family is full of abuse. Rotten with it, in fact."

"Mrs. Bragg had kids into her house all the time. We found dozens of prints from kids' fingers. She tutored them, or they just came to see her."

"But only one hair?"

"Hell, no, but only one foreign hair on Mrs. Bragg's body. On her left breast. Sure suggests that the person who shed it saw her lying on that floor naked. Looked down at her, in fact, and dropped a hair in the process."

Sally held the bag up to the hall light. One brown hair, not very long. Most of the Davis kids had brown hair. One of the girls was a blond. "Could we match this definitely?"

"It's never a positive match with hair. We know that this hair belonged to a Caucasian. As I say, my impression is that it's from a young person. It is from the head." He went into his briefcase. "We've had Houston do a neutron activation analysis." He held out a report. "If we get a hair with the same pattern, or a similar pattern, there's a strong chance it's from the same person. Or, at least, the same nuclear family."

"DNA?"

"No good there. Would've helped if we had the follicle. But this hair wasn't pulled out, it broke off."

"Why would that be?"

"Maybe he ran his fingers through his hair, or he combed it."

The perp was too careful for that, Sally felt. "Could this be from an older person?"

"Age is a guess. It could be from anybody except someone with gray hair."

"Just the one hair?"

He nodded. "You're thinkin' plant?"

"We already believe that the perp knows forensics. So, if he does, what would be more logical than to plant some evidence that would throw us off?"

He nodded again. "We need a match on the hair."

If the perp knew about her interest in the Davis family, maybe this was one hell of a clever deception. She allowed herself to think it: what if the perp was a law enforcement officer?

For example, Ed. But if she opened that door, then why Ed? Because he was a molester? The two crimes didn't necessarily go together, molesting and serial killing. So, what about the other guys? What about Rob?

No, not him, that was impossible.

But why? Why was it? She knew nothing of his background.

Truthfully, this could be a ruse created by a law enforcement officer, and it could be any one of them. It could be Billy or even Tilford, here.

She didn't believe that, though, not a bit of it. She believed that Jeff Davis was the most likely suspect.

She watched Tilford walk off into the foggy late night to his car at the end of the sidewalk. She saw the interior light glow dimly in the fogbound air. He drove off, turned around, and headed back out toward the Interstate.

She slept with her new gun as her companion, and saw Wanda and Glynesse and Mrs. Bragg in her dreams, beckoning to her from far, far away.

The next day started with blue skies and bright sunlight. Sally felt somewhat better, too. She sensed that they were closer, because of Tilford's evidence, to the discovery of the killer, but she did not think that the answer was going to be straightforward.

She felt strangely calm about what must come soon, which was a confrontation with Ed. As far as he was concerned, she'd taken one look at him and run screaming. It could even be thought of as funny. From her long experience in social work and knowledge of abnormal psychology, she also knew that he might not have any clear memories of what he'd done to her. People could be abusers by night and normal by day, and the two personalities might never meet.

On the other hand, if he wasn't in denial, then Ed knew exactly what was up. She had the fleeting thought that he might not be deranged at all, but a methodical killer destroying his former victims who had confronted him, and maybe, also, anybody who knew . . . like a schoolteacher, for example.

If that was true, then she was likely to be next on his list.

Anybody in town would allow Sheriff Ed to come close to them.

She wondered if it would be such a good idea to go to Ed's place alone. Or to be alone anywhere, for that matter. One thing was sure: he would not find it so easy to get through her front door.

She consulted her watch. One thing that needed doing was another confrontation with Waddy. She knew that the principal would resist, but she was prepared to throw her new law enforcement weight around, no problem. She had to get that kid to provide evidence in family court. If Waddy had not yet been assaulted, maybe she could still save him that anguish.

She decided to wait for the school lunch period to see Waddy again, because that had worked well last time. As a social worker, she'd been on the edge of legality interviewing him without a responsible adult present. The only thing that had made it possible even to argue that her actions had been acceptable was the fact that she'd carried them out in a school setting, with the implied permission of the responsible teachers.

The DA wasn't about to pursue Sam Davis's complaint,

but he had let her know that she'd been running way too
close to the limit of the law.

As sheriff, the requirement was ironclad: if she wanted
to interview Waddy about a crime, she needed a parent or
legal guardian present, and that adult could tell Waddy
not to speak, and she could not countermand the parental
order.

So she was going to go past the limit of the law this time,
and misuse her authority into the bargain.

She went to the office and phoned Starlight Community
to get a report on Elizabeth. She had been wanting to do a
rundown of Elizabeth's patients, most of whom were juve-
niles, on the outside chance that the perp was a kid but not
a Davis.

Elizabeth, however, was still in detox and, as the receptionist so diplomatically put it, "unable to talk on the
phone." The DTs do have a tendency to make conversation
difficult.

The receptionist suggested that she attend an AA meeting there this coming weekend, when she would be able to
see Elizabeth for the first time since Rob had taken her to
the facility. Sally accepted gratefully, and remembered to
add Rob's name to the list.

Sitting in Ed's old office, with his citations, his picture
of himself with Governor Dolph Briscoe, his law books
and criminal procedure manuals, even his winter Stetson
on the hat rack, she found that she couldn't think effectively about much of anything except confronting him.
The need to deal with Ed was overwhelming, but so was
the need to do something to save Waddy. And then there
was the added pressure of knowing that the killer would
be going after another woman . . . and the outside chance,
always, that it would be her.

She got the hell out of that damn office. She was eventually going to have it stripped bare, repainted and refur-
nished. She wanted no trace of Ed left in there.

And the hell with him for keeping the cruiser. She
wanted it and she deserved it. If the townspeople found it

hard to get used to her, she'd tell them the real reason Ed had appointed her: to relieve himself of a terrible burden of guilt. He had given her the best thing he had, his position as sheriff, to quiet his own raging guilt.

She had an hour before she needed to see Waddy and she finally understood that she was not going to be able to concentrate on that interview—or anything else—until she faced Ed. Danger or not, she drove out to his house. She had her damn gun and she was prepared to use it.

She went up the drive, stopping at the front porch of the peaceful old house. This time, seeing it didn't make her nostalgic, it called up a wave of nausea. Her dream house had become a nightmare vision. It was no longer a place where she belonged; in fact, there was no such place and never had been. She had no past. She was all future, or she was nothing.

She felt amazingly bitter as she trudged up the front steps. Ed better not be in the shower again. She'd seen that particular man naked for the last time.

She walked in through an unusually neat kitchen, with the breakfast things put away and all the dishes done. The only smell was the scent of Pine-Sol.

When she entered the dim living room, she was startled to see him sitting quietly in a chair, fully dressed, as if he'd been waiting for her.

"Uncle Ed." The familiar phrase escaped her lips before she knew it. She didn't want to think of him as her uncle anymore.

"Sally." At least he didn't call her "darlin'."

"Oh, Ed, how could you!" she said, her voice dropping low, almost to a whisper. She had meant to be strong, to confront him with her rage and her hard-won wisdom. She cleared her throat, and resolved to speak forcefully. After all, she had the power of righteousness behind her. She could even put him in jail, if she wanted to. "Ed, you make me sick!"

He hung his head, and didn't dare to meet her eyes. "I loved you," he mumbled.

"But, Ed, that's not the kind of love a grown-up should have for a child!"

"I didn't know any other way. It was what was done to me." He looked up at her. "Your mother, too."

Her tears started again, and she sat down in a nearby chair with her hands over her eyes. "My poor mother!" she cried. It was the first time in a long while that Sally had let herself feel truly sorry for her mother. She let go of all her resentments about being abandoned.

"I'm sorry."

"You're sorry! Is that all you have to say, you bastard? Do you think that'll wipe out everything you've done to me? I've just discovered my whole childhood was a fake. This was the only place where I remembered being happy, but it was just another lie."

"I truly did love you, Sally, and I do. I just didn't know how to show it the right way."

She wanted to scream at the frustration of it all. Maybe he really didn't know any better, but that knowledge did nothing to help her.

This was a warped man, passing on love the way he'd been taught by the sick abusers of his parents' generation. The only kind of love he knew was a hideous, predatory perversion.

As he sat there, his face expectant, trying out a small smile, she saw that his beloved profession had been merely an acting job. He pranced around in his properly scuffed boots and sweat-stained hats, while the troopers were the ones who really did the work. He was tolerated by the town because he fit right in with the antiques shops and the renovated old courthouse. The bottom line on Sheriff Ed was that he was part of the decor.

And look at her, she was just as useless as he was. She didn't know how to love any better than he did, and every job and personal relationship she'd ever had was a farce.

Whatever her situation was, and however limited her abilities, she couldn't quit this case, though, and she would not be overwhelmed by the black storm of despair that she could feel growing inside her. Her mother had chosen the final alternative, but Sally would not, she swore that, no matter how terrible this all turned out to be. No, she would live, she would find what love she could, and she would break the chain. God only knew how many generations of her family had been clapped in the irons of perversion, but there was one thing that was true: here, now, in her generation, it stopped.

She looked at her watch. She had no more to say to Ed. It was already time to interview Waddy.

She stood up.

"Sally . . . darlin'?"

Look at him, at that stupid grin, those desperate, smiling eyes. His life is over and he knows it.

She turned around and walked out of the house without another word.

Her mouth had a dry taste of metal in it, her skin was crawling under her clothes. The mere sight of Ed was disgusting—no, it was loathsome. And that confrontation—it hadn't solved a thing. In fact, it hadn't even really worked. He should have begged for forgiveness, not slung her that crap about love. At least he hadn't denied anything.

What was the matter with this town? From the Davis place to Ed's house was a distance of five miles, with all of Maryvale in between. In that little space, there was perversion, hate, terror, and murder. Why? Was every little town like this? No, and neither was Maryvale. There were a few rotten people, a few sick families, just like any town. Very rotten, very sick, and in this case, someone among them was very, very dangerous.

She drove to the elementary school and parked in the lot at the side among the rows of teachers' cars. She noticed that most of them were as old and beat-up as her Camry, and figured a Maryvale teacher's salary must be about as low as the sheriff's.

She pushed open one of the big double doors and headed

straight for the basement, where she could smell the spilled milk already. Once she was there, she looked around for Waddy. At first she thought he might be absent, but then she saw him, sitting all alone in his favorite corner. She went over and said hello and saw he had a brightly iced cupcake in front of him.

"What's that for?" she asked.

"It's my birthday," he said proudly. "I'm eleven!"

Was a single cupcake the only celebration he would have? "Did you have a party here at school?" she asked.

"Nope." He looked at her sideways while taking a big bite. He seemed afraid he might have to share. "Mrs. Roberts, she's my teacher, she don't believe in that 'cause it's too messy and takes up too much class time."

She heard the tone in his voice that reminded her of the many teachers she had hated down through the years. "You don't like her very much, do you?"

"She's not so bad. One of my old teachers was a lot worse."

"So you're having a party at home this weekend?"

By now he had a jawful of cake. "I was supposed to, but my daddy says I've been bad lately, so my party's canceled."

Sally remembered Jeff telling her that Sam Davis had been known to cancel his children's birthday parties.

"What did you do that was so bad?" Thank goodness Waddy didn't seem to think it strange that Sally was asking him so many personal questions.

"Well, I guess I killed one of the cats."

The world heaved. She had just damn well solved one part of the case, just like that! She licked dry lips. "You mean you let it outside and it got run over?"

Sally realized she felt protective toward this boy, who seemed so small and slight for his age. She didn't want to hear what she was pretty sure she was about to hear. She'd never thought to ask him before, or he probably would have told her.

He sat there, silently eating.

"So, Waddy, the cat didn't get run over?"

"No, ma'am."

"You killed it on purpose?"

"I guess I did."

"How?"

"Well, I put a rope around its neck and I tied the other end to a hook on the ceiling of the garage and I left it there."

"Why, Waddy? Do you know why you did it? Was it a bad cat?"

"It was just a cat cat."

"Then why kill it?"

He looked at her as if she might have the answer. "Because I felt like it?"

It made Sally shiver to see those big eyes, with their long lashes, looking up at her as if he truly wanted an answer. "You felt angry at your father," she suggested, "but you couldn't hang *him* in the garage, so you did it to the cat instead."

"Why should I be angry at Daddy?"

"Because . . . because of what he does to you."

Waddy looked blank.

"At night, Waddy."

He glanced away. The chewing stopped.

She took the plunge. "I know what your daddy does to you. Jeff told me. He's very worried about you. Your daddy is not supposed to do that, you know. That's only for when you're all grown-up." She felt such compassion for him, after the morning she'd spent with Ed.

"Oh, you mean—that."

"Yes, *that*." She hoped to hell they were talking about the same thing. "When he puts his—his penis inside you."

Waddy licked cake off his lips.

"That's a bad thing for your daddy to do, Waddy."

He put his cupcake down on the little table, elaborately crossed his legs, and leaned back with his hands behind his head. "Oh, it ain't so bad, Miz Hopkins. I can take it." He looked just like Ed sitting in his office chair. He sounded almost proud.

If he was admitting it now, he could probably be persuaded to admit it in front of a sympathetic family court judge, too. Maybe it wasn't going to be as hard to get him out of that house as she thought. "But you shouldn't have to take it, Waddy! That's for grown-ups when they find somebody they love."

"Daddy loves *me*. He says that. Nobody but you, Waddy, I am your lovin' dad."

Sally thought about how she herself had confused being loved with being brutalized. She was halfway through her life now, and was just beginning to remember what had really happened. Waddy would need a lot of counseling before he could even begin to understand what had gone wrong, especially when this really began to trouble him, as it would when he reached puberty.

She decided to take another step. "Waddy, I think we both know who killed Suzette the cat and Harry the Pomeranian."

He looked down at the table. "Are you goin' to arrest me?" he asked. Then he looked up at her and for the first time she saw panic in his moist, staring eyes. "Because it'll make Daddy awful mad if he finds out. I won't have no more birthdays ever!"

"I won't tell him if you'll promise me one thing."

"What's that?"

"You'll tell me all of this again next week. I'll have someone else with me when you do. And then a wonderful thing can happen. You can go be in a place where nobody will wake you up at night for—that kind of stuff. Then, when that happens and you feel safe, you'll stop hurting these poor animals. I know you want to stop, but it just feels so good when you do it—you just, well, you do it."

He looked at her. Sally thought he seemed puzzled, almost as if he didn't really want to quit torturing animals and couldn't understand why she was making such a big fuss about it.

"Don't you want to live in a place where you're safe?"

He shrugged. "I guess so. I'll miss Jeff, though."

"Jeff can come see you. Anyone can, as long as you want them to. Your mother can come and be with you, too."

That didn't seem to interest him much. "I want Jeff."

"Jeff wants you to do this, Waddy. He's the one who sent me here to talk to you about it."

His face twisted suddenly, as if he'd been gut-punched. "Waddy?"

"I guess I'll do it, then. When do I leave?"

"It's not as easy as all that, I'm afraid. This has to be our secret right now, or it may not happen. Your father may fight it, and then maybe it won't ever happen. So it has to be just between you and me." She decided to add a little white lie. "Jeff is going to leave home soon and he wants you to do the same, but you can go with him only if I help. And the only way I can help is if you tell your story again in front of that other person I told you about. But you have to stay absolutely quiet about it until that happens. Promise me that."

He gave her a solemn look, his big eyes wide. Then his face blossomed into a grin. "I promise."

"Good!" She would go to family court tomorrow and get things rolling.

She stood up, then reached down for his hand. He grasped it and they shook hands firmly. "Take care of yourself this weekend, Waddy. Not a word."

"Don't worry, I won't tell him anything."

"Good! And, Waddy—"

"Yes, ma'am?"

"Happy birthday, honey."

She left him there, licking his finger and using it to pick up the last scattered cake crumbs from the table.

So she'd solved the animal mutilation case. Maybe she should be content to leave the rest to the FBI. Except, of course, that they were idiots.

On the way to the office, she reviewed her murder suspects. Jeff and Ed were the leading candidates. She thought the hair was a plant, and therefore that Ed was the most likely suspect. Molesters don't just stop. Sally doubted that she'd even been the first, and she was quite sure she hadn't been the last.

Her theory was that her return to Maryvale had triggered a defensive reaction in Ed, and he'd begun killing off people who knew about his activities. Wanda was probably a sexual victim. Glynesse and Mrs. Bragg may have had some kind of evidence against Ed. It was logical: both of them worked at the school, Mrs. Bragg was the sort of teacher a kid might confide in, Glynesse was the bus driver—who might have also gotten close to the kids, perhaps close enough to learn some dark secrets.

Ed was cleaning house.

She stopped by Flagg's and picked up a dubious-looking frozen dinner, then went home to her dark, empty house to heat it up. On evenings like this, she sure did miss her landlady. It would have been so nice to have someone to share this mess with.

As she arrived at home, the phone was ringing. She ran in, dropped her groceries on the kitchen table, and answered it just in time.

It was Rob. "The FBI has a suspect," he said. "They're questioning him as we speak."

It turned out to be a drifter they'd found in Burnham, a black guy called Walter Waters, who claimed to be an out-of-work golf pro. The problem was, if a nearly seven-foot-tall black man with an ancient set of golf clubs on his back had appeared in Maryvale, he would have been noticed by everybody. Also, he was a wino and weighed over two hundred pounds. And yet, there had been not a footprint, not a broken twig, not the least sign of forced entry at any of the crime scenes. Maryvale had all the prejudices of any small southern town. No way would these women have let such a man into their homes.

Rob's only comment had been, "I guess he's supposed to be the one who did Glynesse. Now they're going to start looking for the copycats."

Sally had an awful feeling growing in her gut. The case was way out of control, obviously, and the FBI was supposed to fix that.

No way did this have anything to do with a black drifter. This was intimate, local stuff, Maryvale stuff. So, while the FBI concentrated on their drifter, Sally got in her car, went back to the office, and got all the case records that had so far been assembled, plus Ed's Rolodex. She took them home with her and gobbled down her dinner as she methodically reread every single word of witness testimony, how each body had been found and by whom, and all the forensics reports.

When she was finished, she was thinking about Jeff again. He had been a student of Mrs. Braggs's. She would have let him in without hesitation. Ditto Glynesse, who would have known him from his days on the bus. And Wanda would certainly have known him, maybe well.

At eleven Rob called to say that Jeff had returned home after an early shift at the Blue Boy. Two troopers were stationed in the woods nearby. They would watch the house until daybreak.

This was all well and good, but none of the murders had been committed at night. That was the strangest part of it: they'd all been done during the day, and in no case had there been any resistance at all.

She went back to the grisly forensics reports, reading again about how the blows had been delivered with an upward swing . . . like a golfer might use, actually. But no, the FBI was wrong, these women had known their killer. Unless—what if the golfer was an expert at breaking and entering? He could be, and a real expert might be able to get in and out undetected, and leave a very minimal forensics trace.

She was brought back to this world by the chiming of the clock. Midnight already. She was learning a lot about the difference between real mysteries and mystery novels, which she'd always loved . . . and had always assumed reflected the real world. But real mysteries were crazy, they were messy, the clues, if there were any, were misleading at best, and mostly the criminals got away. That was the truth of it. Most of the time, police work didn't work.

After putting her gun butt-out between the mattress and the box spring, she slept a restless sleep until about two, when a sudden noise woke her up. She lay there, thinking perhaps it had been the cry of a rabbit being lifted into the sky by an owl. Or the scream of a woman, suddenly interrupted.

As she was getting out of bed to investigate further, she realized that the bedroom door was beginning to open. She grabbed her gun, leaped out of her bed, and shouted, "Freeze, police!" at the top of her lungs.

There was nobody there. She raced through the rooms turning on lights, but there was no sign of anybody and no sign of entry.

Then the scream came again, and she recognized it for what it was: a bobcat prowling in the brush, hungry and having a lean hunt, no doubt.

She was really, really on edge. She heaved the thick case folders onto the kitchen table, then sat down with them and started making a new list of the characteristics of the three women, their appearances, their known associations, their work, all of it, all over again.

She did this because she thought maybe she could come to a final decision about whether she was dealing with a psychotic serial killer or a grudge murderer, or somebody like Ed, protecting a dirty secret, or just what it was she had here.

At first she concentrated on the thing that triggered most serial killers, which was appearance.

Hair: Glynesse, bottle blond, straight; Wanda, natural blond, curly; Mrs. Bragg, gray and waved. No similarities there. She stared at the color photos of their dead faces. Eye colors also different. Shape of faces, also different.

Racial background sometimes figured into it, but these three women were all pretty much standard East Texas. They were white, of European background. Nothing stood out. Unless the black golf pro had a racial motive.

She tried to imagine Wanda letting a seven-foot-tall black stranger into her house, then turning her back on him long enough to get whacked by the baseball bat he was carrying.

No. And the weapon hadn't been a golf club. It was established as a baseball bat.

Could the murders have something to do with politics? She hadn't considered that. But none of them had been politically extreme or a member of a radical religious sect. Mrs. Bragg was a registered Republican. The other two weren't on the voter rolls at all.

She sighed. The case folders hadn't changed, so why was she down here making herself miserable? These were three ordinary women who lived in the same small town and therefore went to the same stores and knew the same people. They didn't stand out, not from each other and not from the rest of the community.

A thrill killer, then, that all three of them knew enough to let into their houses. That would mean that she might not even be close to an identity. All of her suspects could be wrong.

She looked down the list of associations so carefully compiled by the state police. Again, there was nothing to learn: all three women knew virtually everybody in Maryvale and Burnham, and Mrs. Bragg had quite a few associates in the education community statewide. Wanda's older sister and her husband lived in Gladewater, and Wanda knew a fair number of people there, also.

There was an exhaustive alibi list, and a smaller list of twenty local names without alibis for all three murders. Jeff was not on that list, nor was his father, nor was Ed, nor was Jackie—in fact, the only people on it had long since been dismissed as possible suspects.

Could the FBI be right, at least in thinking that the killer was not local?

No, they were not right. There was a secret here in Maryvale—some secret that she had not yet fathomed. It was hiding somewhere in these records . . . and somewhere out there in the night, with the screaming bobcat and the swooping owls.

She lay half awake for the rest of the night. When she

did sleep, she dreamed about Ed, about smothering in the sweaty stink of his body while the bed creaked and groaned. It was the smell she loathed the most, the sourness of Ed in heat.

She got up before dawn and made a pot of coffee, and sat out on the little front porch watching the world slowly emerge out of the shadows. Golden light filled the sky, dew pearled the grass, wrens began to twitter in the bushes, cardinals to sing in the trees.

As she dressed, the miseries of the night passed, and she began to think about the Starlight trip. Rob was picking her up at ten. She dreaded meeting Elizabeth again, after seeing her in a drunken state, but she sensed that her new friend needed her, so she would go. Afterward, she and Rob were scheduled to spend the night at a bed and breakfast.

That part, she decided, she was looking forward to.

The session would start with a buffet lunch at twelve-thirty, then go on into the afternoon until dinnertime, when there was a barbecue held on the grounds.

At nine, she made a call to State Police Dispatch and got the night blotter read to her. An out-of-gas car on the Interstate, stopped to assist. A DWI outside the Bluebonnet Palace in Burnham, cited and driven home. Two speeding tickets on the Maryvale Road, both teens, no drugs, no alcohol.

She thanked the dispatcher and hung up. This didn't mean that there wasn't a bludgeoned woman somewhere in some quiet house out there, known thus far only to the flies.

She wished she felt better about this Starlight business. She really wanted to be there for Elizabeth, but there was work to do here, obviously. Urgent work. Plus, she wasn't sure how to face the situation. There would be a group session, for example, with recovering addicts and alcoholics sitting up front with their families and friends in folding chairs facing them. At some point, she would be called upon to plead publicly with Elizabeth to leave her liquor

behind. She liked and respected Elizabeth, but their friendship was very new. Did she really belong at a gathering
like this?

She considered the fact that Rob had asked her to pack
an overnight bag. His little country inn had sounded lovely
yesterday, but she found herself thinking now about exactly what the invitation meant . . . and what she wanted it
to mean.

He'd said that the inn was called Cootchins and it was
run by an old high school buddy of his and his wife. "We
can get up early and get in some fishing, if we want. Jeb
fixes a mean breakfast, too."

These country people just did not have a sense of ur-
gency. How could they possibly fish when lives were in
danger? They had to be on the case twenty-four/seven, as
far as she was concerned.

But when she heard Rob's horn, she grabbed her bag and
sprinted down the stairs. She got in his truck, responding
with a shudder of inner pleasure to the happiness in his
greeting. He was genuinely glad to see her, and that was
very nice.

He backed out of the drive and headed for the highway.
"You look great," he said.

"I'm glad. I didn't get much sleep. A bobcat kept
screaming."

"They'll do that."

"I spent the night with the case, Rob."

"Me, too."

"What did you look at?"

"The blows. They were so alike, up from behind like a
golf swing, almost. Not all that much velocity, but coming
up at the base of the skull like that, damn effective. Like,
he stood behind them and took his swing . . . almost while
they waited for it, Sally."

She thought about that. "What are you implying? Was it
the golf pro?"

"I have to tell you, I kept hoping that it would be him.

Because otherwise there's somebody living here in Maryville right next to us who is very, very different from what he seems."

"It's always that way," Sally said. "It always turns out to be the local clown who performs for children's parties, the Eagle Scout who seemed like the perfect young man."

"Trouble is, that Eagle Scout doesn't live in Maryvale. Our kids are a bunch of hell-raisers, always have been. Wildcat football and underage drinking, not campfires and merit badges. But also, no real crime, certainly no killing."

"Rob, this guy is going to be nonthreatening, capable of putting people completely at their ease. And almost certainly known to everybody in town."

"The FBI is searching for the weapon."

"In the drifter's golf bag, I assume."

"God only knows. Maybe they're looking for a bazooka on Neptune."

"You knew this would happen, but you didn't stop me from calling them in."

"You did right, Sally, you followed correct procedure. We were stuck—still are. It's just that the best agents don't exactly end up in backwater stations. You're looking at guys who mostly deal with immigration cases and drug problems. Probably never had a murder before in their whole careers."

They rode in silence, then. After forty-five minutes, they stopped for Cokes and a fill up at an Exxon station. After another hour, they reached the gate of Starlight. On the way, Sally considered telling Rob about Waddy. She decided that she had to do it, but not just now. Officially, a juvie case was between her and the family court judge. As yet, she could not say to Rob that she had an arrestable crime committed by an adult. She would return to the school on Monday with the judge, and if Waddy repeated his accusation, then she could bring Rob in to arrest Sam Davis.

Maybe she'd tell him later tonight, after they'd finished with Elizabeth. It was not urgent, though. The maddening thing was that all they could do about the urgent part, the murders, was to talk and wait.

Two stone pillars flanked the entrance to the facility, with an arch of black iron stretched between them with the words "Starlight Ranch" emblazoned on it. Iron outlines of the ranch's original brands, a triangle, a star, a horseshoe, surrounded the letters. This had been a working ranch before it became a drunk farm.

They pulled up in front of an enormous old homestead built out of tan Texas limestone. Rob parked his truck out back on the grass, among at least twenty other vehicles. Everyone was strolling over to the front porch, and Sally and Rob followed along. A friendly-looking lady in jeans stood by the door, greeting everyone and waving them in.

Sally and Rob soon found Elizabeth. She drew them out onto the porch that stretched across the back of the house.

Once outside, they both gave Elizabeth hugs, then pulled up rocking chairs and sat down to chat. "So how do you like it here?" Sally asked. "Is it awful? Tell me the truth."

Elizabeth's eyes twinkled. "This is a big change for me," she said. "Coming here, staying."

"I miss you back at home."

"Oh, Sally, you don't know how good it is to know I've got someone waiting at home for me."

In that moment, all of Sally's doubts about coming here evaporated. Elizabeth turned to Rob. "Any luck catching your killer?"

When she heard about the murder inquiry, Elizabeth shivered. "The FBI, in our little town. Who would have believed it?"

Sally held off telling Elizabeth what she'd discovered about Ed, even though she'd been ready to pour her heart out a few days ago. She still wanted to share the pain, but she figured Elizabeth had enough troubles of her own to deal with.

Sally was also planning to ask about Elizabeth's teenage clients, but she began speaking about how much she needed her little boy, and Rob told her he'd support her shared custody case as long as Starlight had signed off on her rehab.

She cried quietly for a while, and Sally wondered where her addictions came from—where any addictions come from . . . even the addiction to murder. Ultimately, the motive behind serial killing was a mystery. To say the killers had sexual problems or violence issues wasn't enough. For every serial killer, there were thousands of people with similar problems who never hurt anybody.

Elizabeth had been watching them carefully. She asked, "Are you two becoming a couple? What's been happening in my little house while I wasn't there?"

"No, not at all! We're just—we're friends!"

Rob said, "I thought—well—" He laughed a little.

Sally felt her face get hot, and her blush sent Elizabeth into gales of laughter. "For God's sake, girl, loosen up! Sex with this man could be lots of fun, and you'll never know till you try. He won't gossip about you, I promise you that, 'cause I'll murder him if he does, and he knows that. He won't beat you up, either. What more do you want?"

Sally was openmouthed. Had Elizabeth and Rob been discussing her sex life—or lack of one—behind her back? "Elizabeth, I'm not ready to settle down yet, I don't know what I want . . ."

"A muscle-bound motorcycle guy, but with a PhD? A lawyer with a thousand-acre hunting lease and a fleet of Escalades?"

"No, somebody—a person that I can . . . you know— that I can trust."

"Well, I guess that leaves me out," Rob said.

They were both making fun of her, and that made her mad. But before she could respond, Elizabeth said softly, "Maybe you need to stop running, Sally. Just like me."

"What are you running from?"

"Myself. Just like you are. Just like everybody does, all the hurt ones."

"You know about Ed."

Elizabeth glanced toward Rob. "Old Sherlock here filled me in."

"Were you abused, too, Elizabeth?"

"I have a lot of alcoholics in my family, but no abusers. I don't really have any excuses. Not like you."

"We can't stay the night," Sally babbled. She was scared now, things were moving too fast, all of a sudden. "We need to get back to town. The case—"

"Sally, hey. The case can wait."

"It cannot wait!"

"It has to," Rob said, "because we don't have anything to go on. So what are we gonna do over in Maryvale that we won't be doing here?"

He reached out to her. She looked at his hand—and Elizabeth took both of their wrists and brought their hands together.

Sally managed to smile. "Bound together," she said, "three friends."

Elizabeth burst out laughing.

"What?"

She kissed Sally's cheek. "You are one tough case, girl!"

The rest of the day was a time of gentle support and forgiveness among the twenty or so families present. In a place like this, there were many terrible stories. She heard a wife ask her husband and two little children for forgiveness. It turned out the court had taken the children away from her after she overdosed on heroin for the third time. An immigrant family was there, trying to understand why their youngest son couldn't seem to stop drinking, after all the sacrifices they'd made crossing the border to a new life.

After the session was over, Elizabeth and Sally reviewed her cases, but there was little information to be gained. None of the local troubled teens fit the profile of a serial killer, not even close . . . except, once again, Jeff. But he wasn't one of her clients.

When it was time to leave, Rob and Sally each gave Elizabeth another big hug, then found themselves being hugged by employees and other patients and family members, as well. It would once have been an embarrassing situation for Sally, but after all the truth-telling of the afternoon, she found herself responding to this intimacy with less discomfort than she had ever known.

She understood that Elizabeth hadn't invited them here only for her own sake, but also for Sally's. A part of her, deep inside, that had been frozen solid for so long that she'd forgotten it was even there, was thawing and coming to rich life. Her heart, closed up tight for so long, was beginning to awaken, to feel, to hope.

In the car, Rob said, "I've been calling in every hour. All quiet on the Maryvale front."

"You know what we need to do? We need to get the names of every paperboy, every kid who does summer gardening or chores for money, especially all the nice ones, the ones folks really like."

He drove silently for a while, then sighed a long sigh. "Makes sense."

Sally continued. "But we obviously can't do that on a Saturday night."

"No, we can't."

"So let's go to Cootchies, or whatever the heck that house of ill repute you booked us in is called."

"Cootchins. And the only bad thing I plan to do there is fish out of season."

"Drive on, Trooper."

Smiling quietly to himself, he did just that.

After half an hour's drive on a road lit only by stars, Rob
turned into an open metal gate. They drove up a white
stone drive just like the one at Starlight, and soon arrived
at a low-slung ranch house. Soft yellow light glowed from
its windows.

"Is that candlelight?"

"Lanterns. They're still kind of edging into modern
times."

As they hauled their bags out of the car, Sally could hear
horses stamping and snorting over in the barn.

There were big swings on the broad porch, and moths
whirling around two lanterns hung beside the wide front
door. A breeze crossing the porch brought with it the scent
of night-blooming jasmine.

Sally felt goose bumps rise on her arms. Rob was tall beside her, so tall that he instinctively ducked his head as he
pushed open the screen door and called out, "Jeb!"

A nice-looking woman came into the hall, carrying a
skillet. "I've been trying to get the egg off this damned

thing," she said. "Jeb forgot to soak it this morning. He's out feeding the horses. Welcome, Rob."

She turned toward Sally, eyebrows raised. Rob just stood there.

"I'm Sally Hopkins," Sally said. She could feel her face getting hot. Hopefully, her embarrassment wouldn't be noticeable in the dim light.

"Oh! This is my friend, uh, Sally Hopkins," he said, "Sheriff Hopkins!"

"Will you and the sheriff be looking for two rooms or one?"

"One," Rob said.

Now Sally really started to blush. "Actually," she murmured, "uh, I'm staying the night, too."

The woman smiled.

"One room for me and one for, uh, the sheriff."

The woman laughed a little.

"Sally," Rob said, "this is Martha Callisher, Jeb's wife."

"Hi, Martha."

"A woman sheriff! Well, if that isn't delightful to see," Martha said, shaking Sally's hand.

"I just wish I could solve something, so I could get a chance to show how tough I really am," Sally heard herself saying. Of course, she had solved something. She just hadn't told Rob yet, perhaps because she was disappointed that the solution to the animal killings had confirmed that the murders were being done by somebody else. There would be no neatly wrapped package, and that, she was finding, was a bitter thing to face.

"I heard about your problem down there. But the news said you've got the FBI on it now."

Neither of them could think of any response.

Martha led them upstairs to their rooms, which were indeed separate, but side by side. "You'll have to share a bathroom," she said, "end of the hall. If that's okay with you, Sheriff."

Rob hurried to apologize, but Sally had become a bit

less uneasy. "I don't mind sharing a bathroom with you," she said. "Just leave the seat down."

"Hey, I'm not that good."

They went to their rooms to unpack.

Sally hoped she hadn't hurt Rob's feelings, not wanting to share a room. Maybe, in some big, anonymous hotel, she would have felt differently, but this was way too small and intimate, she couldn't just—well, not in front of his friends, not like that.

Her room was blue, with a bed canopied in light blue, a navy bedspread, and eggshell-blue walls. Very pretty, even sort of country-sophisticated. There was a kerosene lamp ready for use, but the lighting itself was electric.

She opened the top drawer of the old dresser, was greeted by a sharp sachet of cedar. She looked at the girl in the dresser mirror. Hollow, tired eyes, tension around the lips.

Rob was right to bring her here. She needed this.

She'd brought her coziest pair of flannel pajamas, in red and green plaid, and some nice, warm, fluffy slippers. Should she put them on now, or was he expecting something different? Well, he wasn't knocking on her door, was he?

Taking off her blouse and jeans was pure heaven. She was real tired, and it felt just great to be out of her clothes.

Once she got her pajamas on, she looked at herself in the mirror again, and had to admit she didn't look too sexy. All she needed was a teddy bear under her arm to complete the picture. Had she unconsciously done this, to send a message to Rob: do not touch?

Which, she realized, was something that she wanted him to do. And why not, Rob was close to being movie-star handsome. In fact, he was way ahead of the Billy Bob Thorntons and the Steve Buscemis of this world. North of them, she decided, south of Jude Law. Just a little south of Jude Law.

Oh, no, he wasn't, he was north of Jude Law, *way* north of him, and she was an *idiot*!

She stood there looking at the girl sheriff in the mirror, now all fluffy, and thinking that maybe—well, if he wasn't knocking, which he sure was not, then maybe it was up to her to let him know that she was not a lost cause.

She went out into the hall.

Quiet, dim, one kerosene lantern glowing on a table at the far end, its wick cut low.

She stepped up to Rob's door, raised her hand, closed her fist. Hesitated.

Maybe she should wait a little longer. Maybe he needed to get past all the obstacles she'd thrown in his path and come to her anyway.

But if he didn't?

He would.

But *if he didn't*?

She knocked—tapped really softly, actually.

"Come in," he called, his voice oddly high, as if he'd been holding his breath. She peered in tentatively, in case he only wore briefs to bed. He was sitting in an easy chair, still fully dressed, although he had taken his boots off.

"Hey, sexxxy," he said, in mock appreciation.

Was he serious? "Little Miss Muffet isn't sexy," she responded.

"And Little Miss Muffet didn't just walk into my bedroom. Sally Hopkins did."

She sat on his bed, curling her legs up under her. He looked at her. She looked at him. Smiled a little, to let him know she was glad to be here.

"Sally?"

"Yes?"

There was a moment. Right there. If she just moved toward him, he'd get up out of that chair and—

"I have an issue I need to discuss," she heard herself say. "Case related."

Idiot!

"Oh," he said, his voice, and his face, full of surprise. "Okay, a case issue. So, let's hear it."

She sighed at her own incredible resistance to intimacy. She could have choked herself, but she plunged on. "As a matter of fact, there's something you don't know yet. But you have to promise me you won't act on it without getting clearance from me first."

"I don't know if a law enforcement officer can make a promise like that. Is there a crime involved?"

"The situation has to be handled carefully, if we're going to get enough proof to get a conviction."

"So tell me." He put his feet up on the edge of the bed and waited.

She told him about Waddy. "He's admitted to me that he tortured those pets," she said. "He also claimed that his father was abusing him, and I'm gonna go back with family court Monday."

Rob was silent, lost in thought. "This gets us no closer to the murderer—or does it?"

"Well, it's not a child of eleven, that's for sure."

"No, I don't mean that. And we're pretty sure it's not Jeff."

"You know where he was when Mrs. Bragg was killed, then?"

"The Blue Boy alibi worked on that one. But there are other Davis boys. What about the middle ones? Sam Junior and—what's his name?"

"Kenny. They're certainly possibilities."

He was silent for a time. "With the house under surveillance," he said at last, "we're going to see if any of them do anything unusual. It's just, if you think about it, with two parents and all those brothers and sisters, how could—" He stopped abruptly.

"Rob?"

"God, Sally, maybe it's Ed."

The room shifted, the lights literally seemed to dim.

"Rob, I've been thinking that, too. But I would hardly . . . allow myself."

"Could it be him, Sally? Because if you think it's possible, I'm gonna get a warrant on him, and search his house for that bat or whatever it is, and that is gonna be hard."

"Hard?"

"Because of the betrayal involved, of the man who brought me into law enforcement and mentored me and, up until just these past few very hard and very sad days, has been the best friend I have ever known. I want to be damned sure I'm right before I do it."

"I feel the same way," she said carefully, "but Ed's a sick man." She considered maybe she should have been more aggressive about him. "I've been thinking he could have done this." Her voice was soft, almost as if speaking too loud might be dangerous. "Anybody would let him in. He knows everybody."

"We can take him into custody. Should we do that? Go back right now and do that?"

The truth was, Ed could be extremely dangerous right now, and she was horrified at herself for not reacting more appropriately earlier. She had come here and let an entire day pass without addressing the issue of this major suspect. She was still in his thrall, somehow, still thinking of him, at least in part, as a mentor and friend. That was the power of Ed's easygoing charm and affable, fatherly manner.

So many really vicious criminals conceal their evil behind a curtain of charm.

"How long could you keep him?" she asked in what was almost a whisper.

"Suspicion of murder? Without any direct evidence, maybe a day. Depends on the judge."

"But he'd get bail?"

"Oh, yes. But it wouldn't go that far, not unless we could charge him, and we're far from that right now."

"Instead of locking him up for the safety of the community, we'd tip our hand, and maybe he'd flee."

"That'd be my thought."

They could not risk leaving Ed without surveillance. And Rob couldn't simply order one of the troopers to do it. These men had also grown up respecting Sheriff Ed. They might not understand, and if they didn't, he just might end up being tipped off by some well-meaning fool.

Sally realized that the two of them really, absolutely, had to return to Maryvale. As tempting as Cootchins was, this was not going to be their night. "We better get back," she said.

Rob stood up. "I'll meet you downstairs."

Martha and Jeb had gone to bed, so Rob left a note on the hall table.

They left quietly, stepping out into the still, star-filled night, thick with the scent of the night-blooming jasmine that choked the house's front porch. When Rob started his truck, a deer whistled off in the dark, and tiny hooves clattered away into the pines.

Driving back, Sally thought more about Ed. "The most dangerous thing about this is that he might not be aware that he's doing it."

"Oh?"

"He might have nightmares, or periods of blackout. If he's a dual personality."

"Meaning what?"

"Meaning that the Ed we confront might be innocent, in the sense that he's unaware of his own crimes."

"I don't believe stuff like that. It's my job to arrest the guilty."

"It might make our task easier if you'd take it on advisement. Because you might not need to get a warrant. If Ed is unaware of his own acts, he's going to consent to a search of his property. No problem."

Rob considered that. "But what reason would we give?"

"We'll think of something." She paused, considered further. "But do not let him near any kind of a weapon during the search, because inside him there will be somebody who does know, who is ruthless, who is terrified, who will kill us both in a heartbeat." And she thought, *At last, I've just faced the truth about Ed.*

They arrived on the outskirts of Maryvale around four A.M. Rob shook Sally's shoulder to wake her, and she was amazed to find that she'd been sleeping. They had to come in along Pinewoods Lane, and as they passed the Davis house, they both noticed two state police cruisers in the drive, light bars flashing.

"I hope that's not supposed to be surveillance," Sally said.

"Nope, that's a call." Rob pulled in behind them.

The entire Davis family was on the porch, all except Jeff and Waddy. Two troopers were with them.

"Thank God you're here!" Lana said to Rob as soon as she saw him.

"Have you found him yet?" It was Sam Davis who spoke, coming down onto the driveway. His eyes were hollow, his face tight with worry.

Rob looked to one of the troopers. "What's the complaint, here?"

"It's my little brother, Winchell," said a voice Sally recognized. Jeff came out of the house. "When I came home from work, I went into his room to say good night." *And to check that he was still all right,* thought Sally. "His bed hadn't been slept in. Some of his clothes and his backpack are missing." He glanced at his parents. "I woke up my folks when I realized what had happened. That was about half an hour ago."

"I want you guys out on the roads, looking for him!" Sam said.

Lana was twisting her hands together. They looked red and wet, as if they'd been twisting for a lot longer than thirty minutes. "He must be out in the woods," she whispered. "He's gone out in the woods before."

"This isn't the first time he's run away?" Sally asked.

Lana was about to reply, when Jeff interrupted her. "He's done it lots of times. But usually we can find him when we take our dogs out. He's got a fort he's made out there, from some old logs he found lying around. But I just came back from searching there and I can't find him." Sally noticed that there were dried leaves stuck to his pant legs.

"That goddamned kid!" Sam Davis exploded.

You goddamned hypocrite, she thought, but she kept silent when Rob gave her a long look.

"Maybe we can get those FBI agents to look for Waddy," Sam suggested. "It's their job to look for kidnappers, isn't it?"

"I doubt he's been kidnapped," Rob said.

"How can you be so sure?"

For once, Lana ignored her husband. "I'm afraid he's gone over to the highway," she said to Rob and Sally. "Maybe he's hitched a ride, gotten into a truck—oh, God, anything could happen to him, he's so little!"

"We'll conduct an immediate search, ma'am," Rob said. "I'll turn out the whole squad. We'll get the dog team from over in Gladewater, they'll be down within the hour." He started back toward the truck.

Quickly Sally said, "If it's all right with you, Mr. Davis, we'd like to have a quick glance at his room. We might find some useful information there."

Sam Davis looked at her, she thought, like a cornered tiger might look at its oppressor, eyes probing for any weakness, any way out. "Yeah," he mumbled, "sure. Of course."

They went upstairs to a small, dark room at the end of the hall, that seemed to be packed, top to bottom, with junk. There were baseball cards and a beer bottle cap collection (courtesy of Jeff, Sally suspected) and model airplanes gathering dust on the top shelf of the cheap bookcase. Some picture books and model dinosaurs were heaped in a corner, relics of earlier phases of childhood.

"What are we looking for?" Rob asked.

"Any evidence that would help us get him fostered, if he turns out to be unwilling to testify against his father. If we could show hard evidence that he was the torturer, that'd support a neglect finding." Sally looked under the messy bed, almost crawled under it. She opened the closet, searched among the clothes, on the floor. She thought she might find a snapshot or maybe a digital camera that might have some images in it. People who did terrible things did them for pleasure, and liked to keep souvenirs, and kids were no different. But there was nothing here, not so much as a length of rope.

There was something about the room that she couldn't quite put her finger on. She looked around again. There was a basketball, deflated, a pair of sneakers tossed down beside it. There was a cupcake cup that had been carefully scraped clean of crumbs. Other sports equipment included a miniature football and a bright pink softball.

"Oh, Rob, this all feels very wrong. Something is very wrong!"

"Well, yeah, the little boy ran away, plus we've had three women murdered and Ed might be a serial killer. I'd say that scenario qualifies as very wrong."

Sally looked around again. "I guess I'm just really spooked by this runaway. He seemed so . . . calm. Calm, that's it, when I talked to him. Wary, but eager to comply with whatever I asked. And now this."

They went back downstairs.

"Find anything?" Sam Davis asked.

Rob shook his head. Sally said to Jeff, "We'd like to take a look at Waddy's fort."

"Jeff told you he's not out there!" Sam exploded.

"Mr. Davis, will you let us do our work!"

"My boy is gone so you look in places where he isn't. How stupid is that, girl?"

A sheriff cannot just haul off and belt jerks like this, but Sally really, really wanted to put this gentleman's lights out. "Mr. Davis," she said, her voice tightly controlled, "we need evidence. There could be evidence out there."

"Right," Rob echoed, backing her up.

"Jeff," Sally said, "please lead us to Winchell's fort."

The trees were like ghosts in the gray light of predawn, the air heavy with fragrant dew, as they moved quickly along behind Jeff Davis.

From time to time, Jeff cupped his hands and shouted, "Waddy, boy, come out! These folks are on your side. We're going to take you somewhere safe. Dad's not with us!" He glanced at Sally. "If he's hiding out here, he'll be scared to come out if he thinks Dad's along."

"Good thought," she said. She doubted that Waddy was out in these woods, but you never knew. Sally and Rob exchanged glances. Either Jeff truly didn't know where Waddy had gone, or else he was a damned good actor.

"Jeff," Sally said, "we want to find your brother, but we're also looking for something else."

"Something else? What are you talking about?"

Rob intervened. "Jeff, he admitted to Sally that he's been killing people's pets. He's disturbed, Jeff, very disturbed. Apparently his relationship with his father is extremely unhealthy."

Jeff sighed. "When I first heard about it, I was afraid it was him. I knew he couldn't lie to me, but I didn't like to ask him about it. He's got so many problems already. Are you going to arrest him for something like that?"

"At the least, he needs fostering, Jeff. I think all the kids in your family do."

"That's for sure."

Rob said, "Where's this fort, anyway?"

"We're almost there."

Jeff led them through so many twists and turns that Sally doubted she'd be able to make it back to the Davis place on her own.

Soon they came to a wall of logs, built from old, weathered trees that had been brought down naturally, by old age or lightning. Leaves were stuffed into the cracks between them and a green plastic drop cloth was stretched over the top.

There was no sign of Waddy inside, but they found old, opened bags of potato chips and empty soda pop bottles piled in one corner. This must be where Waddy took food forbidden by his dad. There was also a ragged black blanket with some comic books stowed underneath it. No doubt the comics were also forbidden by Sam. But hard as they searched, they couldn't come up with anything that suggested where Waddy might have gone, or gave them any more insights into his torture games.

They covered the woods to the highway and back, but there was no sign of the boy. By the time they returned to the Davis place, Sally was feeling serious fatigue. A fitful nap was not enough sleep for her, but she could not stop, not now. The Rite Aid in Maryvale opened at eight. She'd get a bottle of No-Doz.

As they walked up to the Davis place, they saw a state-issue Ford Explorer standing in the driveway. "The dogs are here," Rob said.

There were four of them, all shepherds, all superb, their faces full of intelligence, their eyes sparkling with eagerness.

"Sheriff," Rob said, "meet Joe Hemphill."

Joe, a rangy guy in state police fatigues, stuck out his hand. "Hey there, Sheriff." He blinked, then turned back to his animals.

Sam Davis trotted down the driveway with a handful of Waddy's clothes.

Sally told Jeff, "Please go inside and get some clothes from Waddy's room."

"I've got some right here."

"No. I want Jeff to get them."

"What are you, crazy? These are Waddy's clothes!" He thrust them toward the dogs, who did not move an inch. They only responded to Joe's commands, that was clear.

Jeff trotted into the house.

"Lady, these are Waddy's."

"Maybe they are, but I want to be certain they're taking the scent of the right child."

"And you don't trust me? The boy's father?"

Again, Sally looked into his brown, scared beads of eyes. She had to literally choke back the wave of loathing that she felt. "No, sir," she said carefully, "I do not."

"Lady—"

"Mr. Davis," Rob said, "you'd better back down, here."

"Back down! She as much as called me—"

"Let it go! Now!"

"But, Officer—"

"Mr. Davis, I'll have to restrain you."

"I have a lost child so I'm a criminal? That's the biggest load of—"

Now it was Rob's turn to stare him down. "Mr. Davis, if you imagine that we don't know anything about the depths of this case, you are mistaken. And while I am not reading you your rights at this time, you are of interest, here."

Davis's mouth opened, then snapped shut. The little eyes looked left, right. He backed away a step, as if he were standing too close to a fire.

Jeff came back with more clothes, and Joe put the dogs on the scent. The animals rushed up to the house.

"Oh, great," Sam said, "that's all we need."

It crossed Sally's mind that the child might be hidden in there, might even be dead. Sam could kill if he felt threatened, she had no doubt of it, and child molesters who felt threatened by discovery were notorious for killing their victims.

Why had she ever sent this little boy back to this household? Another sickening, wet-behind-the-ears mistake. Or no, it hadn't been a mistake. Under the law, she had acted appropriately. She could not separate Winchell Davis from his family, not yet.

The dogs turned and went back down the driveway, moving close to the brush, clearly on a good scent.

The group trotted behind them, all except Sam Davis, who stood in silence, staring after them.

As they reached Pinewoods Lane, dawn came, brilliant and hard, the early sun turning the dewy wildflowers along the road to shimmering, multicolored crystals.

Then the dogs stopped. They had reached the end of the track. And here was a disturbing finding: Waddy's scent ended.

"Lana was right," Sally said, "he got in a vehicle."

"But this isn't the highway. Who's going to be driving down Pinewoods Lane in the middle of the night?"

"Rob, it was planned. Almost certainly. A planned pickup—a rescue."

He thought about that. "But who would do that except Jeff?"

"Let's talk to him."

Jeff gasped when he heard that Waddy must have been met by somebody. His mouth opened as if he was about to speak, then closed.

"Jeff," Sally said, "you tell us what you know!"

He shook his head. "That's the problem, I don't know. Frankly, I can't imagine."

"Somebody sent by you, Jeff," Rob said, his voice surprisingly gentle, "helping you save him from your dad."

Jeff shook his head. "Not anybody connected with me. I mean, I haven't told a soul. But how could he arrange it himself? Who would he call?"

"He got picked up," Sally said, "that's the bottom line."

The guys had already issued the Amber Alert, and all of East Texas was soon looking for little Winchell Davis. Privately, Sally was tremendously relieved that the dogs had not found a body. She'd been sick with fear that Waddy had let something about her interview with him slip out, and Sam had killed him to shut him up. She told herself: *In the future, woman,* think. *Being a sheriff is extremely serious business. Lives depend on your decisions.* She could only hope to God that she'd never expose another person to a danger like that, or that she'd be foolish enough to leave a terrified and threatened child on his own.

Her correct procedure would have been to go to the county attorney beforehand and seek advice about how to move Waddy into state custody immediately after the interview. But how was she to know what the boy was about to tell her?

Whatever, she desperately wanted to find him and to help him, but she also knew that their main focus had to remain on catching the murderer. For her, that now meant going in two different investigative directions: the older Davis boys and Uncle Ed.

When Rob let her off at home, it was just pushing six A.M. They had to shower and fill themselves with coffee. They agreed to meet at the sheriff's office at seven.

Sally threw herself on her bed, just for a second. The next thing she knew, the sun was shining on her face. She leaped up, grabbed the clock. Incredibly, it was ten to seven. She'd been deeply asleep.

Feeling almost sick with fatigue, she washed her face, brushed her hair in a few quick strokes, then threw on some fresh clothes.

As she reached the office, Rob was just getting out of his cruiser.

"You look like a million bucks," she said. "How do you do it?" His face was smooth-shaved, his uniform crisp. You'd never believe that this man was running on zero sleep. They hurried into the office. "What in hell?" Sally said as she opened the door to her office.

It had been stripped of every single trace of Ed.

"Sally, you work fast."

"Rob, I didn't do this. Ed must've. I think this is his final message to us—it's a rejection of his past, and of me. He probably thinks of himself as a spurned lover."

"You're kidding."

"It's his justification. We were lovers. I invited his attentions."

"You were a little girl!"

"That's the nature of the sickness. That kind of justification."

Rob dropped into the chair across from the desk. "Listen, I think we need to move, here. I think he could be taking a flier on us." He shook his head. "Ed a suspect on the lam. Unbelievable."

"We have to stay with the Davis situation. That little boy is in some kind of trouble."

"You know, I don't think so. I think that Waddy has an ally. I mean, nobody would just happen to be driving along Pinewoods Lane at that hour, and just happen to want to kidnap a little boy. First off, you don't find strangers out there, not even during the day. The FedEx truck, UPS, that's about it. Second, you said yourself he was highly intelligent. He's got resources, Sally, and he's trying to use them to escape a very frightening, out-of-control situation."

She wished she was more comfortable with that theory. But what if he was wrong? It had already been six hours. The horrible reality of stranger abduction was that for every hour that passed, the likelihood of finding the victim alive dropped by about five percent. After a day, they were almost always either found dead or not at all. "You know the odds against Waddy," Sally said, "if it's a stranger abduction."

"And I also know that your uncle and my dearest friend is probably a dangerous felon, and we have reason to believe that he may be in flight or preparing to flee, and our first obligation is to deal with that situation. The more so, given that the whole trooper force is now on the child case."

"Okay, makes sense. I have to tell you, though, the idea of confronting him makes me feel literally sick. I'm not over it, Rob, not nearly. Just the smells in that house—I go in there, and I start to suffocate."

He looked at her, looked long. "Sheriff, we need to search the Walker place for the murder weapon, and we need to do that right now."

They drove across town in the blushing light of morning, past Cantor's and the courthouse and out the long, shady road to Ed's. When they reached his house, Sally said, "Let me go in first."

"No," Rob said. "You don't need to face him again."

"Rob, I have to."

Suddenly he took her face in his hands and kissed her very quickly. A thrill went through her, right down to her toes. Then he stood silently on the stoop while Sally pressed the door . . . which opened easily. This time, it was unlocked.

Inside, there was a faint smell of cold grease . . . and something else. Air freshener. Ed had realized that the smell of his cooking disgusted her. He had also known that she would come.

The only sound was the old clock in the front hall, ticking slowly, as if time itself in this house had a different meaning. Many a night, she'd laid in bed listening to that clock, and its slow tolling of the hours.

She told herself, *Sheriffs don't cry.* But little girls do, and she remembered, now, the desperate tears that flooded the nights of long ago, in the part of her that knew everything and forgot nothing.

She went into the front hall. "Ed?"

Rob came up behind her. "I'm gonna be right with you," he whispered.

She called again, "Ed, it's me, Sally. Ed, I need to talk."

"I know you do, darlin'."

They both turned, shocked that he'd come up behind them so quietly. Sally thought, *He can move like a ghost.* He must have been outside the whole time, watching them, them come around the side of the house.

If Sally had been alone, would he have a baseball bat in his hands right now?

"Hi, Ed," she said. "Doing some gardening?"

"I take a little walk, mornings, before I go in. Used to go in."

"You cleaned out your office for me," Sally said, "I appreciate that."

"I bet you do," he said. Then again, as if to himself, "I bet you do."

Soft as they were, Sally knew that the words were bullets of bitter hatred. Behind her, she could feel Rob stirring. She thought he'd slid his hand onto the butt of his pistol.

It could still end like that in Texas, in a fast-draw gunfight, right here, very suddenly, right now.

"Come on in," Ed said. He went ahead of them into the living room, with its yellow lampshades and worn furniture, most of it dating back to the days when the house had been expanded, back in the 1880s. There was a Barcalounger, however, angled toward the old Sylvania TV.

The Walkers had been farmers, pulling onions and corn

and what was known as "truck," consisting of anything from tomatoes to melons, up out of the yielding East Texas earth. It was good land, too, well watered, not like the western half of the state, where it took twenty acres and more to feed a single cow, and farming had to be done with irrigation.

"Winchell Davis has gone missing," Rob said. "But that's not why we're here."

At that instant, Ed glanced upward, and a shock went through Sally. As a social worker, she'd been taught to watch carefully when she asked a client if there was any-body else in the house, since they were always trying to root out boyfriends and husbands who weren't supposed to be around. People's eyes invariably glanced toward the room where the person was hiding.

Her mind began moving fast. Had the car Waddy had gotten into out on Pinewoods Lane been Ed's?

Oh, God, no. But Ed was a child molester, and they never stopped, and Waddy would have been open to seduc-tion, made that way by his own father.

"Ed," she said, leaning forward, "if you know anything about this boy's disappearance, you have to tell us. We know he's the one who's been killing those animals. He's a very troubled little boy."

Rob looked sharply at her, frowned. "Sally, that isn't the issue—"

She shook her head, tight and quick. "Ed, what do you know?"

He looked from one of them to the other, his eyes hooded, his lips forming what was almost a sneer. She knew that she was looking at the Ed of darkness, now, the Ed who had come to her, and laid on her until she couldn't move a muscle and she was suffocating—

"Waddy? That little doll. Sweet little old doll." The sneer parted into a smile, full of ugly memory. "That little boy has got some moves on him, you would be amazed. He came to me looking for protection from his dad. I'm his friend—the only one he has!" He shook his head, as if he could not understand what problem they could possibly have with that.

It was the victim's fault, of course. If asked, Ed would describe just how sexy little Waddy had seduced him. Sally worked to contain her loathing, to keep it out of her body language, out of her voice.

Rob leaned forward. "Ed, did you really do this? Tell me the truth."

Here it comes, Sally thought.

"It's not like it sounds, Rob," Ed said with calm reason in his voice. "The boy seduced me. Hell, he threw his little body right at me, time and again. I tried to resist, but he started coming over here every day. He liked to sit on my lap, he wanted to be held . . . and he told me his father was already loving him that way, so how could it be wrong if I did, too?"

Sally wanted to go for her gun. She wanted to pull it up out of its holster. She imagined how that smile would look with a bullet in it, shattered by a fist of lead.

"You bastard."

He shrugged. "God made me, too, darlin'."

"Don't you call her that. Don't you dare."

Ed's mouth snapped shut. "Why, Rob, these kids are regular little seducers. They want it. *She* did. She was a real little whore. She used to come to me, tell me to hurry up washin' the dishes, she needed her sleepin' pill."

Sally was on her feet. She wanted to scream at him, to howl down the lie.

But Rob was there first. "And you raped her. You're a rapist, Ed. Scum, my friend. My old friend. Scum."

His voice was so even, so unnaturally calm, that Sally thought again of the danger of a gun. And Ed's caution to her, *The gun always comes out of nowhere, darlin'. You gotta remember that, the gun could come, always.*

He would be carrying, she thought, probably in the small of his back. There was nothing in his pockets or the tops of his boots, she could see that.

As she glared at Ed, Sally felt Rob's strong arm come around her shoulders.

"Ed, we're going to set that aside for now," he said. "We'll deal with it later, once the boy is found, and maybe the law will address what you did to your niece as well. We've got something more important to discuss with you. But first, we've got to locate Waddy. Is he here in this house right now?"

Ed nodded, still looking down at the floor. "He comes here a lot when things get hard at home, when he's frightened and needs some loving."

But Sally was already heading toward the stairs.

"Sally?"

"He's upstairs, Rob."

"Is he?" Ed asked. "Hey, Waddy—"

"Keep it down, you," Rob snapped. Ed shut up.

There were two stairways, the main staircase that she was about to use, and an outside stairs that went out the back. The property lay along the Crockett River, and a kid who knew his way around could get lost back in there for a long, long time.

"Watch the back stairs," Sally told Rob. "If you see him, grab him."

Rob stayed near Ed, but watched through the doors that led out onto the porch that Ed had added twenty years ago. Sally remembered the fun she'd had with the old Mexican carpenter, Steve Rangel, who used to fry grasshoppers with little peppers called Chili Petines. The two of them would eat them out of Steve's tiny black skillet. Sally remembered them as being salty and spicy and delicious, and how horrified Ed had been when he saw grasshopper legs sticking out between her lips.

They'd sipped iced tea together here, she and Ed, in the evening, in breezes tickled with coolness from their journey across the nearby river.

She reached the head of the stairs. She halfway expected to see Waddy curled up in Ed's bed, or in hers, but both rooms were empty.

In Ed's, though, there were two suitcases, an open one full of Ed's stuff, the other, much smaller, lying closed.

They had been planning to run, the two of them, go over to Houston, maybe, or off into Louisiana, maybe down to the Easy where they'd take a shambling old flat in the Garden District, and Waddy would go to school as an orphaned grandson.

They had their dreams, the innocent child and the demon.

She looked at the closed door that led up to the attic. The back stairs went all the way up, so unless she was very quiet, Waddy was liable to take off for the Crockett River.

How resourceful could he be?

Very, was Sally's thought.

If he ran for it, they might not find him, maybe not for days, maybe never.

Those big barges full of pine logs that were pushed down the Crockett on their way to pulp mills in Houston could make an excellent means of escape. If he jumped from a bridge, or a high bank, he could land among the logs and hide there.

What would happen to a little boy off in the world, alone like that?

She put her hand on the knob and tried to remember what the attic looked like. There had been a big vent fan up there, stuck into the far end of the space. Just beyond the door were three trunks, one of them full of her mother's childhood things. She'd spent many heartfelt afternoons going through that trunk, trying on dresses, reading the yellowing Camp Waldemar newspaper with its stories of exploits via canoe and its hunter's stew recipes, and the Sports Report that had been, over three lost summers in the very long ago, written by her mother.

The attic had been dark, but she remembered it as being full of sunlight, the happiness she found in that trunk, in the dust that she loved the most, in the few moments when she no longer felt like an orphan.

She turned the knob, opened the door, listened.

Little boys are not quiet, not normal ones. But she was dealing here with a child who could creep up to a house in broad daylight and catch and kill its elusive cats, like a little cat himself.

There were two broken dining chairs there now, along with a three-legged table, and the three trunks. Sally remembered the wonderful sweet smell of dying paper that came out of the one that was filled with sheet music. "God Our Help in Ages Past," "Speak to Me Only with Thine Eyes," "The Old Texas Trail," the songs that had defined life in this house once, before she had come, bringing along her little collection of worn-down Elvis forty-fives.

The fondness of the memories was agonizing. Why was tragedy touched with such beauty, almost unbearable, like a butterfly being lost in the autumn sky, among the gaudy leaves?

She came fully into the attic, looked from one end of the shadowy space to the other. There was a whiff of garbage, as if someone hadn't been too careful about disposing of their food. In a dim corner she saw what looked like a shower curtain. It was attached to a rod anchored to the low ceiling. When the curtain was closed, as it was now, it concealed the far end of the space, the one where the fan was housed . . . and where a rear dormer opened onto the top of the outside stairs.

She moved across the space, coming closer and closer to the curtain. Nothing was stirring within. She could smell him, though, smell the sickly sweet odor of bubble gum.

She touched the black curtain, the plastic cool against her fingers. Then she pushed it aside a little, just enough to see.

His little body lay splayed out in the heat, one pudgy hand dangling off the pallet where he slept. He wore baggy jeans and a T-shirt. His hair was a brown tangle. His face, slightly rosy and flecked with freckles, spoke so eloquently of boyhood that it almost made her sob aloud. *The days of innocence are precious days, and if they are stolen, the theft lasts for life.*

Her throat closed, tears welled. *Poor Waddy! And poor damn me . . .*

Elizabeth's voice came to her, now, her wisdom singing through her own hurt: "You're healing, girl! Hold on to that."

She observed him carefully, that one hand dangling, the other closed in a terrible fist. There were two discarded candy-bar wrappers crumpled up next to him, a Butterfinger wrapper and a Snickers wrapper. The Snickers wrapper had been twisted inside out, to get at some candy stuck to the paper.

She used to do the same thing, with the same candy bars, in this same house.

Like so many abused children, Waddy did not sleep deeply, and she was not surprised when his eyes suddenly opened. She was still like that. They called it "guarded sleep," the curse of the abused and the attacked.

He smiled, then yawned, an elaborate affectation. Still, she could use it as an opening. She came in and went down to his pallet, sitting beside him with her knees up, between him and the window.

"You found me." He propped himself up on his elbows. "I got Ed to take care of me now, and he's got a gun." He sighed. "I wanted a puppy for my birthday."

She held out her arms and he snuggled into her embrace. She pulled him onto her lap and kissed the wet, sweaty hair above his ear. "You'll be all right, baby," she whispered to him, "you'll be just fine."

She didn't believe it, though. No, Texas had slashed the budgets that the public didn't care about or want to know about, money for the orphans, the crippled, the mad. After a stint in juvie rehab where he'd get maybe a half hour of counseling a week, he'd be fostered, and would sink into the system, and maybe be broken by it and maybe not.

She continued to rock him gently.

His big eyes, with their incredibly long lashes, gazed up into hers. "Lady," he said, "you know something?"

"What?"

"Lady, I gotta piss. Then you can take me to jail."

She laughed a little. "Nobody's taking you to jail."

"Ed said you were gonna. And he said you'd lie about it."

"I'm not lying. I'm here to help you."

He scampered out into the attic.

Silence fell.

She waited. No faint tinkling, no sound at all.

She leaped to her feet, threw back the curtain—and was stopped dead in her tracks by the single most terrible thing she had ever witnessed.

Standing there was Waddy. His face was flaming red . . . and poised over his shoulder was a baseball bat. But it wasn't just any old bat—this one was beaten up along one side, as if it had been used for pounding nails. There were dark stains all along the length of it.

Sally sucked in her breath sharply. They stayed like that, two statues.

"Waddy?" Her voice was a bare whisper. She could make no more sound. "You put that down, that's Ed's and you mustn't touch it."

His eyes showed their whites, the muscles in his short arms pulsed. A cry came, then was stifled behind tight shut lips.

She gasped as the bat whistled toward her. She raised her hand to ward off the blow—an inch more and he would have smashed her wrist.

He muttered under his breath, a voice that sounded tough and older than seemed possible, deep with an adult's awful fury.

The bat went back, reset to aim at the side of her head as she frantically sought to rise to her feet. Choking, she tried to make a sound, couldn't. He raised the bat high, far behind him, tangling it for an instant in the curtain—which he brought down with a furious shake.

She drew breath, opened her mouth, somehow found her voice, and screamed as loud as she could.

The bat whistled past her face, blasting it with air.

"Damn you, lady, will you stop that!"

He was ordering her not to move, ordering her to let him kill her. The poor, crazy child was that far from understanding what he was doing.

"Waddy, no, it's wrong, you mustn't!"

His face reddened again, deeper, his eyes stood out in his head, so that he had the popped, lunatic expression of a cartoon madman. "You gonna put me in jail, you dirty *bitch*!"

Two sets of boots came running swiftly up the stairs.

The bat swung toward her, and she was still reeling, and she knew he had her.

He knew it, too, and he paused for an instant, to watch the suffering of his victim, as he must have when he was playing hell with the poor animals. His lips parted and his eyes flickered, and she saw something there that was truly terrible, a monster that had been birthed inside this innocent child by his life in hell.

She knew she could not turn aside, not in time. She raised her hands, but this blow would get past them, and he would smash her head in.

Oh, he was good. He was an expert with that bat.

And then he screamed, a high, thin wail, all the monster gone, replaced entirely and in an instant by a terrified child.

Ed was behind him and had him around the waist. The bat came down, slicing the air, and smashed into the floor at Sally's feet.

Waddy shrieked and fought Ed off, but then Rob appeared. He pried the bat from Waddy's fingers. Then he took his wrists, and as Ed held him, he pulled them behind Waddy and got him into his handcuffs. The little boy fought and snarled like a trapped bobcat.

Rob held the bat by his fingertips, in order to preserve the forensics harvest. "Looks like we found the murder weapon," he said. "Help me get my jacket off." He wrapped the bat carefully in the cloth.

"But . . . How did he know about Ed's weapon?" She turned her attention to Ed. "What have you done, here? Why does this little boy know, Ed? *What have you done?*"

Hell marched in Ed's glaring, sorrowful eyes. "You think I killed those women?" As if her gaze was too agonizing to bear, he looked away from her. He bowed his head. "Sally . . . Sally, darlin' . . ."

The truth struck her then, with more force than one of the terrible blows that Waddy had used to kill his victims. She heard herself cry out as if gut-punched—and heard Rob draw air in between his teeth as he, also, realized that he was cradling the murderer in his arms.

Then Ed raised his eyes, looked at her with the suspicion, the danger, of a cornered tiger . . . just like Sam Davis, the other member of this unholy trinity. She still did not see a pistol, but kept one hand on the butt of her own gun.

He snorted. "I ain't gonna kill nobody," he muttered. "I'm not the type." He glanced at Waddy. "He's too young. He's gonna spend his life in a cage and he's too damn young for that."

"Ed," Sally gasped, "you knew. That's why you stopped working on the investigation."

Ed looked at Waddy with eyes now melting with tears. "He just got a temper on him, needs a little work."

Rob literally gagged. Sally said nothing. The remark was beyond comment.

They went downstairs, with Waddy fighting and scrabbling the whole time. Rob held him under one arm while he carried the bat, still carefully wrapped, under the other. He set Waddy down in a chair, then pushed his face so close to the boy that Waddy could probably smell the coffee on his breath, and said, "Now sit still, or I'll find a way to make sure you can't move." Waddy's struggles subsided. He sat with his knees up to his chin, his arms still fastened behind him.

Ed held out his own hands. "You got cuffs, girl. You remember the Miranda warning?"

She ignored him. She knew enough about the law to know that an arrest right at this moment could lead to an acquittal. They would have to take this thing to the DA and let him decide when to arrest Ed.

"You figured it out, and you just walked away."

"I've been keeping a close watch on the boy." He gazed down at Waddy "You said you'd stop, right, honey? We talked through all that."

Rob asked, "Why these three women? What's the connection?"

"They were a bunch a bitches!" Waddy screamed. "They ain't no loss, Mr. Cop."

"Ed, do you understand why he did it?" Sally asked.

"I couldn't see any connection between the three women, except that Mrs. Bragg and Glynesse Sunderland both worked for the school. Then I discovered Wanda had filed a complaint with us that Waddy had stolen some comics. And I knew."

Waddy's voice piped, "She told my daddy and he punished me bad! And Mrs. Bragg hated me! She hated me because I didn't learn my times tables! She told on me, too! And you did, too, lady!" His voice rose. *"You did, too!"* The cuffs jangled and the little body threw itself back and forth in the chair. His eyes were wild, his lips spraying spit. He shrieked, *"You told my daddy somethin', bitch! And he was after me, he was after me becausa you!"*

Sam must have suspected that Waddy had confessed his abuse to Sally. And Waddy, confused and afraid that Sally had betrayed him, had been about to make her his next victim.

If he'd showed up at her house, she would have certainly let him in . . . and she would have died just like the others.

"What about Glynesse?" she asked Waddy in a voice so tiny and shocked that she cleared her throat and asked again, "Why her?"

"She tole him I took my dick out on the bus." Tears sprang into his eyes. "I was just showin' some cat it's bigger'n his'll ever be, and *I got this!*"

He twisted, he shook, and a little hand came free—the cuffs were too big—and he jumped up and raised his T-shirt.

His back looked like the surface of the moon, so covered it was with red, angry craters.

Sally opened her arms to him.

"Sally—" Rob cautioned her.

"Come here, honey, come to me."

He burst into tears and fell into her arms. She held him, his baby flesh soft against her breast, his soft hair tickling her nose. She glared over his head at Ed and said to Waddy, "It's not your fault, baby . . . not your fault."

"Ed," Rob said, "you won't leave town on me, will you?"

"You aren't arresting me?"

"Harboring a juvenile fugitive isn't an arrestable offense in Texas, as I'm sure you know, if it can't be proved that you were a direct witness to the crime."

"But child abuse is," Sally said.

"Waddy won't testify." Ed's eyes flashed sudden defiance. "Even if he does, who's gonna believe him over me?"

"Ed," Sally said carefully, "my testimony is going to support his."

"You'll admit that? That you spent your summers as my dirty little whore?"

Were it not for the badge on her chest, she would have spat on him. As it was, she didn't bother to respond.

They left Ed rocking in his living room, staring into space.

Rob put Waddy in the backseat of the cruiser, with the cage locked.

They had the problem of what to do with him on a Sunday in a small community like Maryvale. The parents had to be informed. He had to be charged in juvenile court, but it didn't open until Monday.

"We can't hold him in the jail in Burnham, it has no juvenile facility," Rob said.

"I want to go with Jeff," Waddy announced from the back.

Waddy didn't understand that his life was over, but his fate was clear to Sally: he would be detained until his twenty-first birthday, whereupon his case would be reviewed. Given that he'd murdered three people in cold blood, he wouldn't be released unless there was an absolute certainty that he was no risk to society. In fact, it was not likely that he would ever be released. He would graduate into an adult facility and spend the rest of his days there. And experience much more abuse.

Sally said to Rob, "You could keep him at your place overnight. Cuff him to a bed."

"Not practical, not legal. No, I need to track down those feds and remand him. This is officially their case." He hit the radio, and soon had them on the horn. "We have the perp in custody and the weapon in our possession," he said. Sally noticed he didn't reveal it was an eleven-year-old boy. He was saving that little surprise for the moment that they saw him, and he had to overcome what would, inevitably, be their disbelief.

Sally felt a tap on her shoulder from a little hand poking through the wire mesh. "Can we stop for McDonald's?" Waddy asked.

Sally looked at Rob and he nodded. "Why not? We could use some breakfast."

"Where are we going?" Waddy asked.

"Gladewater. They have the closest J.D. unit. The feds will meet us there . . . and your parents, and their lawyer."

"Good, 'cause I self-defended myself from those friggin' bitches," Waddy said.

"You killed innocent people," Sally blurted.

Rob glanced at her, shook his head sharply.

Waddy rattled the cage, his little fingers twining in the mesh that isolated him in the backseat. "My daddy's gonna sue you, you dirty cops! *I self-defended myself!*" He howled and hammered at the mesh, and the car shook, such was the power of this child's rage.

As they waited in the McDonald's drive-through lane, Sally wept for Waddy, slow, silent tears. She wept, also, for herself and for abused children everywhere, and for those poor dead women.

The little fingers came through the cage again. "Hey, lady, that's okay," Waddy cooed, "you're okay, lady, you ain't killed." He pressed his face against the mesh, and made a smacking noise, as if to kiss her. His lips were pushed back by the pressure, and his teeth showed.

Hard days followed, and harder nights. Sally would wake up in a sweat of fear, hearing the whistle of that bat passing an inch from her face. She had been so vulnerable, so *available*. If Waddy had appeared at her door, she would have opened her arms to him, would have offered him hot chocolate . . . and turned her back to make it.

The national media hadn't been interested in the Maryvale murders, but they sure *were* interested in an eleven-year-old serial killer, and Sally had to hold a press conference. Her office was too small, so Cantor's got a few minutes of dubious fame as a hollering crowd of reporters and TV newshounds peppered her with questions.

She was the "Lady Sheriff" who had caught the "Child Psycho." There were pictures of her in a brand-new Stetson and her ladies' Levi's from Rank's on the front pages of all the Texas papers. The story even made the *New York Times,* but without pictures.

The press said that she had "courageously subdued" her "attacker." She had "narrowly escaped" being his fourth victim.

Rob worried that Sam Davis or Ed might come after her. She didn't believe that Ed was a threat, and Sam was unlikely to do anything rash, given that his case was before the grand jury and he was likely to be charged with some very serious crimes.

Sally attended Waddy's maturity hearing in Gladewater. She was not all that surprised when Frank Whatley, the district attorney, moved to try the little boy as an adult. She could do nothing but provide testimony, though, and she could see the DA's position. The case had gained national attention. He couldn't afford to be seen to be soft on crime, not given the depravity involved.

The entire Davis family was there, sitting in a row: neat, clean, and disciplined. Jeff testified about his scarring, and Waddy's injuries were shown to the court. Lee Holmes, acting for the defense, brought in none other than Elizabeth to testify that Waddy had been driven insane by his father's actions. But she could not say that he would be able to be safely handled in a juvenile setting.

The court sent him to prison pending a determination on the issue, so Waddy ended up in solitary confinement in the Bradley Correctional Facility over in Leland County.

Afterward, Judge Letty Raymond Ward confided to Sally that she felt helpless. She didn't want to release Waddy into the adult criminal system, but she didn't feel that juvenile justice was capable of handling—or of helping—him.

Sally didn't want to think about what would happen to a scared kid in a prison population with hardened criminals.

In the end, Letty had to keep him in the juvenile process. He was not yet eleven when he'd committed his final crime—he'd been just a few days short of that critical birthday. So the state couldn't remove him from the juvie process even if it had wanted to. Had he killed his teacher forty-eight hours later, he could certainly have been tried as an adult, given that his crimes fit the law's definition of "extreme and indifferent depravity, with premeditated malice." Those few hours were all that had kept a child out of adult detention.

Now, whether it wanted to or not, the state was required to make an effort to repair this broken soul, but the one thing that would be absent would be the only thing that might enable a real recovery: love.

Sally's bad nights were always made worse when she thought about this. She imagined the poor little boy, who probably would have been a perfectly nice kid if he had not literally been tormented like a dog tortured by a cruel master until it turns mean. She could picture him sitting in his tiny cell, playing the same little video game over and over, and not really understanding why he couldn't go outside. Sometimes she pictured him being sexually abused by hardened prisoners and flinched from those thoughts.

One night over dinner at Cantor's, she told Rob that she had made a decision about Waddy. "I'm going to have to give him the love he needs, if he's ever going to heal."

Rob looked into her eyes. "How?"

Leave it to Rob to get right to the point. "I'm going to visit him every week from now on, and form a relationship with him."

Rob toyed with his Salisbury steak. He stared across the room to where the Valette sisters sat quietly eating their nightly fish dinners.

"Rob?"

"As a law enforcement officer, you're going to come across a lot of hard cases and a lot of sad cases, and there are going to be many times when you'll want to help more than you can."

"If he doesn't get that love, he'll never be well enough to leave the system, and you know it."

"Sally, what you're really saying is that because you, as a first-time sheriff operating under virtually impossible circumstances, did not see this incredibly difficult case with the eyes of some kind of genius, which, God love you, you are not, and three innocent people died, and a little boy was destroyed, you should also spend the next ten years of your life paying a penalty. Sally, I have to tell you, I don't think so. I just plain do not."

They ate their dinner in silence for a time.

"What about your own family?"

"Forget my dad. Suffice to say he's happy to pretend that Sally doesn't exist. I don't really have any family."

"But what if you get one? Marry, have kids, I mean."

He was not asking, not quite, but she knew waters were being tested. She reached across the table and touched his hand, and he slid it over hers. Nothing more was said. Nothing needed to be. They tried eating one-handed until they started laughing, and then they finished their meal in a happy mood, chattering about this and that. She knew that they were at the beginning of the long, intimate conversation that creates a marriage, and binds it, and makes it true.

At least, so she hoped.

She did not take his advice about Waddy, though. She drove over to the prison, down the long, narrow road to the low buildings surrounded by Cyclone fences. Razor wire gleamed in the sharp autumn sun.

She went through the ID and search process, consigning her weapon to the guard at the entry station. They directed her down a long hallway to a little booth that was separate from the larger room where inmates met their visitors in a fairly open setting.

Here, there was a glass wall with a telephone. This was where dangerous prisoners spoke to their lawyers, the men who'd been too free with their guns, with their knives, the kind of violent men whose numbers in Texas were an echo of the anarchy that had followed the Civil War, that the public had romanticized as "the Wild West."

They brought him out, a miserable little baby in an orange jumpsuit two sizes too big. "Can you get me some M&M's, lady?"

Maybe the reason she wanted so badly to rescue Waddy wasn't that she felt guilty about what had happened to him, but rather because nobody had rescued her, and she did not want that to happen to him.

She said to him, "Waddy, I am going to be your special

friend. I am going to be the one who's always on your side no matter what."

"Then get me outta here."

"I will, Waddy, one day I will."

Waddy was tried in a juvenile proceeding. In the testimony, evidence was presented that indicated that Sam Davis had tortured both him and Jeff. The DA got an order that compelled all of the children in the family to be examined for signs of torture, and it turned out that all the boys were scarred in one way or another.

Sam Davis's children were removed from his custody. To prevent her whole family from going into the fostering program, Lana divorced her husband.

He was charged with eleven counts of child endangerment, six of depraved indifference to the welfare of a minor, and four of depraved acts with a minor.

When Sally made her daily rounds in Maryvale, everybody who saw her waved. She was the hero of the moment, and unless hell froze over, she'd be sheriff here for as long as she wanted.

Some of the teachers formed a support group for Waddy. Tom Keener put it best when he said, simply, "This whole community failed that little boy."

Maryvale, she realized, was indeed a community—quiet, drawn into itself, and wounded, but a real community, and they could stand together when they needed to.

Sam Davis went to Huntsville for fifteen years, the maximum term allowed. It meant that he wouldn't see a parole hearing for six years—time enough, the judge had made sure, for all his children to be grown.

Another criminal was brought to justice in those weeks, but his story never got past the local news media. Ex-sheriff Edward Walker turned himself in to the DA and confessed to multiple counts of endangering the welfare of a minor and depraved acts with a minor.

Ed mounted a defense of innocent by reason of insanity. It did not work, and there came a day when he stood before a judge whose diapers he could have changed, and received his sentence.

In the reedy little voice of a man suddenly very, very old, he read a statement. "I have very little clear memory of my crimes against these children. I know that they happened, though, and I have decided not to defend them. The truth is, I need assistance in remembering them, and I need to be confined until, and if, I am able to be free of the desires that led to them. Until that time comes, I cannot tell you, in all honesty, that I will not offend again. Although I can tell you, before God as my witness, that I am sorry to the depths of my soul for the injuries I have done."

He was sent to Huntsville for six years to contemplate his errors. During this time, rehabilitation would be attempted, but Sally knew the odds, and she feared that if Ed lived long enough to get out, he would still be dangerous to children—or as dangerous as any man of seventy-six could be.

After sentence was passed, Ed turned slowly around and faced Sally.

She was shocked, seeing, up close, just how small he had become, how white his hair had gotten. She noticed a continuing tremor in his left hand, as it compulsively worked against his handcuffs.

This was Uncle Ed, tall Uncle Ed, beloved Uncle Ed. And in the soft of memory, she remembered him singing to her, "Yes, sir, that's my baby, no, sir, I don't mean maybe . . ."

Now, the old voice said, "I want to say I'm sorry, darlin'. I am so very, very sorry."

She nodded. Rob, beside her, took her arm in his. It was good to feel him next to her.

From prison, Ed deeded his little bungalow to her, and gave her what money he had, just under ten thousand dollars invested in a mutual fund. Crime might or might not pay, but sheriffing certainly didn't. Sally decided to rent it out; she couldn't bear living there again.

Sally and Elizabeth e-mailed each other daily, but Elizabeth would never commit herself to coming home. Finally, Sally decided that no alcoholic could need that much therapy, so she carved out a Saturday and took the long drive to Starlight.

Most of the faces had changed, but the same contradictory sense of peace and desperation defined the place. You'd see somebody walking beneath the huge oaks that surrounded the wide ranch house . . . walking and walking, up and down, up and down, and you'd feel the human spirit there, locked in its struggle with the hunger that devours its victims.

Elizabeth spotted her car and came out the front door. She'd easily lost fifty pounds. She was tan, her hair was beautifully waved, she wore a nice skirt and a pretty blue blouse. Her eyes, always lovely, now positively sparkled.

"Well, now, girl, you are a sight for sore eyes," Elizabeth said. "Come on in here and have some of our coffee." She winked. "It's almost as addictive as heroin."

They went down the long hall, past a room where a new arrival, dead drunk and roaring the Gettysburg Address, was being videotaped for his own future consumption.

"That's step one," Elizabeth said. "You get to watch yourself the way you are when you're blasted. Starlight prefers its customers to come drunk. It's always the best start."

The guy reeled over and tried to paw Sally. She slapped him away and he stood roaring curses into the camera.

She and Elizabeth went out onto a side porch with big mugs of coffee.

"You're not a drunk anymore," Sally said.

Elizabeth smiled. "Vivé la difference."

They just sat together for a time, enjoying each other's presence, smiling a lot. "If we were a little younger," Sally said at last, "we'd be giggling like crazy."

"Did you do that, too? Giggle for no reason whatsoever?"

"Truthfully, Elizabeth, I've only seen it in the movies."

There was another silence. Sally realized that something was missing here, something was not being said. "So, I miss you."

"I miss you."

"So when are you coming back?"

"I'm not."

Had Sally heard that right? "Excuse me?"

"I've decided to stay here at Starlight, for now."

Sally was baffled. Elizabeth had licked her addiction.

"As a counselor. They can use me here. And if I stay, I know I won't be tempted to fall off the wagon."

Sally felt tears coming. She was annoyed at herself—sheriffs don't cry—except, of course, when they do. "Elizabeth, I'll miss you too much! Please come home. You're strong enough to resist temptation. I'll help you."

"You don't understand, Sally. I'm really needed here. This is where I belong, where my work is. Do you realize that half of our patients are under the age of twenty-five, and half of those are under the age of eighteen? I can help those kids, Sally. I understand the forces that lead them to drink and do drugs."

I have to talk her out of this, Sally thought. *I know I'm being selfish, but I don't know how I'll be able to go on without her.*

"I want you to continue to live in my house," Elizabeth continued. "You take care of it for me. And I want you to keep it in good shape!"

"Elizabeth—"

Elizabeth began ticking things off on her fingers. "I want you to get the furnace checked out thoroughly before you even think about turning it on. And the stone wall in the back-yard needs to be repaired. Get Rob to help you with that."

Sally took her notebook out of her purse, and began writing things down. "Anything else?"

"And get Rob to move in with you."

"Uh, what?"

"I'm telling you to take the step you've been longing to take. Do it, girl!"

"Rob—I mean, I like Rob, but—"

She looked stern. "If you don't let Rob move in with you, I'll kick you out and rent it to someone else."

Sally just stared at her. What was this about?

"You absolute idiot, *marry the guy*. Or at least shack up with him! He loves you, Sally, can't you see that?"

"I—I'm not sure."

"Are you the last person in Maryvale to see that the two of you have become a *couple*?"

Sally squirmed, but she had to admit that it was true. They were together during most of their free time and a lot of their working hours too. They ate dinner together most nights. And the issue of marriage hovered between them, unspoken.

"Have you ever been in love before?"

"Yes!"

"Don't say yes when you mean no. It's a bad habit. The answer is, you haven't but you are now, and you are scared stiff because there is a real commitment waiting for you, and the love of a damn good man. A fine man. And that is very scary to an emotionally beat-up little lady like you, who's running as hard as she can just to keep from becoming a basket case."

"Elizabeth, that isn't me."

She threw back her head and laughed. "Listen, girl, we get real direct around here. No more East Texas lady, I'm sorry. You are loved and you are in love, and you have to face it."

Sally just sat there. Stunned. It was true, every word. She was madly in love with Rob, and he was in love with her. Crazy about her. But holding back out of respect for her fragile heart.

"Now, listen, I have a little surprise for you. You can't go home tonight, it's too late, and you won't get back until after midnight. So I've reserved a room for you over at Cootchies." She stopped, bent forward, shaking with silent laughter. "Sorry, but everybody calls it that. The poor damn Cootchins. Anyway, you go over there and they'll give you a good supper and put you to bed for a proper sleep. Then you go home and continue your life."

"Without the only really good friend I've ever had."

"You are not experienced in the art of friendship. You will find that no matter where you and I are, this dialog will continue until the day one of us croaks, and probably after, in the heart of the other."

As evening fell the visitors' bell began its soft tolling, and the wives and husbands, mothers and fathers and friends, trailed slowly off to the parking lot.

Sally drove through the golden autumn evening, along the winding roads, to the lovely old inn. As she pulled up into the empty parking area, she realized that she'd be the Cootchins' only guest.

The front door was open, so she went on in. She stopped at the desk that stood at the edge of the large sitting room with its big stone fireplace and its antlers, and filled in her name and address on the card that had been placed there.

The whole place smelled delicious. Somebody was cooking something really, really good back there in that kitchen.

"Woo-hoo," Sally called.

There was no response. She could hear a radio playing faintly, so she just went on back.

The kitchen was done in red Saltillo tile. Its counters were black granite. Dozens of beautifully polished copper pots hung from the ceiling, and a tall man stood over the big professional stove frying something in a pan.

"I hope you like quail," Rob said as he turned around. "They left us a whole mess of 'em."

She just stood there. She couldn't talk. Her face got hot. Tears swam in her eyes.

He laid the skillet aside and came to her in two large strides. "Hey now," he said, taking her in his arms, "don't get overwhelmed here, it's just a bunch of quail." She laughed then, and they kissed, and that felt very right.

"The Cootchins have a habit of getting kind of scarce at times," Rob said as they made dinner together. "In particular, times like this."

They ate together at the big dining table, already set for two in a corner close to a dancing little fire. The clock ticked, the candles glowed, and she thought that Rob was definitely the best man she had ever known.

He cleared his throat. "Sally," he began.

She held up a hand. It wasn't something that needed words. She moved her chair closer to his. He took her in his arms and dinner was forgotten in this kiss, long and deep, the kind of kiss that reaches deep into the heart.

He kissed her face, her neck, then, suddenly turning courtly, her hands. He continued, "I'm not much of a catch, I know, compared to men you've met before. But I have something they don't have."

"Oh, you do, do you?" she teased. "Will I ever get to see it?"

He blushed. "Sally, don't make this into a joke."

"I'm sorry, Rob. What do you have?"

"I'm never going to hurt you," he said. "I'm never going to leave—I'll always be here for you. I keep my promises."

She knew it was true, and her heart rushed with the joy of it. But she heard herself say, "Oh, Rob, I'm sorry, but I guess I can't believe that somebody who says he loves me today won't get tired of me tomorrow. I just don't think I'm very lovable." And her heart screamed, *Woman, are you crazy?*

Rob took her words—frightened, distancing, and false—at face value. "I haven't gotten tired of you yet," he said firmly, "and I don't intend to. I'm past getting tired of you, Sally." He dug into his quail, ate for a moment, then took a sip of wine.

She was silent, struggling to be warm, to relate, feeling the scars of her ordeal that were preventing her.

He took another sip of wine. A pull, actually. Then he reached over and lifted her face. She realized that she'd been looking down at the table. Dear God, she was fine with casual dates, but when it was serious she was almost autistic! She knew why, too, but she just could not break through.

"Sally," he said, "I know you have trouble with this."

"I'm sorry."

"No, this is very serious stuff. I mean, I'm a man who loves you and I think you love me too and I'm asking you, right now, Sally, to marry me, and that is a very serious moment." He smiled a little. "So you have to look me in the eye, and tell me what you're gonna tell me."

Her heart was hammering, she felt sweat bead out all over her body, and instinct made her push her knees tightly together. And then a little voice from deep within did something completely unexpected. The little voice of her heart, struggling down there to do its job, laughed.

And the laughter filled her, the bubbling joy of yes, the promise of happiness, the simplicity of love. Sally heard a voice that sounded like it belonged to somebody else squeak out, "Yes!"

Rob looked stunned. "Yes? You mean yes, you'll get married?"

Suddenly a huge weight, as big as a boulder, seemed to lift right off her heart. "I mean yes—*yes!*"

"Oh, Sally, you—we—we've both wanted this? I mean, I'm not . . . forcing you?"

She jumped up out of her chair and just literally fell on him, and the kisses poured out of her like a rainstorm that had been trying and trying to break and could not, and now at last it could, and the healing rains came, tears and kisses and kisses and kisses.

And then a voice full of the crying of happiness said, "You marry me, Trooper. That's an order."

Rob got up. They faced each other. "When are the Cootchins coming back?" she asked.

"Tomorrow at noon."

"Really?"

"They have to. They're doing your engagement party, Sheriff."

"Who in the world would come to an engagement party for me?"

"Well, if there's a single soul in Maryvale who doesn't come, I'm going to be very surprised."

"The whole town?"

"The party itself's going to be down at the dance hall. Barbecue and champagne, Texas style."

"Oh, Rob, what if I'd said no?"

He looked toward the stairs. "Oh, I'd've spanked you and sent you off to bed by yourself, then taken you anyway."

She broke away, headed for the stairs. Now it was his turn to feel a little challenged. "Come on," she said, looking back over her shoulder.

"Where are you going?"

"Up to where you've been trying to go for months . . . and don't tell me you haven't, or I'll be insulted."

Rob blushed. "I was about to put a soufflé in the oven!"

She'd reached the stairs. "You get your little tail up here," she said. This time, he didn't hesitate.

And it was a sweet time, sweet with discovery of a kind that she didn't know existed, the magic that comes between two people when real love is added to the equation.

Afterward, Rob slept against Sally's side. She lay gazing at the moonlight on the ceiling as Rob snored softly in deep sleep.

She looked down at him, touched his face. This was the truth, finally, wasn't it? Love, in the end, was the truth.

Maryvale, she knew, would go on as it always had, a town of secrets and the lies that hide them. But that was the way of little towns left to themselves in the deep country.

So be it. When the lies got dangerous, the sheriff would be there to put things right. But not in one little house, her house, not where she and Rob would pass their blessed nights, and make and raise their kids.

In that one little corner of Maryvale, at least, there would be no more lies.